PRAISE FOR

THE

SHOE

ON THE

ROOF

INSTANT NATIONAL BESTSELLER

A *GLOBE AND MAIL* BOOK OF THE YEAR

"Ferguson is a skillful and original writer, and over all, the novel is full of life. . . . *The Shoe on the Roof*'s lasting strength is in such sly jabs at the 'alternative facts' and deep divisions we're now reckoning with, making it a tale for the times."

The Globe and Mail

"Often laugh-out-loud funny despite its serious and tragic underpinnings. But it's also thought-provoking, occasionally violent, and will likely stay with readers long after the last page is read."

Calgary Herald

"Absurdly funny."

Quill & Quire

"Another gem from this Giller Prize–winning author."

Canadian Living

THE
SHOE
ON THE
ROOF

WILL FERGUSON

Published by Simon & Schuster

New York   London   Toronto   Sydney   New Delhi

SIMON &
SCHUSTER
CANADA

Simon & Schuster Canada
An Imprint of Simon & Schuster, Inc.
166 King Street East, Suite 300
Toronto, Ontario M5A 1J3

This Simon & Schuster Canada edition April 2018

SIMON & SCHUSTER CANADA and colophon are
trademarks of Simon & Schuster, Inc.

For information about special discounts for bulk purchases,
please contact Simon & Schuster Special Sales at 1-800-268-3216
or CustomerService@simonandschuster.ca.

Interior design by Carly Loman

Manufactured in the United States of America

10   9   8   7   6   5   4   3   2

Library and Archives Canada Cataloguing in Publication

Ferguson, Will, author
      The shoe on the roof / Will Ferguson.
Previously published: 2017.
ISBN 978-1-5011-7358-5 (softcover)
      I. Title.
PS8561.E7593S56 2018   C813'.54
C2017-907599-3

ISBN 978-1-5011-7355-4
ISBN 978-1-5011-7358-5 (pbk)
ISBN 978-1-5011-7356-1 (ebook)

THE
SHOE
ON THE
ROOF

IN THE CORONARY CARE UNIT of Seattle's Harborview Hospital, a woman identified as M. goes into full cardiac arrest. She dies on the operating table. With no vital signs—no pulse, no respiration—an emergency EEG reveals that her brain activity has flatlined. But the doctors and nurses at Harborview do not give up. They work frantically to resuscitate her and, even more remarkably, they succeed. They bring the patient back from a state of clinical death.

When she regains consciousness, M. tells the doctors that she could hear what they were saying the entire time, every word. She'd felt herself floating above the operating table, calm and at peace, had watched the doctors as they tried to revive her. She'd drifted upward into a tunnel of light—but was then pulled back down, into her body, felt the pain and panic return.

When she told them this, the doctors nodded. It was a common hallucination. The light, they explained, was a symptom of cerebral hypoxia: with oxygen cut off to the brain, peripheral vision goes first, closing inward toward the centre of the optic nerve, creating a distinct tunnel effect. The sense of calm would have come from a sudden release of endorphins. The feelings of separation from her body would have occurred as her brain's parietal lobes shut down.

But it seemed so *real*, she said. I could feel myself lifting up, through the ceiling, above the hospital, I could see the roof, could see the ledge, the shoe in one corner.

The shoe?

Yes, a tennis shoe.

The patient described the shoe in detail: the frayed toe, the matted laces caught under one heel. I saw it, she said. It's there, on the roof. The doctors exchanged looks, then sent a janitor up. They found it, tucked out of sight, exactly where she said it would be: a single shoe, on the roof.

PART ONE

THE WINE,
THE BLOOD,
AND THE SEA

CHAPTER ONE

THE ONE ALMIGHTY FACT about love affairs is that they end. How they end and why, although of crucial interest—indeed, agony—to the participants, is less important than that they end. Marriages might linger like a chest cold, and there are friendships that plod along simply because we forget to cancel the subscription. But when love affairs collapse, they do so suddenly: they drop like swollen mangoes, they shatter like saucers, they drown in the undertow, they fall apart like a wasp's nest in winter. They end.

Thomas knew this, and yet . . .

There is a story, often told, possibly apocryphal, certainly apropos, of a seasoned skydiver who, in what can only be described as a monumental lapse of judgment, forgot to strap on his parachute before flinging himself from a plane. As one might imagine, he went through all five stages of Kübler-Ross in quick order, *shock, denial, anger, dismay*, until, in *accepting* his fate, he chose to embrace it. The skydiver spread his arms, turned pirouettes and somersaults while he tumbled, performing acrobatic death-defying feats all the way down.

But none of that makes the landing any softer.

Thomas was in his late twenties when he hit the ground. He'd begun his swan dive without realizing it, in an artist's loft in Boston's West End on a sleepy cirrus Sunday. A muted morning. The curtains were moving; he remembers that, the ripples of cream-coloured cloth: long inhalations, slow exhalations. Sunlight on the floor. A messy room (not his), lined with equally messy canvases. Oil paintings mostly: thickly textured renderings of angular faces spattered with stars. An overstuffed laundry hamper in one corner was spilling clothes like the world's worst piñata. Bricks-and-board bookshelves, overdue art volumes splayed every which way. A telescope by the window, leaning on drunken legs, squinting upward into nothingness. Wine bottles on the windowsills, multicoloured candle wax dripping down the sides—still *de rigueur* among the university set. Wind and curtain and canvas. And now, this: the sound of church bells.

Amy, scrambling out of her dishevelled bed. Amy, dashing about, baffled by the very concept of time. She was always late, which was not remarkable in itself, but she was always *surprised* she was late, and Thomas found this both annoying and oddly endearing. She seemed to think that time was liquid, a substance that filled the available forms it was poured into, when in fact it sliced the air with a metronymic predictability.

Moments before, Thomas and Amy had been playing doctor, a favourite game of theirs, with Amy astride his lap, dressed in a man's shirt—not his. (Where did it come from, this oversized shirt? Why did she have it? Was it a souvenir of other phosphorous love affairs? Best not to think about it.) She wore it loosely, like a pajama top, mis-buttoned, un-ironed.

He remembers the loose cotton. The warmth of her.

Amy, laughing. "Stop it."

It would be the last happy conversation they would ever have.

"Stop what?"

"Stop *that*."

Thomas is in a white lab coat with boxers pooled around his ankles. He slides a stethoscope down the inside of her shirt, and then *slowwwwly* across her chest. Pretends to listen.

Amy, voice hushed. "What is it, doc? Somethin' bad? You can tell me, I can take it."

Thomas frowns. A practiced frown. A *medical* frown. Listens more attentively. "Can't seem . . . to find . . . a heartbeat."

He was scarcely a year older than Amy, but looked ten years younger, as though his face had never grown up, as though it were still trapped in the first flush of postpubescence. It's something she'd often commented on, how young he looked. Later, she would notice how old he had become.

So there they are, the two of them: Amy, with a raven's wing of hair fanning across her shoulder; Thomas in his Sunday-morning stubble. Straw-blond hair that refused to hold a part, eyes so pale they were barely there. "Grey? Or blue?" Amy had asked this early on, studying him carefully before deciding. "Blue. Definitely blue."

Our intrepid young medical student has now slipped the stethoscope further down, cupping Amy's breasts, first one, then the other. She shivers at the touch of it. "Can't you warm those up first?"

Now it was Amy's turn.

She pulled the end of the stethoscope free, flipped it over, held it up to Thomas's chest. A thin chest, almost hairless.

"So?" she asked.

He tilted his head, listened for his own heartbeat.

"Anything?" she asked.

"Nothing." He looked at her. "That can't be good. Can it?"

She laughed, a snort, really. "Are you *sure* you're a real doctor?"

"A real doctor?"

She leaned closer, held him with her thighs. "I've heard rumours."

"Rumours?"

"Med students, passing themselves off as physicians, taking advantage of impressionable young women."

"I resent that! A slanderous accusation! Slanderous and scurrilous! Now then, take off all your clothes and say 'Ahh.'"

Amy leaned in closer, whispered in his ear. *"Ahhhhh . . ."*

And then—and then, the goddamn sound of the goddamn church bells. Dull peals, distant but ever-present.

"We're late! C'mon!" She leapt from his lap, hurried about, searching for underwear. She pulled on a pair, more or less at random, grabbed her jeans and hopped into them on the way to the bathroom.

Thomas fell back onto the bed, frustrated, annoyed, erect. He could see Amy brushing her teeth—or rather, chewing on the toothbrush as she unbuttoned the man's shirt she was wearing. She tossed it to one side like a flag on the play, tried to disentangle a bra from a knot of laundry on the counter.

"Amy," he said (sighed).

She packed her breasts into her bra like eggs into a carton, gave her teeth two decisive back-and-forths, spit into the sink, pulled back her hair with an elastic.

Thomas leaned up on his elbows, boxers still around his ankles. "Listen. About this whole church thing . . ."

She stopped. Stepped out of the bathroom with her toothbrush clenched in her mouth, glared at him. They'd had this conversation before.

CHAPTER TWO

NEW ENGLAND IN AUTUMN. Blue skies. Air as crisp as a celery stalk snapped in two. A dry wind, stirring the trees. Leaves spiralling down: deep reds and unrhymeable orange, twirling on eddies, layering the streets.

And above this calico quilt of trees: the sharpened spire of Our Lady of Constant Sorrow, marking the spot as cleanly as a pin on a map. *Today's field trip will be to an anachronistic remnant of pre-industrial Bronze Age mythology. Hurry along, class.* Amy was churning a trail through the leaves, with Thomas, as always, following in her wake. They passed a playground on the way with strollers parallel-parked out front, babies held on hips like plump packages by thumb-texting mothers. A grinning toddler wobbled across the grounds, giddily enamoured with the power of his own locomotion, pursued by a woman, presumably his mother.

Amy was worried they'd be late, but when they got to the church, a bottleneck of elderly parishioners with canes and walkers had formed on the steps. They filed in slowly, heads bobbing, bowing, as they went.

"We're always the youngest people here," Thomas complained as they waited to make their way through the heavy, medieval doors.

His gaze drifted back across the street.

A man stood on the other side. Ratty hair and a tangled beard, dressed in rags, he was holding up a sign written on a piece of cardboard. It read: I AM THE LORD GOD, SON OF MAN.

Thomas caught Amy's elbow as she was about to step over the threshold. "Hey. I think I found your guy."

"What?"

"You've been looking for him. Well, there he is." He gestured with his chin toward the homeless man.

Amy scowled at Thomas, said nothing—loudly.

He gave her what he hoped was a disarmingly boyish grin, but she'd already pushed past him, had disappeared into the darkness, into that realm of incense and candles, of stained glass vignettes and matronly choirs. Thomas looked back one last time at the tatterdemalion saviour on the other side of the street.

I know you.

Thomas had seen that man before. Where?

It gnawed on him throughout the service. At one point, he leaned in closer to Amy and said, "That guy, the one outside, holding the sign. I've seen him somewhere."

"Shhh."

It was one extended session of Simon Says, these Catholic masses. Stand up. Sit down. Repeat after me. Incantations and swaying chains trailing smoke. The apostles and the martyrs, the miracles and the make-believe. Benedictions and exaltations. Homilies and parables. *"We believe in the Seven Sacraments, in Christ everlasting."* Thomas stifled a yawn, shifted his buttocks on the pew. *Numb enough you could perform rectal surgery on my ass without the need for anaesthetics.*

The interior of the church was vast but largely empty, and the

10

dwindling numbers and sea of silver hair added a funereal feel to the proceedings. *Eventually churches will become little more than curiosities.* It was a satisfying thought. *"Can you believe what we used to believe?"* This is what people would say, looking back at the hymnals and sermons of yesteryear. *"Can you believe it?"*

Amy had a rosary on her wrist. This was for meditation on the Fifteen Mysteries: Annunciation, Coronation, Crucifixion, the Agony in the Garden of Gethsemane, and so on. *Of the Fifteen Mysteries, five are joyous, five are glorious, five are sorrowful.* Thomas had tried to educate himself about the arcane intricacies of her faith, but he still couldn't tell the difference of effect between an Our Father and a Hail Mary. *One was liturgical, one devotional.* And damned if he knew what that meant.

The sermon had ended and the silver-haired set were now shuffling out again, stopping to dip their hands a final time, making the Sign of the Cross over their body before departing. *Spectacles, testicles, wallet, and watch.* Several of the elderly parishioners clasped hands along the way. "Peace be with you." "And with you." The first time Amy had dragged Thomas to a service, he'd misheard the salutation as "Pleased to meet you!" and had gone about shaking hands accordingly.

Virgin and child. Sundry saints. The lacquer-like patina of history. A God that needed constant reassurances: flattery and praise, bribery and placation. Thomas was sitting alone on a pew. Above the altar, with arms outstretched somewhere between embrace and surrender, was Christ in crucifix. On the ceiling, rising into the sky, was Christ ascendant. And in a side alcove, illuminated in a liquid shimmer of candles, stood another Jesus, draped in royal hues: Christ returned, eyes downward cast, robe opened to reveal a heart enshrined

11

in thorns. The Sacred Heart, radiating splinters of light. It reminded Thomas of the plastic overlay pages in his anatomy textbooks, where one could peel back the layers of the human body, one at a time: muscular, circulatory, skeletal. The world's most thorough striptease. It brought to mind autopsy hearts and med school organs floating in formaldehyde, those pale grey lava lamps lit from below for the morbidly curious. It brought to mind cadavers as well. The wet weight of the human brain, the dark gravity well of the chest, the aortas and arteries that his instructors had pulled back in layers.

He could see Amy through a gap in the confessional curtains, on her knees, lips moving. You didn't have to kneel, but she always did. Somewhere, he could hear music, even though the choir had departed.

She was a long time confessing, and when she finally came out, she hurried past him, buttoning up her navy overcoat and pulling her scarf in closer.

Thomas stopped her on the steps outside. "You didn't tell him *everything*, right? The priest, I mean. It's only been a week since your last confession. How much sin could one person possibly have gotten up to? Wait. Don't answer that."

Amy gave him an artfully enigmatic look. "Maybe I'm not confessing what I've done. Maybe I'm confessing what I'm *going* to do."

"Ooooh. Sounds good. Are handcuffs involved? Because I warn you, I bruise easily."

Amy rolled her eyes, almost audibly. Down the stairs, clatter and step, onto the sidewalk, quick-walking, kicking aside leaves as she went. *I gave you a chance. I tried to warn you.*

Thomas caught up with her again outside a corner-store pharmacy where the Coca-Cola sign had faded to pink.

"He's still there," Thomas said.

"Who?"

"The guy with the sign."

She looked past Thomas, down the street to where the man stood, maintaining his vigil, silently proclaiming his divinity.

"Do you think he believes it?" Thomas asked.

"Believes what?"

"That he's really Jesus. Or do you figure at some level he knows it's a lie? I mean, medically speaking, religious delusions are basically a manifestation of—"

"Why does it matter so fucking much? Huh?"

Now, *that* was a showstopper. Amy so rarely resorted to profanity that Thomas had no idea how to respond.

"Why do you care, Thomas? Really. I want to know. Why does it matter to you what he believes?"

"Um. No reason, I guess. Just scientific curiosity."

She gestured toward the man with the sign without actually looking at him.

"That's a real person. That's somebody's son, somebody's brother. Why does it— They aren't lab rats, you know. You can't talk about people like that."

Her reaction seemed so disproportionate to whatever it was Thomas had been saying (he could barely remember what he had been saying) that he knew instinctively: *This is about something else.*

"Hey hey hey," he said, voice laden with concern. "You're talking to the original lab rat, remember? Listen. I'm sorry for whatever it is you think I may or may not have—"

"Don't. Don't do that."

"Do what?"

"One of those jujitsu apologies of yours, where you try to turn it back on me. This isn't about me. This isn't even about *him*, okay?"

"Truth be told, I don't know what any of this is about. All I said was—"

"Wait. Here."

She entered the store on the angry jangle of a bell above the door, leaving Thomas outside, still baffled by her outburst. He looked back at the street-corner prophet. And . . .

Thomas laughed. *I know who you are.*

By the time Amy returned, on a less angry but still strident jangle of bell, Thomas had forgotten they were fighting.

"Hynes Station," he said. "By the overpass, playing three-card monte. That's where I've seen him! You know the game, where you try to pick the queen of hearts. 'Find the lady!' He takes sucker bets at the station. This must be his Sunday gig. Brilliant, don't you think?"

Amy wasn't listening.

"Are you okay?" he asked.

"Can we go? Please?"

There was a chill in the air. He pulled her closer as they walked. She resisted at first, then relented, and he threw one last look to the shyster on the street corner, his three-card Messiah, his trickster god. *Find the lady.*

Somewhere in the distance he could hear a siren, an ambulance from the sound of it.

CHAPTER THREE

Oil paint is poorly named. It doesn't smell like oil—neither cooking, nor automotive—but carries instead the scent of licorice and furniture polish, with a hint of Vicks VapoRub thrown in. It's a smell that is almost tactile.

It reminded Thomas of the balm they prescribed to burn victims. It was only when Amy splashed turpentine into jars and swished the brushes clean that the smell became overpowering. She'd keep the windows open, even in the rain, as she let the turpentine settle in her eclectic array of glass containers, pickle and jam, mainly. She would later pour off the clearer upper levels of turpentine for reuse later, would separate them from the silted pigments at the bottom.

"There's a real science to this, isn't there?" Thomas had said, assuming this was the highest compliment one could give.

He once watched Amy spend an entire afternoon searching for perfect blue. He'd been sitting on her futon, textbook open, trying to get through a passage on neurotransmitters, but he kept going over the same paragraph again and again. His eyes would drift off the page, would turn to Amy at her easel. She often grabbed whatever was at hand to act as a palette—a saucer, a plate, a piece of tile, even wax paper—and would at times work so frantically that she eschewed brushes entirely, smearing the paint directly onto the canvas with a palette knife, thick impasto textures, wet into wet.

"I have this blue in mind," she said, "but I don't know if it actually exists."

She started with titanium white and Prussian blue, added a hint of yellow. Too bright. So she added a dab of raw umber, blended it with Payne's grey, created a more stormy blue, richer, almost smoky. But now it was too dark. So she mixed in translucent green and a softer shade of white and added a touch of alizarin red. But still it wasn't right.

She wiped her knife on a rag, started in again, this time with cerulean blue, adding more green, less umber. A daub here. A tad there. Ochre and eggshell. Burnt sienna. Cobalt blue. More cerulean, less alizarin. But every time Thomas thought she was finished, she would step back, shake her head, and begin anew. Thomas watched her as she eased colours out of the crusted tubes—Amy squeezed her paint the way she squeezed her toothpaste: unapologetically, right down the middle—looking for that one shade of blue among all the endless variations. There seemed to be more alchemy than chemistry involved at this point. He'd gone over to her with a cup of tea—black currant, scented like spiced wood; it tasted the way cedar chests smelled—but she let the tea go cold in the cup. Amy never found it, that perfect blue, but she kept searching.

Thomas had never uttered The Word From Which There Is No Return, that one word, that single puff of a syllable on which so much turns. Thomas knew full well that to be the first to say The Word out loud is to cede advantage. It was a bloated word, that puff of air, one that telegraphed itself in pop songs and poetry; when you heard "up above" or "like a glove," you knew what was coming. A breathy insubstantial abstract noun, a transitive verb, a chemical imbalance in the brain: four letters signifying nothing (and everything). He'd never spoken it, but he came awfully close that afternoon as she searched for her elusive blue. In the end, he didn't speak it but held it instead in his mouth, felt it dissolve on his tongue like a sugar cube, doomed and sweet.

Thomas could map Amy's body by scent alone.

The vinegary tang of turpentine may have clung to her chapped hands, but the corners of her mouth tasted of herbal tea and toothpaste—a strange mix of hibiscus and mint, *the essence of Amy*— and her earlobes smelled (faintly) of soap. Dove's moisturizing, to be specific. (She never rinsed enough behind her neck when she took a shower, was rather slapdash about the whole thing, if you asked Thomas.) She couldn't cook, either. Early on, she'd invited him over for lasagna and he'd pictured layers of parboiled pasta laid down in succulent strata of spinach and eggplant, diced peppers and cottage cheese. Instead, she'd produced a box of Hamburger Helper's "Olde-Fashioned Home-Style Lasagna™" which she then proceeded to overcook while chattering away about art school. Only in the most ironic sense could it have been dubbed "lasagna." From a young age, Thomas's education had included cuisine; he could blend spices and caramelize Spanish onions with an undeniable élan. So when Amy dolloped her rendition of a home-cooked meal onto his plate, he was perturbed, to say the least. "I made it just for you," she said. It was the best lasagna he'd ever tasted.

As Amy and Thomas walked back through the fallen leaves, he said, "Let's go for lunch. My treat. Thai?"

But when they got to her studio, Amy headed straight for the bathroom and Thomas was left to wait around, bored and vaguely curious. An industrial loft in an industrial building, Amy's apartment featured elaborate arrangements of beams and joinery. And windows. Lots of windows.

"You're the only girl I know who owns a telescope," he shouted, but the bathroom door was closed and he wasn't sure she could hear him.

Chipped china plates were laid out everywhere, blotted with paints that had dried and darkened, the reds turning to black, the whites to a muddy grey. She was the first artist he'd ever spent time with, and he'd been disappointed to discover she didn't use a proper palette— the sort that painters in French berets and smocks might don. He'd never once seen her hold up her thumb or paint flowers in a vase, either. She didn't even own a beret.

The walls of Amy's studio were suffering from architectural eczema, flaking off in layers, revealing contour maps of failed colour schemes beneath. *Here's a suggestion! Maybe use some of yer paintin' skills to slap on a coat of latex, spruce the ol' place up a bit.*

Photographs of her family were lined up along the fireplace, a fireplace he had never seen lit. The usual collection of images: Christmas trees. A lake. Someone's graduation. One photo stood out, though: it was of a young priest smiling at the camera as Amy's head rested softly on his shoulder. A priest with Amy's eyes.

"How come I've never met your brother?" he asked.

No response.

"Is it because I'm a heathen? Invite me for supper. I promise I'll behave. Won't utter any blasphemy until at least the second course." He looked closer at the photograph. "Does your brother take confession as well? We couldn't really tell him what we've been up to, though, could we? Might be awkward." *How many Hail Marys does it take to erase a double-fingered G-spot massage to completion in front of an open window?* "I know a nun," he said. "I ever mention that? Kind of a miserable old woman, but she knew my mom. Used to babysit me when I was little. She was like the anti–Julie Andrews."

Thomas began flipping listlessly through her leaning stack of canvases, 24 by 36, mainly. Thickly rendered images, more cut from the paint than coaxed. He stopped at one, looked closer. It was a thin, pale face. Sharp angles and empty eye sockets.

"Is that me?"

It was.

At which point the bathroom door opened, throwing a secondary source of light across the paintings. Thomas turned to say something glib—but the smile drained from his face. Amy was standing in the doorway, backlit by the bathroom. One hand was clasped loosely over her mouth, the other was at her side, holding a home pregnancy test.

He didn't need to ask.

"Wait. No. Listen," he said. "Listen." He took a step, stopped. Tried to breathe. He would later recall that it felt as though he were falling. "I can't. Not with everything that's going on in my life right now, with school, my father." And then: "I can take care of this, Amy. I know a guy. Your brother, your family—they never need to find out."

Thomas wasn't so much propelled from Amy's apartment as flung. His lab coat and stethoscope followed, sailing out like a parachute and a toy-store rubber snake, after which her door slammed shut.

"Amy, wait!"

Silence from the other side.

"Amy."

The door opened halfway and Amy's arm appeared. She handed

Thomas his toothbrush and then slammed the door closed again. He could hear the locks going up inside.

"This isn't even my toothbrush. It's the one you used to clean between the tiles."

In the hallway, a security camera peered down at Thomas from behind its dark plastic dome. He could see himself reflected like a figure in a fun-house mirror, and he realized that this moment was being captured and recorded, was undoubtedly being stored on a hard drive somewhere. *How long do they keep security tapes before they erase them?* He could hear music playing, a faint aria from somewhere else. He quietly retrieved his lab coat and stethoscope. As Thomas walked down the hallway, he could feel the camera on his back the entire way. He tried to take comfort in the fact that this entire scene was probably playing to an empty room. He just couldn't decide which was worse—that someone was watching, or that no one was.

CHAPTER FOUR

BERNIE ON THE PHONE, out of breath. Traffic in the background.

"Where are you?" Thomas asked.

"Don't know. Somewhere. Downtown, I think. What's going on? Don't tell me there's trouble at the lab. I sent Igor out for a brain ages ago! That asshole should have been back by now."

The reference to Frankenstein was a running joke of theirs. Bernie was Thomas's unofficial lab partner, fleshy faced and rounded at the corners. Even his glasses were round. He reminded Thomas of a cherub that had eluded its fate and grown up. "Cherub and the scarecrow" is how Bernie described their partnership. They'd been running tests on brain tissues, dying them various colours, trying to trace patterns of thought in the neural pathways, and it wasn't going well. They'd taken to blaming every setback on their imaginary and highly culpable assistant Igor.

"I'll be in tomorrow," said Bernie, still out of breath. "We'll sort it out then. There's a problem with the protocols. I swear there's a step missing. Talk to the lab tech, she'll know."

"I'm not at the lab," Thomas said. "I'm standing in front of Amy's building. Her lights are still on, but she's not answering the phone. I walked an hour, ended up back where I started."

"So what happened? She finally smarten up and dump your sorry ass?"

There was a long pause.

"Oh, shit. I'm sorry. Look, let me wash up. We can meet at O'Malley's. We'll get drunk, diss the bitch. You can say, 'Fuck it, I'm better off without her' as many times as you like, and I'll say, 'Amen to that!' every time. We'll stagger home and you can sleep it off. It's a time-honoured prescription. Goes back to Hippocrates, I believe. Up there with 'First, do no harm.' *Thou shalt drink away a heartache.* It'll do you good, Thomas. I could use a drink as well." Bernie could always use a drink.

And so they met, and so it went.

The night unfolded exactly as predicted. Bernie was in fine form, mocking their profs and fellow med students with equal aplomb (the students above them were all idiots, the ones below them all morons), while raising toasts and laughing large. They drank until the tavern began to turn, slowly at first, like a dimly lit carousel, then speeding up as the night went on. Bernie leaned in, caught Thomas as he was going by, shouted at him through the haze, "You're too good for her! You're practically a celebrity! I always told you, 'You're too good for her.' Didn't I always tell you that?"

"You did."

"So why are you pining away over some second-rate, pissant *artiste*?"

At this, Thomas protested. "No, not second-rate. She's good. Good painter."

"Really? And what the hell do you know about art?"

"Not a goddamn thing." But that wasn't true. Thomas had once been an artist, as have we all: *Finger paintings. Play-Doh figurines,*

22

squished into shape. Watercolour portraits of imaginary friends, paint-
ings disappearing from the playroom—very strange—then reappearing
later on.

Bernie turned, called for more drinks in much the same manner as
one might call for a medic.

The heightened jocularity of the evening rambled on, self-
consciously loud as though performed for an audience. The façade
fell away only for a moment, when Bernie said, "At least you have
someone."

"*Had* someone," Thomas corrected.

"Better to have loved and lost, right?" It was a snatch of poetry
from Bernie's youth. He left the coda unstated: *Than never to have*
loved at all.

There was a sadness there that Thomas chose to ignore. "Did you
know," Thomas said, slurring his words as well as his sentiments,
"that rats dream about mazes?"

"What?"

"Is true. Rats dream about mazes, birds dream about singing."

"How could you ever know what a bird is dreaming?"

"Lissen. When a rat runs a maze, the location synapses in the . . .
in the . . ."

"Hippocampus."

"Right. Inna hippocampus. Those synapses fire in sequence.
Every time the rat retraces the maze, same sequence. An' when he's
sleeping, guess what? The same sequence fires in his brain. He's re-
playing the maze in his dreams, over and over again, trying to figure it
out. With songbirds, when they're sleepin', the same muscle tensions
in their throat occur as when they're singing. Is true. They dream
about singing."

"And cats?"

"Cats dream about fighting. Is true. If y'remove the—what do you call it?—the inhibitory centre from a cat's brain stem, that cat'll go wild when it's sleeping." The inhibitory centre causes sleep paralysis; keeps cats and humans and other mammals from sleepwalking or flailing about at night. "Remove that and the cat will arch its back when it's asleep, will hiss and claw and bite. They're playing out battles in their little feline brains."

Bernie took off his glasses, cleaned them on a damp pull of sweater (which only made things worse; his glasses were permanently fogged), and the drinks kept coming. Thomas downed another, then another, shouted into Bernie's ear, "To hell with her, right? Dozen madder. Emotions, who cares? Dozen madder, right? Just neurochemical pathways in the brain. I need to cauterize 'em, is all."

"You said it, brother. We're all just molecules."

"Damn straight, 'm better off without her."

"Amen to that."

They left O'Malley's and stagger-walked to Thomas's apartment building, a tony two-storey arrangement of brick and vine, set amid the requisite tree-lined avenue. With one final shoulder-clasping back-slap, Bernie sent Thomas up the front stairs, and when Thomas reeled about to say "S'long," Bernie was already gone.

It took several tries, but Thomas eventually got his key into the front foyer door. Inside, four separate townhouse-style apartments faced a central hallway. Professional people, for the most part.

Thomas entered his own apartment in a swirl of darkness, groped around for a light switch—the switch was apparently of a migratory nature—before giving up. He stumbled across the living room, opened the blinds to let the moon in. He could see the distant silhouette of Constant Sorrow, a spire with a smudge up top that must have been a cross. *X marks the spot.*

Thomas turned, faced the empty room.

"My *sanctum sanctorum*," he said with a flourish—and a sigh.

Sharp corners of silver and chrome caught the moonlight. Thomas had spent a small fortune outfitting this open-concept space with the latest European home décor, only to have everyone who entered say, "Hey! Ikea!"

"No," he would reply, testily, "it's *Finnish.*"

"Exactly! Ikea."

"Ikea is *Swedish*. This is—" Oh, but what was the point. (Amy's furniture, meanwhile, was little more than a collage of thrift store finds and second-hand giveaways, even—egads!—at least one curbside rescue operation. After she told him—proudly!—where she'd found it, Thomas was never able to sit on that swaybacked, threadbare corduroy couch again. "It was just there by a dumpster! Can you imagine?" she'd asked. Yes. Yes he could. He could imagine it vividly. Who knew what sort of guest, rodent or microbiological, what sort of trace DNA those cushions might host. As far as Thomas was concerned, that couch was little more than a petri dish with side cushions, and his flesh itched psychosomatically for days after sitting on it. "You remember Lars?" she'd asked. "From the gallery? He helped me carry it up." *You're a better man than I am, Lars from the gallery.*)

"And I'm better off without her," Thomas muttered. Any mantra, repeated often enough, becomes true. That was the theory, anyway.

Staggering through his modular Finnish world—and aren't those clean corners ideal for the hitting of one's shins?—he gave a desultory pull on his desktop lamp, shoved some papers out of the way, flopped down on the chair, rolled himself backward.

"Hello, Sully," he said to the skeleton dangling in the corner. "Nice hat."

Sully was wearing a novelty store pilgrim-style cap, green with a large tinfoil buckle: a souvenir of Saint Patrick's Days past.

Thomas's room was cluttered with medical charts, files, textbooks. ("I love it!" Amy had said the first time he'd brought her back to his place. "You've got this whole mad-scientist thing going on.") A microscope, a box of glass slides, chemical dyes. A real brain floating in a container on a high shelf. Another, plastic brain being used as a paperweight. The plastic brain had hinges, and Thomas opened it up like a book. Each layer was carefully labelled: the reptilian brain stem and cerebellum; the mammalian limbic system in midbrain; the convoluted outer cortex of our higher functions. Slice a brain in half and human evolution reveals itself to you, like the rings in a tree, from the higher-order primates of the outer cerebrum to the lower-order mammals in the middle to the dark serpentine appetites coiled in the core. It was all there, our past, our present, ourselves. *Snake, vole, ape.*

"And what evolutionary purpose," he asked Sully, "does love serve? Temporary madness, when all is said and done. Good to be rid of her."

He closed his eyes and turned a slow dervish twirl in his chair. He might have slept like that, head back, mouth slack, had someone not started playing music in the next room. Faint, but clear.

Who the hell plays church music at this time of night?

Then, below the music, a whisper, a warning: *"Thomassss."* He jolted awake, looked around the dull confines of his room.

But there was no one there. Only Sully and the darkness.

CHAPTER FIVE

Confronting your ex at their workplace is never a particularly *good* idea, less so on four hours' sleep whilst sporting an apocalyptic hangover and dressed in the clothes you slept in.

Undaunted by the ravages of dehydration, and with residual alcohol still sloshing about in his bloodstream, Thomas made his way with a grim determination, past the winos huddled in doorways beneath their oily sleeping bags, past shopping carts filled with worldly goods. Refugees from Tent City.

Down here. That was the neighbourhood's unofficial name. Rents were cheaper *down here*, hence the proliferation of dollar stores, payday loans, pawnshops, and—equally insolvent—artist's studios. But a larger gentrification process had already begun, and the gallery Amy worked at was just edgy enough to be hip, and just hip enough to be expensive.

She was holding up a Cubist painting by a Cuban artist ("Cubanist," as it was known) for a local dowager to consider—"This would go well in any room, really"—when she saw Thomas coming directly at her, like an arrow.

Poor Thomas. In the instant their eyes met, his determination collapsed. Instead of striding forth with a confident air, he rushed headlong into it, spilling out his words unchecked.

"I texted," he said, voice unnaturally high. "I called and I called and I texted, and I waited outside your building and you never answered. We need to talk."

"No," she said. "We don't."

She turned to leave but Thomas blocked her way. The customer, caught in the crossfire, slipped aside with an embarrassed look. "I'll, ah, come back later . . ." she said.

Amy tried again to slip free, Thomas again stopped her. He could see the doors closing, one by one, in her eyes, behind her gaze. "Please," he said. "Not like this." He tried to explain (to her, to the others, to himself most of all) that what had happened was only a misstep, a hiccup, not fatal. "There's nothing between us that can't be fixed."

He was remarkably handsome, the man who stepped between them. Streamlined facial features, artfully tousled hair. A fucking turtleneck, no less. *Who the fuck wears a fucking turtleneck?* He worked at the gallery with Amy. *What was his name? Larry? Lewis? Something forgettable, anyway.*

The man put his fingers, lightly, against Thomas's chest. "Easy now . . ."

Thomas caught the trace of an accent. German? Dutch? Something insufferable. Even his haircut had an accent.

Thomas talked past him. "Amy, we need to work this out."

"No," she said. "We don't. We really don't."

Thomas tried to get closer, but the handsome man blocked his way. "Relax, okay?"

"*You* relax." Not the best retort, admittedly. What Thomas might have said, should have said, was *Hey, dickwad, why don't you transfer your sexual inadequacies onto someone else? She doesn't need rescuing.*

But instead he pushed on, pleading his case—badly. "Amy, we need to talk about the baby."

At this, the other man's arm dropped away. Even he was taken aback by this.

Amy stepped in, face distraught. "There was no baby. Don't you see? I drew it, with a pen. The blue line on the— I had to know. And now I do."

Thomas felt his knees give out. She kept talking but he couldn't hear. It was the ocean in a conch shell, the static between stations. He turned away, drunkenly, left the way he'd come. *If a plane crashes on the border, where do you bury the survivors?*

CHAPTER SIX

You don't bury survivors.

It was a riddle from Thomas's youth, one asked of him by men with clipboards who nodded approvingly at his answer.

But that was a long, long time ago. Today, a cartoon sun in sunglasses was giving viewers a cheery thumbs-up. *"Good morning, Boston! Your local forecast is next. Warm fall weather is on its way!"*

Thomas always wondered why cartoon suns wore sunglasses. It made no sense. The winter forecasts featured a snowman with a scarf. Rain was a duck with an umbrella. Snowmen might get cold, and ducks might get wet. But a sun radiates light. Why would it need sunglasses? He never could figure that out.

Thomas was waiting in the muffled silence of City TV's morning show. It had been years since Thomas had been inside a television studio, but it was still a familiar world. He was always struck by the empty intimacy of such places, cavernous and crowded at the same time. Thomas hung back, beside a wall of television monitors. Various feeds showed interchangeable reporters standing by. No sound. He looked for a volume control, but found none. Illuminated in the liquid glow of television screens, he watched as the monitors rolled over, one by one, onto a single image: a well-dressed gentleman with stone-cut features, heavy brow and greying hair, a lapel mic, pinned appropriately. Here was a man awaiting his moment. Here was a man sitting imperiously, posture perfect, back straight, without a flicker of doubt or a fidget of worry. A title appeared on the screen: *DR. ROSANOFF, author of "The Good Son."*

A predictably perky blonde with bulletproof hair was reading an intro off the teleprompter. She turned to Dr. Rosanoff with a practiced smile and Dr. Rosanoff began to speak. Thomas turned his attention away from the monitors to the studio itself, but he still couldn't hear what was being said. The host and her guest sat ringed by a circle of light, and Thomas could catch only the occasional interjection from the host, delivered with more punch than necessary. "Really?" "Wow!"

The floor manager walked past, a balding man with headphones; every floor manager that ever lived. When he spotted Thomas, he hurried over.

"What are you doing here? We're live. The greenroom's that way. We'll call you when it's time."

"I'm not a guest." Then, referring to the monitors: "How do I get sound?"

"What? No, no, no, out you go. I don't know how you managed to get in, but—" He was interrupted by the voice of Dr. Rosanoff echoing behind them.

"Tommy? Is that you?"

On set, they'd gone to commercial and Dr. Rosanoff was peering through the darkness, shielding his eyes with his book. "It is!"

Thomas stepped into a pool of light, lifted his hand in greeting. "Hey, Dad."

And that was when the floor manager realized who he'd been hectoring. "Oh my God. If you're his son, then you must be the . . ."

Dr. Rosanoff was calling to Thomas, eyes still shielded. "We've got one more segment. It won't take long. It's good to see you."

They began the countdown out of commercial. "Five . . . four . . ." and then, silently, on fingers, *three . . . two . . . one.*

"And we're back!"

The floor manager sidled closer to Thomas, whispered breathlessly, "So you must be . . . You're the . . ."

"You can say it."

"The Boy in the Box. My God, I feel like I know you. Don't go anywhere. I have a copy of the book, it's right here. One of our giveaways." He fumbled with the same heavy book that Thomas's father had been holding up: *The Good Son*, by Dr. Thomas Rosanoff, PhD. His father's face filled the entire front cover. The floor manager clicked his pen at Thomas, smiled awkwardly. "Would you mind? Murray. That's my name. My wife and I, when we had the twins, this was like our Bible. Would you write something?"

Thomas signed the book while barely looking. Later, when Murray checked what had been written, he would find the following message: *"Dear Murray, Fuck off. Best wishes, Thomas."*

Sound was leaking out of one of the monitors, faint but audible, and Thomas leaned in to listen, so closely that the image on the screen became pixelated and began to break up.

The host with the helmet of hair was asking, "It's been twenty years since the first edition. Ten years since the second. Does it *feel* that long? Or do you figure, 'What the heck, I'm not going to worry about—' "

"And still in print," Dr. Rosanoff noted. "Twenty years and still in print." He smiled, teeth brilliantly white in the studio light. Nice teeth. Expensive teeth. "It's been revised several times, of course, but overall, the crux of the matter, the approach to early childhood development and socialization, that hasn't changed. This new edition includes all the latest developments in the fields of nutrition, neurobiology, juvenile medication, and so forth. I'm quite pleased with how it holds up."

"That's the real test, isn't it? The test of time. How does that make you *feel*? To know that you've written—well, a classic, really. And Tommy. How does *he* feel? It's his childhood on display, after all."

Dr. Rosanoff looked off-camera, to where he imagined Thomas might be standing, lost in the glare, and he smiled with fatherly—and academic—pride. "The success of young Tommy speaks for itself. I truly have raised 'the good son.'"

The host turned back to the camera. "We've been speaking with renowned psychiatrist and author Dr. Thomas Rosanoff "—then, as a laughing aside thrown his way—"and I like how you worked the title in right at the end." She smiled again at the camera. "We have two copies to give away. No? Only the one? Okay, we have one copy of *The Good Son* to give away, so don't go anywhere! We'll be right back after traffic and weather."

The interview ended with Dr. Rosanoff caught in a close-up, still looking offscreen, still pixelated.

Later on, in the dressing room, Dr. Rosanoff would sit like an Easter Island rendering, head surrounded by a voluminous drape of cloth while the hair-and-make-up artist, spray-bottles slung about her waist, circled around him, wiping off his TV tan with soothing creams and hand towels. The mirror that he was enthroned before was outlined in prima donna lights. With Thomas standing behind the chair, they spoke to each other via the mirror.

"What brings you to this side of the river, Tommy? Studies going well, I trust? You look tired."

"Well," Thomas admitted. "That's sort of why I'm here." *I can't sleep, and when I do, I can't dream. I can't concentrate in class and I feel like I'm going to cry and I'm worried that if I do, I won't be able to stop. It feels like there's nothing inside me, not even emptiness. It feels like I'm on the other side of a wall, shouting to be heard. Like a dancer at odds with the dance.* "It's my thesis. I'm supposed to see Professor Cerletti this afternoon and, to be honest, I'm not ready."

Dr. Rosanoff nodded. "Bio-psych is a tough field, Tommy. I pioneered it. I should know."

"See, that's the thing. I'm not in bio-psych anymore. I switched to experimental neurology. Lab work, mainly, but still—still med school. Unfortunately, it's not going well, either."

"Neurology? When did this happen?"

"A few months ago. Well, last year, actually. I meant to tell you."

"You let me worry about Anton. That man owes me more than he can ever repay. It's hard enough for you as it is, living under my shadow. The expectations, the weight of your name." The make-up woman was now methodically wiping Dr. Rosanoff's neckline. "I should never have done that to you, Tommy. I should never have saddled you with 'Junior.' I'm a tough act to follow, I know that. I'll talk to Anton, sort it out. A new submission date?"

"A do-over. My research has stalled. I need to start again. A fresh thesis. Another year, at least."

"I'll take care of it. You concentrate on developing something good, something big. Something that will make a real name for yourself."

"I'll do my best."

"Everyone's watching you, Tommy."

"I know."

"Hoping you'll fail."

"I know."

"Prove them wrong."

"I will."

The make-up lady removed the cloth around Dr. Rosanoff's shoulders with a magician's flourish and he rose, body emerging from Easter Island, a towering figure in every sense.

"Other than that, life is good?"

No. "Yup."

"And how is she? The new one. Emily."

"Amy. We aren't together anymore."

Dr. Rosanoff held his arms outward while the woman brushed his sleeves, whisking him clean. "That's a shame. I liked her. Reminded me of your mother. Your mother had a spiritual side as well. I find it . . ." he searched for the right word, ". . . *endearing*." He said, "Walk with me," and Thomas did. Down endless hallways, past cramped recording studios and editing suites. "I remember Emily—"

"Amy."

"Amy. Saying grace, going on and on and on—at Red Lobster, no less. Do you remember how hard it was for us to keep a straight face? I liked her. It's a shame it didn't work out." He stopped at the receptionist's desk. "Tommy, I still have some things to wrap up here at the station. A panel discussion. Satellite relay, national. So, I'll have to say goodbye to you here. The Prius is running well?"

"It is."

He nodded. "Good. Let me worry about Cerletti. You concentrate on your research."

"Thanks." Thomas turned to go, then stopped. "Hey, Dad. You know how we were laughing? At Amy, when her eyes were closed?"

"She didn't hear anything, Tommy. She never noticed."

"I know. But we shouldn't have done that. It wasn't kind. We shouldn't have done that."

CHAPTER SEVEN

FOR ALL ITS APPARENT VARIATIONS, there are only two types of fame: the type that can get you laid, and the other kind. If you fell down a well as a child, that would be an example of the latter. Appearing on a second-rate reality cooking show—Season Two, the one with the mussels!—that would be an example of the former. Thomas's fame, paltry as it was, was of the fallen-down-a-well category. It was the "former-child-actor-arrested-in-a-liquor-store-holdup" variety of fame. The "one-hit-wonder-where-are-they-now?" or "baby on the Gerber bottle" style of celebrity. Perhaps because of this, Thomas had always held an affinity for those relics of past lives, the former child stars staring out at the world through their mug-shot freeze frames. You could see the bewilderment in their eyes. Thomas would study them whenever they appeared, in a magazine or on a screen, would search for signs of hope, of youth, buried somewhere in their gaze, but he never found it. Only that same stunned bewilderment you see with people who find themselves on the receiving end of an elaborate and unusually cruel practical joke.

In his second year of med school, Thomas had altered his identity, dropping his father's surname, adopting his mother's instead. *Thomas*

Alexander: two first names, yet somehow less than the sum of their parts. He'd started in experimental psychiatry and then switched to bio-psych, then to neuroscience and neurology, tunneling his way ever deeper into the human mind. *How far can you walk into a forest?* Another riddle from his youth. *Halfway. After that, you're walking* out *of the forest*. How far would Thomas have to tunnel before he came out the other side?

For such a complex knot of wiring, the brain itself is surprisingly easy to fool. Inept therapists have no problem planting false memories, optical illusions can trick the brain's visual perceptions with a breezy nonchalance, a brick to the noggin can scramble the circuitry and a tumour in the frontal lobe can turn a God-fearing parson into a sensual libertine. Thomas found this fascinating. He wanted to use his knowledge of the brain for the betterment of mankind, and he wanted to do it one person at a time. Starting with himself.

He first had an inkling that he could use his knowledge of the brain to get women to sleep with him when he was sitting through a particularly dull lecture. It was an idle thought, something to muse about while Professor Cerletti droned on and on about less and less interesting things. The lecture was on "mirror neurons." These lie at the heart of human empathy. That was the theory, anyway. Mirror neurons fire in reaction to other people's situations. Watch a game of basketball on TV and your own leg will twitch. Hear someone weep and your own eyes will well up. Witness a daredevil leap off a cliff in Acapulco and your own chest will tighten, your breath will catch in your throat, as though you yourself were about to take the plunge. True, mirror neurons are not *consciously* controlled, but . . . *what if?* What if you faked it? What if you consciously mimicked the facial expressions of someone else, their speech patterns, their turns of phrase? Wouldn't that trigger their own mirror neurons, make them feel closer to you, lower their defences?

Thomas doodled a note to himself about this; he would later learn that police interrogators and used-car salesmen employ the same technique, imitating the body language of suspects and potential customers, smiling when they smile, frowning when they frown, crossing their arms when they cross theirs, leaning forward, sitting up, looking down. A subconscious game of Simon Says, not unlike the Catholic masses he would later attend. If you could use mirror neurons to nab a murder suspect or net a sale, why not use this technique for more, shall we say, pleasurable goals? This was before he met Amy.

The way to a woman's heart, he realized, was through her brain.

At which moment, Thomas's phone vibrated. Bernie had sent him a text, even though he was sitting right next to him. It read: *"Booorrring."*

Professor Cerletti had brought up an overhead image of the limbic system, that interconnected series of organs that fits snugly into the brain's inner reaches like the pieces of a jigsaw puzzle. "The hypothalamus, located here in midbrain, is the primary pleasure centre."

Bernie sent another text. *"Not the clitoris?"*

Thomas: *"Apparently not."*

Bernie: *"Dammit. Now they tell me. Here I've been searching all this time for nothing."*

Thomas: *"The hypothalamus is probably easier to find."*

Bernie laughed. They hadn't noticed that Professor Cerletti was no longer talking, had in fact turned his baleful gaze upon them, nor that the lecture hall was now deathly quiet.

"Something amusing happening in the back?" Cerletti asked, locking his eyes onto Thomas with an undisguised animus.

"No, sir." *Nothing amusing at all.*

Thomas's first successful neurological seduction occurred soon after, almost by accident. He was living in a dormitory at the time and had, against his better judgment, attended a Friday-night party in the Common Room. *This is what normal students do. They hang out in the Common Room. I am a normal student; therefore, I will hang out in the Common Room.* A fairly straightforward syllogism, but one built on a false premise. Thomas would never be a "normal student."

He regretted coming as soon as he entered. The room was fogged with the skunkweed aroma of cannabis, was crowded and noisy with regrettable indie music bleating from someone's speakers. Bodies squeezed past, hands clutching bottles of cider and beer like security blankets. Navigating the room was like trying to wade through a swamp. Everyone was shouting to be heard. It was the rhetoric of dorm rooms, wherein the passion of one's opinions and the logic with which they were presented were inversely proportional. Here was the baffled rage of strident young men and women confounded by the fact that injustices were allowed to exist in this world. (They were not yet old enough to realize that injustice, like longing, gravity, taxes, or air, will always be a part of our world, not an anomaly. Not a tumourous outgrowth to be excised, but an inevitability.)

Competing punch lines and self-aggrandizing anecdotes, shrieks and sudden bursts of unprovoked laughter: the room became louder and louder as the students tried harder and harder to convince themselves they were having fun. Or maybe they *were* having fun. Maybe the problem was not with them, but with Thomas. The notion irritated him and he retreated to a corner, staked out a spot near the window. The window itself was open, though only a few inches (it could

go no farther; to prevent indie music–inspired suicides, he imagined).
The faint breeze it afforded was a welcome reprieve.

"Not a fan?"

He looked up. A young woman in a frosh-week sweatshirt and
a crooked smile was waiting for his response. *Not a fan?* For a moment he thought she was referring to mechanical fans and artificially
induced air circulation (he was standing by an open window, after
all). But no, she was referring to the music or maybe the cannabis or
maybe dorm parties in general.

"Nope," he said. "Can't say that I am. It'll pop your brain cells
like bubble wrap. You're almost guaranteed to come out with a lower
IQ than when you started."

"The weed?"

"The music."

She laughed. "Wendy," she said, presenting her hand.

"Like in Peter Pan," he noted.

"Yes! That's who I was named after. You're the first person not to
make a crack about hamburgers."

He offered his hand in turn. "Thomas," he said, "like the Tank
Engine."

"Thomas what?" she asked, shouting as the music built to an
ennui-fuelled crescendo.

He hesitated, then said, "Alexander." It was the first time he would
adopt his mother's maiden name.

"Nice to meet you, Thomas Alexander." She hadn't told him her
own last name. It was Burke, but he wouldn't learn that until two
sweaty sexual encounters and several sticky orgasms later.

For all its complexity, the human brain—as noted—can be tricked
with the simplest sleight of mind, and this would prove beneficial.

Thomas had come from an evening seminar on suggestibility, where they'd discussed the tenacity of certain ideas, the way in which an image or a notion, once planted in the cerebral cortex, can prove remarkably difficult to shake. He was about to learn the power of planting an idea in someone's mind firsthand.

"Want to go somewhere else?" he asked.

Wendy's lopsided smile was already sending electrical currents running through his autonomic nervous system, pumping blood—rather optimistically, all things considered—into his penile tissues, causing a slight but undeniable swelling. (You really have to admire the penis; it has absolutely no common sense whatsoever. *"Aye, aye! Reporting for duty, sir!"*)

"Sure," she said, still shouting. "Where do you want to go?"

"My room?" he said, a little too quickly.

"And what could you possibly have in your room that we don't already have here?"

"Board games," he said, and she laughed.

Laughter is good. A release of endorphins loosens inhibitions, momentarily disengages the critical functions of the brain's prefrontal lobe. (A woman's prefrontal lobe is the enemy of seduction. Emotional responses reside in the brain's limbic system, proper behaviour in the prefrontal lobes. Man's attempts at mating were largely a dogged effort in circumventing the prefrontal lobes and appealing directly to the limbic system.)

He leaned forward till his breath touched her neck, "Here's what I propose."

The word *propose* is always a good one to use when flirting. It resonates with images of diamond rings and Jumbotron swains, of a humbled man kneeling before a woman, a cheering crowd. "We go back to my place," he said, "put on some music, turn down the lights, get undressed, rub baby oil all over our bodies, and"—just as she was about to pull back, just as her face hardened—"we break out the Parcheesi."

She wasn't sure she'd heard correctly. "Parcheesi?"

"That's right. The board game. You haven't played nude Parcheesi? It's the best. There's also nude Sorry!, nude Battleship, nude Snakes and Ladders, nude Candy Land. I have a wide repertoire."

She laughed again, openmouthed and unrestrained.

They ended up back in Thomas's room, sitting cross-legged on the floor, speaking profoundly about trivial things (as you do) whilst drinking cheap college-dorm wine by the gallon—and is there anything sweeter in this world than the memory of cheap college-dorm wine? (Not the wine itself, which is horrid, but the memory of it.) Wendy was studying linguistics; Thomas was already considering the switch to neurological medicine. "A brain surgeon!" she said.

"Well," he admitted, "it's not exactly rocket science."

They never did play Parcheesi. But they did end up naked. The image he'd planted in Wendy's mind, of bodies unrobed and sheened in oil, had taken hold, had sent currents down her own autonomic nervous system, had tingled areas that lived for the tingling.

It's about reversal of expectations, Thomas realized as she grappled with his belt, sproinging him free from the tyranny of his trousers. *That's where the tension lies, in the reversal of expectations.* And what is it that tension demands? Release.

She pulled him into her. "Give it to me," she said, flustered and pink, for she was new at this as well and was trying her best. "Give it to me *hard*."

And . . . he didn't.

Instead, he pulled back. He slowed down, reduced his touch to the faintest of flutters, to ghostlike caresses and butterfly kisses. He slowed down until she was *out of her mind*—almost literally. She was now operating on brain stem alone, in the thrall of that reptilian structure in the base of our skull. Her desire was primal, as were her frustrations and her hoarse laugh, her final surrender. Afterward, sweaty and sated, she would admonish him, "You're awful." It was an accusation he would often hear. *You're awful.*

That first encounter would set the tone for the course of their time together. They'd study beside each other late into the night, and then, when their brains were tired and their bodies were demanding equal time, they would slither into each other's arms. Thomas would whisper, "How do you want it?" and no matter what she said—"gentle" or "slow," "hard" or "fast"—he would do the exact opposite. If she wanted it *now*, he would be agonizingly tender. If she wanted it languid and loving, he would drive it home to the hilt without pretext, would deny her the tenderness she thought she wanted. *Tension and release.*

Another game they played was "holding your breath when an intruder enters the room." Wendy's dorm room was two floors down, and sometimes, late at night, she would stretch and say she was going to bed, and Thomas would feign indifference, except to remind her, "Don't forget to lock your door."

He would then wait ten minutes, maybe twenty, sometimes half an hour, and would tiptoe down the stairwell, would find her door unlocked, would open it slowly—if only the hinge creaked to have made the moment complete! Wendy would be lying in bed, facing the wall, pretending to sleep. Looming above her, Thomas would slide his belt free, would crawl in beside her, and then—hand over her mouth—would tell her not to move, not to make a sound. He would churn into her from behind, pushing her to the brink . . . and then over. And when he was finished, he would slip away, leaving her in a heap, always making sure to lock the door behind him.

And then, one day, Wendy came bounding over after class with her textbook open to page 145 and it was all over. She was taking an intro course in psychology, and she asked excitedly, "Is this you? It is, isn't it! Why didn't you tell me your real name?"

Thomas felt his jaw clench, his face burn. He ended it soon after.

The following spring, Thomas moved out of the dormitory and into the townhouse apartment his father had arranged for him. Dr. Rosanoff would have purchased a condo for his son—a better investment, building up equity rather than throwing money away in rent—but the market was inflated and the timing wasn't right. As his father often reminded him, "Every major decision you make in life needs to be carefully weighed." (Wendy, meanwhile, would lie in her room, door unlocked, facing the wall, waiting for someone who never showed. Sometimes, late at night, she would sob.)

It had only ever been an experiment, Thomas living in a dormitory: a way to experience normal life. And every experiment, like every love affair, must eventually end.

CHAPTER EIGHT

"TICKLING THEIR HYPOTHALAMUS is all fine and good," Bernie had said, peering over his glasses at his lab partner. Thomas had been regaling him with the details of his ongoing neuropsychological experiments in the Science of Seduction, but Bernie had remained skeptical. "To be really effective," said Bernie, "you have to learn to read a potential conquest's facial expressions."

This was true. Thomas did sometimes misread the situation. On occasion, his more exuberant test subjects would pounce before he'd even gotten to the moment of reversal. *"Listen, why don't we go back to my place, get undressed, rub baby oil over our naked bodies, and—" "Cool! Let me grab my jacket."* Those were pleasant revelations when they occurred, but at other times Thomas would mistime his pitch, and the target of his would-be seduction would cut him off before he could finish. He would see frost crackle across their gaze and no matter how hurriedly he exclaimed, *"Parcheesi!"* (a magical word, akin to *alakazam* or *abracadabra*—*"Hocus pocus! Clothes be gone!"*), it was too late. Their prefrontal lobes had taken over, were now guarding the gates. Oh, how he resented those damnable prefrontal lobes!

Bernie had been doing research for Professor Cerletti on "microexpressions," tiny facial shifts—flashes of fear, lust, anger, despair—

barely perceptible, wholly involuntary, and often lasting less than a hundredth of a second, appearing when someone suppresses their true feelings. Although not usually discernible to the conscious mind, these micro-expressions can be picked up on tape. Slow the footage down, and they will jump out at you. A test subject is happily describing her day-to-day life when the topic of, say, her marriage comes up, and there it is in stark relief: a face filled with pain and anguish, a flutter, gone in an instant.

"Want to know what makes us human?" asked Bernie.

"Opposable thumbs?"

"The fake smile. The *social* smile. That's what separates us. Other animals express their emotions openly, all the time. Only humans have learned to mask them." But a mask is still a mask, and the real feelings are still there, trying to get out. "You can see a clear difference, for example, between a spontaneous smile and a forced smile. It's in the eyes. Here, let me show you."

They were in the cafeteria, peering into the faces (souls?) of various test subjects who were stored on Bernie's laptop. "See? We ask her if she's happy in her relationship and she says 'Sure!' Big smile, but slow it down and . . . *there*. Her mouth is smiling but her eyes tell a different story. That's a fake smile, my friend. A spontaneous smile will linger longer as well. See how quickly that one falls away? If I were her husband, I'd be worried."

"So poker tells are really micro-expressions?" Thomas asked.

"Basically, yes. They're very hard to suppress, even harder to read. But break down any facial expression into its component parts and you can crack the code."

Bernie pulled up a map of the human face with various groupings labelled.

"The face is basically a communications device. There are forty-four facial muscles, and a full forty of those are used to express emotions. Certain groups fire in sync, others in opposition. It's called the Ekman Facial Action Coding System. So, a contraction in the lateral cheek muscles, together with a flattening of the upper lip and expansion of the outer nostrils? That would signify repulsion. If you catch that, you might as well move on. A constriction at the *sides* of the mouth—signifying a suppressed smile—with slightly raised eyebrows and a dimpling effect in the chin, well, that's promising." There was a pause. "I don't see that one very often."

Thomas had better luck.

Following Bernie's tutorial, he was able to adjust his presentations depending on the signals he was receiving, sometimes going into greater and even more lurid detail (watching the arc of their eyebrows expand and expand). With one young woman he managed to add whipped cream, honey, and a feather duster to his proposed scenario before uttering the magic word. "Sounds messy." She laughed. "Aren't you afraid of ruining your Parcheesi board?" "That's a chance I'm willing to take," he said. Having ratcheted up the tension, the night had ended in greater fury than usual. With expectations raised to such heady heights, the onus had been on her to deliver— and she'd come through admirably. *Thank you, Bernie!* he'd grinned as he walked home. (He never learned her name. Or if he did, he didn't remember it.)

Once he had his test subjects in bed, or on the dining room table or holding on to the balcony rails, it was always the same question, whispered in their ear: "How do you want it?" *Ask and ye shall receive the exact opposite.*

Word, however, has a way of spreading, and when one attractive pre-med student stopped him in mid-incantation to say, "Are you the Parcheesi guy?" he knew his study had run its course.

He discovered his next set of subjects soon after.

Having once again slept in a strange bed, Thomas woke alone, cotton-mouthed and groggy, to a silent room, had gotten dressed, left a scribbled note (the extent of modern etiquette in such matters), and then slipped out into a bleary-eyed morning, feeling empty and alive. He would've killed for a coffee, so when he passed a bookstore café, he ducked inside. But the shop had just opened—the coffee was still brewing—so Thomas wandered the stacks awhile, avoiding Self-Help, looking for Science, when he spotted something remarkable. Although the bookstore as a whole was largely empty, the Travel Section was not. Three different women were running their fingers along the spines of guidebooks and travel memoirs. Soccer moms, from the looks of it, women who had dropped their kids off at school and then stopped here to dream awhile before returning to the everyday mundanities of life. *Paris. Paraguay. Portugal. Qatar. Cambodia.* A world so far away it hardly seemed real. Here, he realized, was an aching, a *longing*, that he might be able to assist with.

And so it was that the Travel Sections of Boston's bookstores became Thomas's hunting grounds. He would arrive as soon as they opened (the moms always came in first thing in the morning to sip lattes and sigh among the atlases) and Thomas would watch and wait, select one of the moms as a test subject, and then take note of where she lingered: Okinawa or Macao, Morocco or Istanbul—you could almost taste the desire and loneliness—and then, using his phone, he would look up a few salient points about the destination in question. From there it was an easy step to choose a similar guidebook. "I've always wanted to visit Morocco, too! The walled city of _____ or the markets of _____. But," and here he used the Ekman Facial Action Coding System to create a wistful self-deprecating smile, "I'm only a broke university student, so who knows if I'll ever make it. Maybe someday . . ." His voice would trail off, pregnant with possibility, at which point the soccer mom's own mirror neurons would kick in. "Oh, don't say that. You're so young. You still have time."

The longing for travel is, of course, the longing for escape, and while he couldn't whisk the soccer moms off to Istanbul, he could at least offer a few hours' idyll in the afternoon. (He often skipped classes to do so; he was something of a philanthropist that way.)

Doctors can identify a brain as male or female simply by looking at it: female brains are more symmetrical, with greater interconnections between the emotional and the cognitive. The male brain, in contrast, looks as though someone took a normal brain and gave it a sharp twist: the lobes don't line up with the same precision, and the areas that connect the right brain to the left—and the rational frontal cortex with the emotional limbic system—are smaller, less tightly woven. Fewer connections means fewer distractions, better focus; it also means less nuance.

Female brains have more surface area, male brains more volume. But when it comes to sexual arousal, brain scans reveal a deeper, even greater divide, with male sexuality more closely linked to those regions that handle aggression, and female sexuality more closely associated with hunger. Thomas had made note of that as well: male, aggression; female, hunger. The trick, then, was to play to that hunger, to that *appetite*, whether physiological, psychological, or emotional.

Thomas drew a circle around the city and by systematically visiting every Barnes & Noble in Boston and the outlying areas, ranging as far as Salem at times (an especially fertile constituency), he quickly worked his way through several PTA rosters. His youthful demeanour appealed to their maternal instincts, and more than one fretted about his finances, asking whether he was "eating properly."

Soccer moms smell of fabric softener. Soccer moms wear lululemon to Whole Foods. Soccer moms close the curtains before they undress, trying to blot out the sunlight (but light will find a way; it seeps in unbidden; eyes adjust and details emerge; although, as Thomas would discover, the gaze goes both ways). Soccer moms are starved for laughter. They laugh easily. They are sardonic and wry. They are embarrassed about their stretch marks, but not ashamed. Soccer moms have tricks they haven't used in years, and they like to finish on top. They would roll Thomas onto his back and stare into his eyes when he was inside them. He learned to avert his gaze, just as he learned to avoid looking at their children's toys on the floor or the report cards on the fridge. (He often wondered what grade they would give him: A for effort?) He preferred to experience the world they inhabited primarily through his peripheral vision. He even managed, having caught a glimpse of *The Good Son* on one shelf, to pretend he was someone else entirely.

Soccer moms didn't take his question seriously the way younger women did—"How do you want it?" They guffawed instead, saw his game for what it was. But they always answered, and they always chose one or the other.

Soccer moms alluded to their husbands but never disparaged them, and even better, they always fed Thomas afterward—usually a sandwich, sometimes a Yoplait, too—and dropped him off at his campus, pulling him in for one final, desperately wet, open-mouth kiss among the minivan ruins of crumpled juice boxes and discarded

Subway wrappers. One final desperate kiss before returning to a tepid world of tennis lessons and Facebook updates. They would text him later, flirting with varying degrees of skill, and a few even arranged repeat performances, but none made heavy demands on his time and none ever offered to leave their husbands for him. He was a diversion and he knew it. (He liked to think he provided a service, much like the Roto-Rooter Man or a furnace cleaning company.) It was a good run, his time among the soccer moms, and it might have continued indefinitely, wrapped in warm comforters and cups of postcoital cocoa and minivan make-out sessions, if it hadn't been for a single slip of the tongue. Not on Thomas's part.

One mom, more frazzled than most, had dragged him into her bedroom, apologizing for the mess even as she was tugging at his clothes. She'd answered his inevitable question by gasping, "I want it deep and slow. Make me *feel*."

Had she misspoken?

Had she inadvertently left off the final pronoun, the "it" or the "you"? Or, worse, had the missing word been "again"? It was hard to say, but either way, Thomas never went back to the Travel Section, and he never had to look up into the steady gaze of soccer moms again.

CHAPTER NINE

WAS IT LOVE AT first sight? Perhaps. The phenomenon of sudden infatuation, or "love at first sight," as it's known, is the result of definable chemical reactions in the brain. It occurs in the *amygdala*, an almond-sized cluster of cells buried deep in the temporal lobe, and the *hippocampus*, a seahorse-shaped structure that curls around the brain's interior. The almond and the seahorse help sort out incoming sensations, assigning emotional importance to each, deciding what matters and what doesn't. They are triggered, in turn, by the visual cortex of the brain's *occipital lobe*. When these three areas fire in sync, a fourth region of the brain, one that specializes in facial recognition, will sometimes *mis*fire. The result? A person you've just met seems instantly familiar, instantly loveable. It's that strange sensation of meeting someone again for the first time, of having known them forever, as though you'd been waiting for them your whole life but hadn't known it. Perhaps this is what happened when Thomas met Amy for the first time, a cascade of chemical reactions. Romantic, yes?

The other symptoms of "love at first sight"—the shiver in the chest, the increased heartbeat, the sense of dizziness, the sudden draining of the temporal lobes, home to our higher language functions (hence the stammering, tongue-tied nature of those stricken)—are simply outward manifestations of what the seahorse in our brain has already set in motion. Alas, not many love sonnets have been written to the hippocampus or the amygdala. More's the pity. Biology does all the work, poets take the credit. In the end, there's nothing mystical about the experience. Except, of course, for the experience itself. *There's the rub*: science still doesn't know how the brain creates mind, how the mind creates self, how the self creates ideas, or how chemistry alone can conjure up something as intangible as a feeling. Does explaining love at first sight also explain it away, or does it only heighten the mystery? These are questions best left for another time.

Amy arrived like an electrical impulse. It had been a bad day; that may have been part of it. Thomas's limbic system was probably searching for some kind of reward, some sort of positive stimulus, anything.

Only moments earlier, he and Bernie had been reigning triumphant, having successfully cornered God in the brain's left temporal lobe. (If you imagine the brain as a pair of boxing gloves with the thumbs turned to the outside, the temporal lobes form the thumbs, situated above the temples, for which they are named.)

The experiment began with an offhand remark by Professor Cerletti. "We don't need to grasp for supernatural explanations to religious impulses," he'd intoned from his lectern. "The conversion of Saint Paul on the Road to Damascus, for example. The bright light, the temporary blindness, the Voice of God. Clearly the result of a physiological disorder, most likely epilepsy. Patients who experience seizures in the left temporal lobe often describe feelings of profound meaning, the presence of an intangible entity. God is a seizure in the temporal lobe. Saint Paul was an epileptic. Joan of Arc was schizophrenic. And what are religious rituals, with their endless repetitions and obsessive attention to details, if not socially sanctioned OCD? There are no psychological problems, only medical ones. Mental illness is a symptom, it's not a diagnosis. Mental illness is simply the outward manifestation of a neurobiological issue."

This got Thomas thinking: *If Saint Paul encountered God not on the Road to Damascus, but in his left temporal lobe, why couldn't you re-create this experience in a laboratory?*

Thus the God helmet was born.

Together with Bernie, Thomas had rigged up a contraption that would pulse low-level electromagnetic currents through a test subject's temporal lobes. They threaded a second magnetic coil over the top of the helmet to stimulate the parietal lobe as well, the area that helps distinguish our sense of self from our surroundings, the "orientation association" area, as it is known. It anchors us in time and place. Interfering with that region can create a sense of floating, of disengagement, of merging with a larger reality. By stimulating these two lobes—the temporal and the parietal—the goal was to recreate an encounter with an otherworldly presence. In a word: God.

Bernie and Thomas commandeered a corner in one of the basement labs for their project, moving—or rather, rearranging—the junk-pile clutter of previous scholarly studies. When he'd first enrolled at the Hawthorne Institute of Brain Sciences, Thomas had expected the laboratories to be sleek, polished affairs, sterile and clean with white-coated scientists striding past to great purpose. Instead, one swam through a series of antechambers, down hallways worthy of a Minotaur—made all the more narrow by an eclectic array of refrigerators squeezing in from either side. Not high-tech cooling containers but dented Frigidaires of dubious provenance in various sizes and shapes, forming a ragtag honour guard, all of them humming different tones, rescued from second-hand stores from the looks of it, with hand-scrawled messages taped on the doors: *"Specimens only!"* and *"Keep this closed!!"*

The labs folded in on themselves, the equipment and cabinets forming snug corridors and cul-de-sacs. Endless beakers and other assorted glassware lined the shelves. There were osmometers to measure salt in the solutions—too much salt and the cells shrink; not enough and they swell—and pH meters to gauge acidity. Brooding fume hoods squatted above loosely coiled ventilators that sucked up mouse dander and chemical contrails. Water distillers drip-drop-dripping. Glass pullers to cut razor-sharp, filament-thin syringes. Eye washes and protective goggles. Tissue box–style containers of disposable gloves. A murky fishbowl, with a fish presumably inside (someone's neglected pet, no doubt). A waxy-leafed plant, probably plastic. (It looked far too healthy to exist in the depths of the catacombs, as the basement labs were referred to by staff and faculty alike.)

"A lovely ambience in this corner of the catacombs," said Bernie as he set up the tripod and video camera. "I like how the smell of ammonia complements the mildew." A small fridge marked LUNCHES ONLY!! contained several ongoing experiments in the effects of bread mould on baloney sandwiches.

Compressed-air tanks were wedged in every which way, with rubber tubings running between the lab's cumbersome confocal microscopes. These microscopes floated on cushions of air, and so precise and minute were the images they collected that the slightest tremor—a door closing on the other side of a wall, footsteps in the hall—could ruin the readings.

Signs, posted: *"Passcards are to be worn at all times!"* (duly ignored), "*If I'm talking, you should be taking notes!*" (likewise), and "*WARNING: Premises Patrolled by Trained Attack Rat.*" Every available patch of wall space in between was layered with photo collages of colleagues on ski trips and holidays, on Cancun beaches and in Vegas lobbies, hamming it up for the cameras with frilly umbrella drinks and hoisted beer mugs, urgent reminders of Life Outside the Laboratory. (These photos had been compiled over several decades, a forensic study of questionable fashion choices and regrettable haircuts, stretching back to sideburns and flare pants: the gap-toothed smiles of Polaroids and faded Kodachrome snapshots. Somewhere in the layers was a younger Cerletti, a younger Rosanoff.)

It was here, in the contained chaos of a university lab, that Bernie and Thomas set up shop. With office hours over, they had the run of the place. Their subjects were drawn from the usual ranks: undergrads who needed the money and were thus ideally pliant. The pay was paltry, but pizza doesn't pay for itself! (A great wealth of our scientific knowledge is based on broke undergrads who are short on cash and, thus, ideally pliant.) The bulletin notice that Bernie and Thomas had posted on campus asked potential participants: *"Would you like to have an encounter with God? Here's your chance!"*

Sessions typically lasted twenty minutes in a dimly lit room with soft music playing. Sure enough, the parade of undergrads that strapped on the helmet reported having spiritual experiences, a "separation of body and soul." "It's like, there's someone here . . . who's not here." "A presence." "A spirit guide." "My dead grandmother. I could feel her near me." "It was calming." "Mystical." "Comforting." "Scary." "It felt like I was lifting out of my body!"

Here was the biological source of religion. God was merely the brain playing tricks on itself.

"We did it!" said Bernie. "We solved the riddle!"

When the last of their test subjects had departed, Thomas plucked a pair of cold beers from a fridge, the same fridge used to store urine samples and plasma. A scattering of magnetic poetry formed the unintentional message *"where biology is bold are curious"* on the refrigerator door, and Bernie and Thomas congratulated themselves on the success of their experiment in what promised to be a paradigm-shifting study. "This will move the field!" said Thomas. Bernie (being a lapsed Catholic) made a sign of the cross (jokingly, of course) and shouted, "Forgive us, Father, for we have sinned!" And then, with a sly grin, "Can you imagine the look on the priests' faces when they find out?" Bernie could already see his name lit up in Nobel Prize announcements. " 'Evidence of God as a Neurochemical Phenomenon Originating in the Brain's Left Temporal and Parietal Lobes,' by Doctors (*in fieri*) Bernard Flanagan and Thomas—" He looked at Thomas, unsure. "What name would you . . . ?"

"Alexander," he said. "Let's stick with that." Thomas tipped back his beer, took a long draw. "How is it an Irishman like you ended up with a name like Bernie anyway?" he asked.

"After the saint. Or maybe the dog. Dad was vague on the details."

"To the end of the saints!" said Thomas, and they clinked their bottles like they were crossing swords—only to have Cerletti show up and ruin everything.

The professor cast his stick-thin figure over the proceedings like an insect Ichabod Crane, although, with his imperious manner and perpetually dour features, he reminded Thomas of one of the lesser Caesars. Not an Augustus or even a Caligula, but a Diocletian or a Galerius. *And that ridiculous streak of white hair running from his widow's peak. That has to be an affectation. No one goes grey like that.*

"Gentlemen," he said.

"Professor," they replied, sitting up straighter reflexively.

"I caught wind of what was going on down here in the catacombs." The professor gestured toward the contraption that was sitting on the table, wires braided into imbedded electrodes. "It looks like a football helmet."

"It, um, is," said Thomas.

"And these tests you're running, double-blind?"

"We're following proper scientific protocols," said Bernie (evading the question).

"And yet, you clearly advertised the opportunity—how was it you put it?—*to meet God*. Calling it a 'God helmet' would suggest you are trying to influence the outcome, no?"

"We never called it a God helmet," Thomas said.

"It's written on the side."

Oh, right. Damn. Bernie had indeed emblazoned the helmet with cool flames and the words B & T'S AWESOME GOD HELMET.

"That was for fun," Bernie explained. "The test subjects probably didn't notice."

"I see."

Thomas could feel his face begin to burn.

Cerletti nodded thoughtfully. They recognized that nod; it was the Nod of Doom. "So," said the professor. "Not double-blind, not randomized, not controlled. And I'm guessing the results are anecdotal rather than statistical. Congratulations, gentlemen. You have discovered suggestibility, something that has been known for six hundred years."

"The science behind this is still sound," Thomas said, "even if—"

"Oh, it's science, all right. It's just not good science. Gentlemen, do it properly or don't do it at all. This"—he waved a hand at the video camera on its tripod, the notebook, the microphone, the helmet itself (which now seemed less magnificent, more ridiculous)—"is a stunt." And with that, Cerletti flung his toga over his shoulder and departed. *Fucking silver streak in your fucking hair.*

"Asshole," said Bernie (after Professor Cerletti had left).

The beer tasted flat now.

Even worse, Cerletti had been right. They had indeed discovered suggestibility. (When they attempted to reproduce their results later on in a double-blind study, wherein neither the people administering the procedure nor those taking part knew what was being tested, and with all the proper controls in place—which is to say, randomized test subjects who received no electrical stimulation to their temporal lobes as well as those who did—the only effect was faint nausea and the occasional headache. God had once again eluded their net, had once again escaped.)

The two of them were packing up their equipment when Amy arrived, out of breath, cheeks as pink as bubble gum. Thomas was feeling deflated and embarrassed: perhaps that's what triggered the cascade of chemicals we call infatuation. His dopamine-depleted brain was yearning for some sort of jolt, and when Amy entered the room it was as though a switch had been thrown. A new neural pathway was carved into the soft tissues of Thomas's inner cerebrum.

She was clutching one of their notices, torn from a hallway bulletin board. "Am I too late?" she asked. "You're the ones looking for God, right? In the brain?"

Of course in the brain. Where else? That's what Thomas wanted to say, but the words wouldn't come. Heart rate: elevated. Chest muscles: contracting. Sudden dampness in the armpits. Vocabulary draining away. "That's, ah— That's right. What you said."

Bernie looked up from the extension cord he was winding into a box. "Sorry," he said. "We're all done."

Thomas shot him a look. "I think we have time for one more."

"But Cerletti told us to . . . Oh. I see."

"Bernie," said Thomas. "Could you pass me one of the forms?"

"The forms?"

"On the desk," Thomas said, through clenched teeth.

"Oh, right, *those* forms." A twitch appeared on Bernie's lips, a hint of a smile, there and then gone. A hell of a tell, that one, and one of the reasons Bernie was so bad at poker and so good at small talk.

It's hard to say what it was specifically about Amy that set the dominoes toppling over in Thomas's mind that day. She wasn't looking particularly attractive. Most of her hair, pulled back, had escaped the scrunchy and was falling forward. Her face was mottled and flushed from running. Perhaps that was it: the fact that she was flushed and out of breath. Perhaps the mirror neurons in Thomas's brain triggered a similar reaction: heightened respiration, a dizzy feeling.

They were lost in a laboratory labyrinth, a decidedly non-erotic milieu, almost the definition of non-erotic (look up *erotic* in a dictionary and it reads: "*antonym, see*: science, lab, laboratory, research, research laboratory, et al."), and yet, Thomas felt that familiar rush of desire. The romance of unlikely places.

"Here you go." Bernie slid a clipboard across the desk to Thomas, facedown. When Thomas turned it over, there was a blank piece of paper on the other side.

"Now then," Thomas said, taking out a pen and pretending to read from a list. "We have a standard set of questions we need to

go through. Age, hobbies . . . telephone number. That sort of thing.
Let's start with your name."

"Amy Lamiell."

"Oh, French?"

"I guess, at some point."

"And can I get your phone number? Perfect. And your email?
Thanks. You're a student? Terrific. What are you studying? Visual
arts. That's wonderful. I've always admired the early Impressionists,
myself. And are you currently in a relationship? No? Great. And what
type of music do you enjoy?"

She was confused. "What does any of this have to do with—"

Bernie interjected, speaking in a *highly* professional manner.
"Ma'am, we need to create a personality profile in order to get a sense
of your emotional state prior to the test. It's standard practice."

"Standard," said Thomas. "And how about food? What type of
restaurants do you like? Thai, you say?"

Thomas was busy analyzing physical clues as well, studying Amy
with a steely Sherlockian resolve. *Fingernails, closely cut.* (A sign of
biting? Anxiety?) *Traces of different colours embedded around the nails.*
(Remnants of various nail polishes, apparently. Insecurity? Or inde-
cision? Either was a good sign, as this added a touch of vulnerability;
self-possessed women were hard to seduce.) *Hair, falling over half her
face.* (An unconscious desire to hide or withdraw? Possible feelings of
alienation? Isolation?)

She had a faint dusting of freckles across her nose, so faint they
looked like they might come off with a warm washcloth. *Beautiful
imperfections.*

Thomas's analysis was precise and methodical, and absolutely
wrong. Thomas had struck out on every item: Amy's nails were kept

short so that when she kneaded clay or mixed glazes nothing would get caught underneath; what Thomas had thought were multiple attempts at choosing nail polish were in fact various colours of paint she hadn't quite scrubbed off her hands; her hair had been pulled back because she'd hurried over to the lab right after her last studio class and her hair had come loose while she was running through the corridors and down the stairs hoping to catch Thomas and Bernie before they left. It was two minutes to five when she arrived. (He was right about the freckles, though. They were indeed beautiful imperfections.)

"Is that the . . . the mechanism?" she asked, referring to the God helmet that Bernie was now setting up.

"It is," Thomas said. "So let's dim the lights, start recording, see what happens."

After the tests, they removed the helmet, and Amy was in tears. "Nothing," she said, trying not to break down in front of them. "I felt nothing. Nothing." Not God. Not even nausea. Amy was an outlier, immune to suggestibility. She pulled on her coat, hands shaking as she buttoned up, and fled.

Thomas would have followed her into the catacombs, would have tried to comfort her, but there was no need.

"Hi! Amy? It's me, Thomas Alexander. You came in for the experiment with the God helmet last week. Listen. I felt bad about how it ended. Can I take you out to dinner to make up for it? There's a Thai restaurant near my place, just down the street from a club that features a terrific jazz trio. No? Are you sure? Well, if not dinner, would you like to come back for a follow-up study? This would be for a brain scan. We use an IV, inject a tracer, follow its path. It allows us to map out your mind, pinpoint where your sense of spirituality resides."

She said no to dinner, but came back for the follow-up test.

Forging Cerletti's signature to gain access to the lab's PET scan after hours was simple enough (and it's not like Thomas and Bernie had attempted to access one of the school's prohibitively expensive MRIs; no, they'd shown a certain amount of restraint).

"But why do we have to do this at night?" she asked.

"Easier access. And hey, afterwards, there's a jazz band playing on campus, if you'd like to go. The food court has Thai as well."

They asked Amy to recite a centering prayer (her choice; a form of Catholic meditation said to bring one's soul into spiritual alignment) while they took a snapshot of her brain, and although the entire procedure was mainly a ruse—that's right, Thomas was willing to inject low-level radioactive material into her bloodstream to get a second chance at a date—he'd watched her brain light up, but not in ways he expected.

"She's engaging her frontal lobes almost exclusively," Bernie pointed out after she'd left (having again turned down Thomas's offer of jazz, even though she had clearly stated that was her preferred choice in music).

The two of them had her scan up on the screen, were—in effect—peering into Amy.

"That's weird."

Faith, they'd been told, originated in the emotional regions of the brain. But not so with Amy.

"It's like she's *choosing* to believe," Bernie said. It was as improbable as *choosing* to fall in love. We're just molecules, after all, and yet, here she was, glowing in the radioactive half-life, *deciding* to believe. And if we could choose something as irrational as faith, thought Thomas, could we also choose madness? Sanity? It was an idea that would linger like a tune caught in his head, and it would set other, larger dominoes in motion.

Amy would eventually say yes to Thomas for dinner (a testament to persistence; he kept asking till she relented). He took her to a jazz bar, where he pretended to enjoy it, and then out for late-night pad thai. (He was banking on all that noodle slurping to trigger subconscious oral fixations.) They ended up back at her messy apartment, where she showed him her canvases and made him a cup of tea. This was followed by conversation with kisses, and then kisses with conversation, until finally it was only kisses; they had replaced conversation entirely: a predictable progression, yet one with endless variation. *Not unlike jazz*, Thomas thought.

The hardest part was hiding who you were. Amy was the first girl he ever told willingly, confessing his Rumpelstiltskin identity to her under the ecclesiastical candlelight of her studio. She'd hardly reacted, had hardly seemed interested, in fact, something he tried to convince himself was refreshing. *She doesn't care! Isn't that wonderful!* (The sad truth is that Amy didn't want to know, didn't want the added burden of Thomas's family history; she had burdens enough of her own, and was worried that in making his confession Thomas had opened the curtain for further disclosures on both sides.)

Sometimes when she was sleeping, Thomas would lie beside her, would softly inhale her breath as she exhaled. Toothpaste and tea.

CHAPTER TEN

IT POURED THE DAY AFTER Thomas saw his father at the television studio: great bucket-throws of water dousing the streets, cars hydroplaning past, fanning water onto pedestrians. So much for the sun in sunglasses. This was duck with an umbrella weather.

Thomas went through his mail before he left, hoping in that sadly deluded way of rejected lovers that Amy might have reached out, but there were only the usual letters from people asking him for advice (because of his father's book) or wanting to share the story of their own childhoods. They came in bundles, two or three times a year, redirected from his father's publisher and they were, by turn, needy, greedy, demanding, exhausting, trivial, heartrending. He never answered any of them. The only unusual entry in this batch was a loose postcard of a generic landscape, instantly forgettable save for the message written on the back: a single sentence in cramped, boxy letters, as though the person who'd sent it was trying to hide their handwriting: REMEMBER ME?

No name or return address, so no. No, I don't remember you.

Thomas sensed a certain anger lurking behind the question, a vague threat. But the feeling quickly passed, and Thomas tossed the postcard in the recycling box with the rest of the letters. It was only as he was pulling on his overcoat that he stopped, went back, retrieved it. The postcard hadn't been forwarded to him by his father's publisher; it had been mailed directly to his apartment. Whoever sent it knew where he lived. A former lover? One of his soccer moms? Not worth worrying about. He discarded the postcard again and stepped out, into the rain.

A long walk brought him past Our Lady of Constant Sorrow. The tattered vagrant was still there, maintaining his vigil, the handwritten sign proclaiming himself Saviour held in front of his chest like a number in a police arrest photograph. A mug-shot Messiah. Jesus on the sidewalk. The tent-like tarp he had set up was sagging under a pool of rain, and the man himself stood out front, hoodie soaked, beard streaming, facing Our Lady of Constant Sorrow. *You'd think the Son of God would have enough sense to come in from the rain.* Thomas hurried past him, leaning into the wind behind an umbrella that threatened to turn inside out at any moment.

The homeless shelter was down an alley from Our Lady, a cinder block building that had once been a juvenile detention centre. The ragged men and bag ladies inside were crowded around long, low tables as volunteers moved through, clearing plates, topping up cups of coffee, teasing patrons.

"Beautiful weather!"

"Did you order this rain?"

Rheumy eyes and waterlogged hearts. The musty smell of wet hair. Thomas shook out his umbrella and approached one of the volunteers, a thin-faced gentleman barely distinguishable from the people he was serving.

"Is Frances in?" Thomas asked.

"Frances?" The man's face clouded over. "Don't know anybody by that name."

"*Sister* Frances," he said. "Frances Mary Bedford. She's a nurse."

"Nurse?"

"And a nun."

"Oh, right. Didn't know her name. She's in the back, in the men's dorm."

Down a sallow hallway into the leaden light of the dormitory. Rows of cots. Damp coughs. Every bed was full: women in the front room, men in the back. It reminded Thomas of a Civil War battlefield triage.

Frances Bedford (*Sister* Frances Bedford) stood in a haze of light with a medical kit open on the cot beside her. Her laminated Community Health ID read "SR. FRANCES," which had earned her the nickname "Sir Frances." She was examining a gaunt old man, more sinew than muscle, who sat with his shirt off, staring into the middle distance. Frances didn't look much like a nun: no Sally Field winged hat, no soft-focus eyes fixed ever-heavenward, no crucifix clutched between praying hands. She wore a plain olive-green dress that looked more like hospital scrubs than a nun's habit. Grey hair, pulled back. Face as creased as linen.

"Hold still, Charlie."

The old man's back was wet with sores, and as Frances applied cotton and gauze, Thomas sauntered up with a big fake smile plastered on his face.

"We could use a drop of golden sun," Thomas said.

She glanced his way. "Look what the cat dragged in. Make yourself useful. Grab me that tape."

He handed her a roll, along with some disinfectant.

"Are you a doctor yet?" she asked.

"Soon."

"Ants," the old man said.

"You have to wash more often, Charlie," she said, speaking slowly. "I'll check in on you, but you have to help." She held up a tube of ointment. "Twice a day, okay? When you wake up and before you go to sleep. Shelley will assist you, but you have to remind her, okay?"

"Ants," he rasped. "They're under my skin."

Thomas looked to Frances. "He needs quetiapine."

"Quetiapine?"

"Maybe lithium."

She gave Thomas a sour look.

"What?" said Thomas. "This patient is clearly hallucinating. He needs to be medicated. Any atypical antipsychotic drug should do the trick."

"What he needs is to get these sores to heal. The ants are in his imagination. The bedsores are real."

"Frances, those bedsores are only a symptom."

"So are the ants, Tommy. So are the ants." She gathered up her supplies. "You sound like your father. How is he anyway? Still famous?"

"Dad? He's still Dad, only more so."

"You're all done, Charlie. You can put on your shirt now."

Frances pushed her cart down the next row of cots. "Grab a bedpan, Tommy." Then, warning him: "Next one's a colostomy. The trick is to pinch the valve *before* you turn it."

The smell, even with the disinfectant, reached down his throat and punched him in the stomach. He gagged. Tried to speak, gagged again.

"Breathe through your mouth," Frances said as they rolled on to the next cot. "It's a trick I learned years ago. Of course, then you end up tasting it."

"Can't you just add a dab of tiger balm inside your nostrils?"

"Not a good idea. It can mask symptoms. If someone is hemorrhaging from their anus, you need to know."

"Busy place," Thomas noted.

"Migrants from Tent City. It's getting bad down there. They found two more bodies this morning. People are running scared."

"ODs?"

"The residents tell a different story. They say the devil is running loose."

Frances mentioned Maggie, a sex trade worker from the overpass, who told her what was happening. "She came in with six cracked ribs," Frances said as she pushed the cart to the next cot. "Bad date."

"What did you do?"

"Not much we could do. Can't tape ribs, the shallow breathing might induce pneumonia. All we could give her was ibuprofen and comfort. While she was recovering, she whispered to me that there's someone haunting Tent City late at night."

"The sex trade is a hell of a business."

"But whoever's killing people isn't targeting women. They're targeting older men. Not that it matters. Everyone is running, male and female, young and old. The Sally Ann, Crosswalk, Mustard Seed: they're overwhelmed. People are crowding in here now as well. This is supposed to be a recovery centre, not a flophouse. Although"—she looked at the rows of cots—"I imagine everyone here is recovering from something. And anyway, it might not be the devil at all. It might simply be a spike in overdoses. It happens."

More cuts, more bandages, more suppurating wounds sticky under gauze. Frances looked over at Thomas. "You should come for a drive-along in the health van sometime. The alleys, the parks, and the projects. You'd learn a lot. Situations not covered in your textbooks." She stretched her neck stiffly one way, then the other. "I've seen it come, I've seen it go. Amphetamines, meth, crack, ecstasy, OxyContin, and now fentanyl. Some have even taken to mainlining cleaning fluids. But I haven't seen anything like what's happening in Tent City right now. Not the ODs, but the fear. It's like they're being picked off, one by one."

"Heroin?"

"Probably. The dealers have started cutting it with horse tranquilizer and Clorox, even industrial-strength rat poison. Gives it that extra kick. Not enough to kill you, just enough to make your lips go numb. That's the idea, anyway. Doesn't always end well." She stared at Thomas with unblinking eyes. "Why are you here?"

"I had a question. You knew my mom. She was with you at the— What do you call it? The convent?"

"College. She never joined the order. She met your dad, remember?"

"Still, she was *almost* a nun. And who becomes a nun in this day and age anyway?"

"Fools like me," said Frances. "Hand me the antiseptic. No, not that. The swabs."

"How did my parents reconcile their opposing beliefs? Something had to give, right? Or was it a stalemate? That's sort of the definition of a marriage, right?"

"You came all the way down here to ask me that?"

"Well, there's this girl."

"Ah, yes. Here it comes."

"She's very . . . 'churchy.'"

"Churchy? You make it sound like an affliction."

"Oh, it is," he assured her. "But don't worry, we're working on a cure."

"Good to know."

"Her name's Amy, comes from good working-class stock, as they say. Her dad is the floor manager or something at a mattress factory, you know the one, down on 3rd. Her mom died when she was young, so we have that in common. Not much else. Like I said, churchy."

They came to an old man with bruises on his face lying on his back, talking to the ceiling. Frances began an assessment.

"Thing is," Thomas said, continuing their conversation as Frances worked. "This girl I mentioned? She lied to me and we had a falling out, and now she's gone and I don't know how to get her back."

"Well, if you want this young woman back—and if she lied to you, think about whether you—"

"I do."

"In that case, you need to ask yourself what really matters. To her."

"Art. She's a painter. That's what matters to her. Art and her family, though I've never met them."

"Maybe that's where you should begin. Pass me a bedpan."

"Can't." He held up his hands. "These are the tools of a future neurosurgeon."

"Or an overpaid pill dispenser."

"Either way, can't take that chance."

"Grab a bedpan, okay?"

He slid a clean one from the cart, exchanged it for the full one

Frances handed him. "You're a mean old woman," he said to her. "I ever tell you that?"

"All the time."

The next morning, he phoned Bernie. "Do you still have those tapes? Of Amy on the first day?"

CHAPTER ELEVEN

"OKAY, SO THERE ARE only seven basic emotions," said Bernie, clearing a space for his laptop on the cafeteria table. "Three of them we're born with: *fear, love, rage.* A newborn baby will demonstrate all three. The primordium of fear, the primordium of love, the primordium of rage. A Holy Trifecta. They're like the primary colours of emotion. The other four—happiness, sadness, surprise, and disgust—those come later. And you can blend any of those seven emotions to create further variations, the social emotions, as they're known."

"Social emotions?" Thomas asked.

"Envy, shame, guilt, pride. Those are taught. Those are inculcated in us. They don't come naturally. Guilt, for example, is disgust turned inward. Pride is love without a secondary subject. Religious awe, the *mysterium tremendum et fascinans*—that's Latin, by the way, you un-couth lout—the formula for religious awe is just fear plus fascination. And so on. We blend old emotions to make new ones."

It reminded Thomas of Amy's painterly palettes and the endless possibilities she was able to call forth from three primary colours. The search for perfect blue.

"It's, like, how there's only five basic tastes, right?" said Bernie, counting them off on his fingers. "Salty, sweet, sour, bitter, and—I forget the other one. But from those five, blended and mixed, we derive an endless, almost infinite variety of flavours, everything from sharp citrus to thick butterscotch, from creamed curries to onion soup, lemon tarts and licorice, fishy seaweeds, cilantro, chocolate ice cream, nutmeg and Nutella. Even—God forbid—olives and feta."

He was trying to chide Thomas on his taste in toppings, but Thomas wanted only one thing: to view the video file labelled GOD HELMET: DAY ONE. TEST SUBJECT: LAMIELL, A.

"Umami!" said Bernie. "That's the other flavour, the one I forgot. It's like a savoury taste, a kind of 'mouth feel.' "

Thomas nodded toward the screen. "About Amy . . ."

"Wanna know which food exhibits all five tastes? Which one has a balance of sweet and salty, bitter and sour, with umami as well?" He waited for Thomas to guess. When he didn't, he said, "Heinz ketchup! Really. It has all five tastes. It's considered 'the perfect food.' Weird, right?"

"Um, I don't know. I don't use ketchup."

"You don't use ketchup? Who doesn't use ketchup? Even on fries?"

"No. Listen, about—"

"Wow. You really did have a deprived childhood. Here." Bernie brought up the file on his laptop. "I think this is the one." He clicked PLAY.

And there it was, like a sledgehammer to the heart: Amy, looking offscreen. Amy, answering questions.

Thomas felt his mouth go dry. She was speaking to a Thomas who was off-camera. *My name? Amy Lamiell. . . . I'm in the visual arts program, postgraduate. . . . Painting, mainly, but some kiln work, too.*

Pottery. Glazes. . . . Whose work do I like? Freud, I guess. . . . No, not him . . . Lucian Freud, the painter. . . ."

Bernie slowed the recording down, and Amy's voice became lower and lower until the words became indecipherable. But even as her words blurred together, her shifting facial expressions became sharper, clearer. It was as though the one had been hiding behind the other. Thomas could see flashes of impatience, confusion, and fatigue as the interview dragged on, until—

"There!" said Bernie. "Did you see it?"

He hadn't. Thomas had been mesmerized by the sheer number of expressions she was capable of. We think of the human face as static, but it's not; it's constantly shifting, constantly in flux.

"There, right there," said Bernie. He scrolled back, slowed it down further, and now Thomas saw it, too: a look of abject pain, there and gone in less than a heartbeat. But he had seen it. It was real.

"You want her back," said Bernie. "That's where you want to start."

CHAPTER TWELVE

The Catholic seminary at Saint Mathurin's sits aloof from the city. Concealed in a forest of elm and oak, amid laquered shade and sudden shards of light, the main building forms a protective wall of rust-red brick. It wraps itself around a courtyard where acolytes and older priests walk in slow circles, mulling enigmatic theological riddles. The seminary reminded Thomas of a university campus on a long weekend: muffled in silence, under-populated, staid and sad at the same time. *University with all the fun sucked out.*

He'd parked his Prius out front (and let's not judge him too harshly for driving a Prius; it wasn't his choice, but a gift from his father), and had waited in the main hall to be ushered into the rector's office. A pair of priests—one older, with thin hair forming a faint outline around his head, the other younger and more richly maned—were waiting for him, dressed in requisite black. They wore white collars around their necks and concerned looks on their faces. What followed was a strangely elliptical conversation.

"Sebastian," Thomas said after a long, awkward pause. "I believe his first name is Sebastian."

"And how is it you know Mr. Lamiell?" asked the older priest. (He didn't say "Father Lamiell." He said "Mister." Thomas should have noted that.)

"I don't, not really. I mean, I know *of* him. I know his sister. I was hoping I might speak with Father Lamiell—just for a moment."

"Unfortunately, Mr. Lamiell is no longer at Saint Mathurin's. He hasn't been for quite some time." Then, because Thomas had identified himself as a medical student, the older priest, Father Patrice, confessed, "I studied medicine myself, before I found my calling. At one point, I thought I might become a doctor, too. But there are many ways to heal."

The younger priest leaned in. "Among some members of the clergy," he said, "a nervous breakdown is considered a sign of sincerity."

"Family? Just me and my dad . . . and my brother. . . . He's studying to be a priest."

There, caught in single-frame video capture: a look of joy when she said "dad," a flash of anguish when she said "brother." It was that moment on the tape that led Thomas to the seminary, and from the seminary here: to the San Hendrin mental asylum (more correctly, "mental health facility").

It looked like a hospital, but didn't smell like one. Where the halls of a hospital might reek of ammonia, the San Hendrin asylum was cloaked in softer scents: vanilla and rosewood spritzed into ventilation systems to help calm and declaw the residents. Blandly institutional.

The walls of San Hendrin were painted in what were presumably "soothing hues": soft salmon and warm peach, pastel pinks and rainforest greens. (The problem, of course, is that any colour disappears the longer you look at it, and what might have been soothing at first soon becomes the visual equivalent of background noise.) And anyway, the soft shades were undercut by the relentless rows of fluorescent lights. There were no shadows to hide in at San Hendrin.

Nurses in the corridors. Candy stripers and interns pushing carts down the passageways like ice cream vendors. Residents in grey sweatpants and limp T-shirts.

Thomas arrived at San Hendrin amid a flurry of bravado. Dressed in a starched white lab coat, he strode down the halls in what he hoped was a confident manner. Accompanying him was an orderly: a heavyset man named Phil or maybe Bill. Thomas couldn't recall. He was too busy remaining calm. (That was the secret of any bluff: to remain calm no matter what, haughty even.)

Here was the power of names. Thomas shared his father's name completely—they were both "Thomas Aaron Rosanoff"; the "Jr." was not on any official documents. Thomas had access to his father's Massachusetts Medical Association profile; his father had asked him to update it (honours won, grants awarded) and had long since forgotten that Thomas still had the password, had in fact set the password in the first place. So it was easy enough for Thomas to log on and revise his father's contact information, replacing it with his own phone number and email account. True, he couldn't access his father's patient files— those were encrypted—but he could pass himself off as Dr. Rosanoff long enough to sign out a patient. That was the plan, anyway. He would reset his dad's contact information as soon as he was done.

The only danger of being discovered was if someone at the San Hendrin asylum who knew his father or recognized the name cross-referenced his date of birth and other information. But why would they bother? He'd shown up as "Thomas Rosanoff" (true), had presented his photo ID (true, true), and had signed a scrawling signature that looked not unlike his father's (okay, so that was forgery, but still). He wasn't pretending to be Thomas Rosanoff; he *was* Thomas Rosanoff . . . just a different version: Thomas Rosanoff 2.0.

All of this had seemed easy enough when he'd rehearsed it in his head, but once inside San Hendrin, he battled his nerves to keep himself from bolting. He'd sent in the request earlier, but showing up in person to interview a patient was a different matter entirely. It's always easier to be brave online. As he walked down the stultifying calm of the north wing, with the orderly at his side, Thomas flipped through the patient's case study. " 'Full name: Sebastian Henri Lamiell. Affective schizophrenia disorder. Akinesia tendencies. Auditory hallucinations. An undue preoccupation with spiritual matters.' " Thomas stopped: " 'Patient experienced negative therapeutic reaction.' What does that mean, exactly? Negative therapeutic reaction."

"It means," said the orderly, "the therapy only made things worse."

"Oh."

As they walked, Thomas read on: " 'Sensitivity to light and loud noises. Moments of lucidity, followed by withdrawal.' . . . Wow. They've got him on L-dopa. A lot of it." This was a Faustian bargain: drugs that reduce schizophrenic delusions can also trigger psychotic episodes and even Parkinson's-like symptoms. The treatment was often worse than the cure. Damned if you do, damned if you don't.

"They ought to give him more of it, if you ask me," said the orderly. "He's a pain in the ass. Obsessed with cleanliness. We caught him scrubbing himself with SOS pads till he bled, stupid fucker. If you can do something with him, more power to you."

Soft music, breathy flutes, minor melodies. Thomas flipped back to the first page. "How long has he been . . . ?"

"At San Hendrin? About a year."

"Any, ah, visitors? Family?"

"Priests from Saint Mathurin's, mostly. They used to come to pray. Don't see them much anymore. He has a sister as well. She comes in once or twice a month. Good-lookin' girl." He gave Thomas a side-long leer. Thomas knew what that leer meant: *eminently fuckable.*

He winced, tried to sound nonchalant. "A sister, you say?"

"Yep. She usually leaves in tears. Which is understandable, I sup-pose. It must be upsetting. I mean"—they stopped outside a cell-like door—"he thinks he's Jesus."

The room was small and tidy, and when the door opened it fanned light across a narrow bed, a small lamp, an open Bible. Sebastian was in one corner, head down. A faint wisp of a man, barely there, thinner than in the family photographs Thomas had seen, but still recogniz-ably Amy's brother. Same profile. Same pale skin. He was mumbling something, rocking back and forth ever so slightly, lips moving. The orderly stayed by the door as Thomas stepped closer, spoke softly. "Sebastian? My name is Thomas Rosanoff. I was at the seminary. Fa-ther Patrice and the others are worried about you."

There is a state of apathy unique to asylums. It's called *abulia*. This was what Thomas faced with Sebastian. He needed to get through to him, and the chisel was Amy.

"Your sister is worried about you. She needs you."

When Sebastian finally spoke, it was with a hollow intonation. "I am the way, the truth, and the light. So it is written, so it is writ-ten. You shall love those who imprison you, you shall love those who would hurt you, who would do you harm." He looked up suddenly, eyes wide. "God's love shall redeem us. It shall redeem us in the wine, the blood, and the sea. It is written, the lamb shall lie down with the lion." And then, retreating inward, he whispered, "This love, this terrible love. I carry it with me."

Thomas could see her in him. He could see Amy in there, trapped and trying to escape, an Amy that did indeed need rescuing. He could see the scars that Sebastian had cut into his wrists and up his forearms, criss-cross patterns reminiscent of thorns.

Thomas knelt beside him, tried his best to make eye contact. "Your name is Sebastian Henri Lamiell. You are at a medical facility in Cambridge, Massachusetts. Do you understand what I am saying?"

Sebastian shook his head. "No. Not Sebastian. He has departed. He has left this body as a shell for me to inhabit."

"If you're not Sebastian, then who are you?"

He turned, eyes shining even more than before. "I am the Son of Man, born anew. Child of Nazareth, beloved of Mary, born of a virgin. Sent down to this hall of mirrors to suffer, to suffer this love . . . this terrible love . . ." He looked up to the small window, meshed with wire, in the wall above his desk. He went quiet, listening.

"Is someone speaking to you?" Thomas asked. "Someone right now?"

"Yes."

"Who?"

"God."

The orderly had been watching, clearly amused by what was going on. "What did I tell you, Doctor? Crazy as a loon."

Thomas shot the orderly a withering look.

"Oh. Right," said the orderly. "Not crazy. *Reality deficient.* Tomato, tomahto. Can we go now?"

Sebastian was speaking so quietly Thomas had to lean in to hear. *"Eloi, eloi, lama sabachthani,"* he said, voice cracking.

Thomas put his hand lightly on Sebastian's shoulder, bones as frail as a bird's wing denuded of feathers. *She never told me. Never told me any of this.* "Your sister misses you," he said. "Please come back."

But there was no answer. Only silence.

When Thomas and the orderly stepped into the hallway and closed the door to Sebastian's room, Thomas exhaled with relief. "That was . . ."

"Intense?" said the orderly.

"That's one way to put it. It's the sheer conviction of it. The *certainty* of his delusions. This isn't the occasional voice he's hearing. It's— It's the core of who he is. It's his identity. And it's wrong. What do you think he meant by that: 'the wine, the blood, and the sea'?"

The orderly shrugged. "Something biblical, probably. Water into wine. Wine into the blood of Christ. Three substances, same essence. That sort of thing."

They walked back along the halls of San Hendrin under the influence of rosewood and soft music. Muffled voices behind closed doors.

"He's not the only one, either," said the orderly. "Place is full of 'em. We've got Napoleon on the fourth floor. Alexander the Great on the fifth. Roosevelt on the third. We even have another Jesus. We keep him in a separate wing, of course. Away from your friend."

They reached a service elevator. The orderly pressed the button.

Thomas looked at him. "Why?"

"Why what?"

"Why do you separate them?"

"Our two resident Messiahs?" He laughed. "Would you want them running into each other?"

The elevator doors opened on a single *ping* and they stepped inside.

"Think about it," said the orderly as they started their descent. "You figure you're the One and Only Jesus, Lord God Almighty. Then you bump into someone else. 'Oh, and what's your name? Jesus, you say? What a coincidence. That's my name, too. Where you from? The Holy Land, you say? No kidding. Born in a manger? Me, too! Wait a sec—you're claiming *you're* the Messiah? I'm the Messiah!' Think what would happen. Everything you believed about yourself turned upside down in an instant. All your assumptions, your sense of identity. Imagine how upsetting that would be. Think what would happen."

And it hit Thomas full force. "You'd be cured," he said.

The orderly stepped out at the ground floor, but Thomas didn't follow. Instead, he held the elevator back with his hand. "Take me to the other Jesus."

CHAPTER THIRTEEN

THEY HEARD ELI BEFORE they saw him.

"Philistines! Pharisees! You sons of whores! You vipers from Hell! Damnation is at hand! Howl! Howl!"

A wild face, full of rage. Thick black beard, streaked with a yellowing grey. Eli, blind in one eye, peering at the world through a clouded cornea.

He stared at Thomas as though he were down a long corridor. *"Do I know you?!"* he roared.

Eli was perched on the edge of his narrow bed, wrists in restraints, ankles secured. Late fifties, but still robust. He was yelling at Thomas at the top of his voice, even though the two of them were scarcely ten feet apart. The corners of the bedframe were padded.

"No," Thomas said. "We haven't met before." He turned to the orderly, asked, "Those restraints, are they . . . ?"

"He's secure, don't worry. Can't reach you."

"Fornicators! Pharisees! The Kingdom of Heaven is at hand! Wild beasts shall cry out in their desolate homes."

Under his breath, Thomas asked, "What's with his eye?"

"Self-inflicted," said the orderly, and then to Eli: "Mr. Wasser!

You have company. This is"—he checked his clipboard—"Dr. Rosanoff. He would like to speak to you."

Thomas had to stop himself from correcting the orderly, from saying, "*Mr.* Rosanoff. Not Dr. Not yet."

"Howl! Howl! I have seen violence and strife in the cities! These chains cannot hold me, for I have seen the truth. And the truth shall set me free!"

"Truth—and a higher dosage," said the orderly with a chuckle.

Thomas took a hesitant half step nearer. "Mr. Wasser . . . May I call you Eli? I'd like to ask you a few questions, if you don't mind."

"The days of calamity are at hand! City against city! Brother against brother! Kingdom against king! Put on the armour of God Our Father, that you may stand against the wiles of the devil. Lucifer reigns! The souls of men are filled with a mighty darkness. There is madness in their hearts."

"You are Eli, correct? Eli Wasser?"

"I am Christ the Lord. Son of God. And I come to you not as a lamb BUT A LION! You scribes! You worms! Howl! Howl at the judgment of Heaven Everlasting!" Then, stopping suddenly in mid-rant: "Got any smokes?"

"Pardon?"

"Smokes. Tobacco. Coffin nails. Got any? They won't let me have cigarettes in this godforsaken place. You got some?"

"Um, no. I don't smoke. Sorry."

And he went instantly back to full Old Testament ire: "Then I shall smite you down! I shall rain fire upon you. Sadducees! Pharisees! You sons of whores!"

The orderly leaned in. "You still want to introduce him to our other Jesus?"

Thomas shook his head.

In the hallway outside Eli's room, the orderly noted the time of their visit in his clipboard file. All patient activities were recorded, including visitors and incidents of "antisocial behaviour." Thomas looked over the orderly's shoulder: no one ever visited Eli, but the list of social transgressions was long.

"Well," the orderly said, capping his pen. "That's that."

"Do you think it starts slowly?" Thomas asked. "With voices and visions. Do they gradually begin to suspect they're someone else, or do you think it happens suddenly?"

"That, I wouldn't know. Maybe one day the Heavens opened up. Hell of a thing, the human mind."

"His background?"

The orderly flipped through the pages. "Homeless. Picked up by the police three months ago. Was dancing naked in Boston Common at night. Detained for evaluation. Admitted to a state hospital."

"And then transferred here? How did someone like Eli end up in a private facility?"

The orderly read further, then looked up. "You should know," he said. "You're the one who had him committed."

"Let me see that."

The orderly pointed to the second page. "'Dr. Rosanoff.' That is your signature, right?" His eyes narrowed. "You are Dr. Rosanoff, right?"

"That's my father. He's at Massachusetts General. He must have signed for it."

"Rosanoff?" He thought about this a moment. "Any relation to—"

"No. No relation. We're a completely different line of Rosanoffs," he lied.

In the background, stifled by the walls between them, but still audible, Eli was shouting.

"Philistines! Fornicators! Sons of whores! Damnation is at hand!"

Thomas and the orderly began the long walk back to the main foyer.

"Too bad it didn't work out," the orderly said. "Your experiment, I mean. Bringing the two of 'em together, face-to-face. Doomed from the start."

"I suppose . . ."

But another possibility was forming in Thomas's mind. Synapses were firing, neurotransmitters were rushing in: an *idea* was taking hold. An idea—and an image. One of a street corner saviour holding a sign.

CHAPTER FOURTEEN

IT LOOKED LIKE A Bedouin camp. The haze of dust. The filaments of smoke uncurling above cooking fires.

Tent City reeked of wet rot, was wreathed in a permanent dusk no matter what the time of day. A figure moved through, lightly, like a shadow that had drifted out of a nightmare and attached itself onto this world. Down the narrow pathways between tarps. Amid the tubercular coughs and mad ravings, past the bottle-pickers and lost souls, down to an addled arrangement of planks and plastic sheeting of somebody's home. The figure slipped inside.

The interior was dark and cramped. It smelled of dank wool, of fermenting straw. The elderly man inside looked up at the shadow standing above him. "Ants," he said. "They're everywhere. They come in at night."

"Hello, Charlie."

The old man's eyes slowly focused. "I know you. You were down here before."

The figure smiled, eyes shining, like an incubus sitting on someone's chest, like an angel, descending. "I'm here for you, Charlie. I'm here to help."

"Is that what you are?" the old man asked. "An angel?"

"An angel? Why, yes, I suppose I am." Left unstated was what type of angel.

Later, when the body was found (an OD, by the looks of it, a common enough occurrence in Tent City), the police would take perfunctory statements from the ragged denizens. *"Witnesses report seeing a 'mysterious figure,' dressed in black. Others say, in white. Their accounts are unreliable: residents couldn't even state whether the figure was male or female."*

But the police report was only a summary of what had been described. Had the officers recorded these accounts word for word, they might have reconsidered their initial, and as it turns out final, assessment. The medical examination concluded: *"Probable cause of death: methadone overdose."* Never mind that Charlie never took narcotics. Never mind that the witnesses didn't say black/white. They said, dressed in black *"like a priest."* In white, *"like a doctor."*

"So there were two figures?"

"No, just the one."

Evil is real. It has a pungent body odour all its own, and the residents of Tent City could feel it, could taste it, could smell it, nearby, ever present.

The rain had stopped and the city was pooled with puddles. Church spires and cobblestones. The liquid leap of squirrels. A flurry of birds scattering across the sky.

Most of the leaves had fallen, raked away by the rain, and the magician was now lying on his side. Eyes half closed. Blanket falling off his shoulders. His breathing was laboured; the cold weather and his vigil had taken their toll. The cup out front was dotted with coins, pennies mostly, and next to the cup was a water-stained Bible, corners well-thumbed. The cardboard sign proclaiming his identity was now almost illegible. On an overturned crate, three creased playing cards were lined up, but there were no takers.

"I've seen you," Thomas said, crouching beside him. "At the station, playing three-card monte. Sleight-of-hand parlour tricks." Thomas looked at the sad squalor that surrounded the magician, the greasy cards, the coins in the cup. "Times are tough, I guess. I only have one question. Who are you? I need to know."

The magician's hand stretched out, asking for alms. His wrist was as thin as a sparrow's bones.

Thomas snapped a crisp $100 bill from his wallet. "This—is yours. All you have to do is tell me you are *not* the Messiah."

The hand withdrew.

Thomas nodded, satisfied. He tucked the bill back into his wallet and the wallet into his coat.

"I've come here because I need your help," said Thomas. "There's a young priest I'd like you to meet. His name is Sebastian and he has a problem. He thinks he's you."

PART TWO

GOD OF THE GAPS

CHAPTER FIFTEEN

THE HAWTHORNE INSTITUTE AT Harvard Medical, midmorning. The clouded windows of a soporific lecture hall. Sunlight through falling dust. A stupor of students, the drone-buzz of fluorescent lights, and Anton Cerletti in front presiding in all his Ichabod glory. . . .

"There are many Bibles out there," Cerletti intones, voice sonorous and slathered with authority. "This one"—he hefts a mammoth textbook onto the lectern—"is ours."

A click of PowerPoint and the book's title appeared on the screen behind him.

"The SDM:III. *Standardized Diagnostic Manual of Mental Disorders: Third Edition, Revised*. Eight hundred pages. More than a million copies sold. Retails for ninety-nine dollars and ninety-nine cents."

(The students welcomed the PowerPoint; the professor's handwriting on the white board was as hard to decipher as it was distinct. It was as though he had his own form of cursive, comprehensible only to himself.)

"When it comes to treating patients," said Cerletti, "this is *the* primary medical reference. Clinical psychiatrists. Family therapists. Psychologists. Counsellors. Lawyers for the defence. Lawyers for the prosecution. Drug companies looking to fine-tune medications for specific disorders. This is the manual they rely on."

A few of the more attentive students jotted this down.

"And all of it prepared under the directives"—he gave a tight smile—"of our illustrious alumnus, Chairman Emeritus of the National Psychiatric Society, Dr. Thomas Rosanoff. Some of you may be familiar with his work on early childhood development."

Scattered nods of recognition.

"Dr. Rosanoff has been so kind as to allow a few lesser mortals, such as myself, to oversee certain sections of the revised edition. If you look under 'Electroconvulsive Therapy,' you will find my own modest contribution."

At which point Professor Cerletti spotted Thomas at the back of the classroom, trying to slip in unnoticed.

"Speak of the devil," Cerletti said, and, with an operatic gesture to the back of the class: "Students, we should feel honoured! Dr. Rosanoff's namesake has decided to grace us with his presence."

Voices rippled through the classroom. Students craned in their seats to gawp.

Professor Cerletti smiled, but not with his eyes. "Yes. There he is. Very much alive. As you can see, the rumours of his demise were greatly exaggerated. Not sure why he's attending one of our lowly first-year graduate classes, but always welcome. Mind you"—and here the professor's smile took on a serrated edge—"at the rate young Thomas is progressing, I imagine some of you here may catch up to him by the time he graduates. *If* he graduates. Thomas is one of our more permanent students. Now then"—annoyed at the interruption—"back to our Bible."

After the class ended, and as the students filed out, stealing glances at Thomas as they went, Thomas approached Professor Cerletti.

"My father called?"

Cerletti nodded. "Your father called."

"I have something new."

"You always have something new."

"But this one is exciting." Thomas could barely contain his enthusiasm, had to fight against allowing it to run free like a tongue-lolling dog. "It's not exactly neuroscience and it's not exactly bio-psych. It's more like a . . . like a new form of identity therapy. So, I won't be able to make it to the lab this week. I'll be too busy setting up the—"

"You're hardly in the lab now as it is. We have experiments that are running without you."

"I know. And I apologize, but this one is big. Really big. I'll be operating out of my apartment, because it's not really a laboratorial situation."

" 'What's It Like to Be a Bat?' by T. Nagel. Have you read it? It was on the required-reading list. A fascinating essay. Nagel argues that, as minutely detailed and precise as we're able to quantify the consciousness of other beings, we will never truly know what it's like to *be* them. We may understand the mechanics of echolocation, but we will never know what it's like to *be* a bat. Tell me, what's it like to be *you*, Thomas? To waltz through life with every obstacle preemptively cleared out of the way, everything taken care of, never having to worry, never having to follow through—on anything. What's that like? It must be remarkable."

Thomas felt his face grow hot. "Professor, with all due respect . . ."

"Yes, Thomas, your father called. And yes, your thesis has been extended *again*. Bravo. Well done." The professor crammed the heavy SDM:III manual into his attaché case.

"I haven't had a chance to put together a formal proposal yet," said Thomas. "I'm still waiting to make sure the test subjects are available, but as soon as I do—"

"Oh, there's no need for that. You carry on, merrily, merrily. And when this latest scheme of yours fails—as it undoubtedly will—have Daddy give us a call and we'll work something out. We always do." And with that, he left, waving aside the proffered, "Thank you, sir, you won't regret this!" that Thomas lobbed at his back.

Thomas stood quietly in the silence of the classroom, excited, insulted, but mainly relieved. He was about to leave when he heard—faint, but unmistakably—the sound of distant music. Not music. Voices. A choir. It rose in unison, then dropped away into an echoing emptiness. Thomas saw something out of the corner of his eye, spun around, but there was no one else in the room, only Thomas.

He took a deep, steadying breath. "Fatigue," he said. A dearth of sleep, a spike in dopamine, memories misfiring in the auditory cortex. Only that, nothing more.

CHAPTER SIXTEEN

THE TOWER OF BABEL is an Old Testament tale in which the descendants of Noah, having settled on the Plains of Shinar, declare, "Come, let us build a city with a great tower that will reach to the Heavens! Let us make a name for ourselves!" Brick by brick, layer by layer, they build their tower. It rises, higher and higher . . . until the Lord intervenes. He confuses and confounds them with the curse of different languages, leaves them speaking incompatible tongues and then scatters them to the four winds. The tower lies in ruins, becomes the focus of pagan rituals and false gods, a testament to grandiose plans gone wrong.

The Tower of Babel was not *accidentally* sacrilegious; it was conceived from the start as an affront to God. This was its very aim. But although presented as a tale of hubris, the real fear was not that God would strike people down as they neared his realm but that on reaching those heady heights, there would be no one there to greet them. It was not a wrathful God they feared, but an absent one.

The Case of Simon Morin is equally unsettling. Simon Morin was a heretic imprisoned in Paris in the 1660s, and his story is recounted in Voltaire's commentary on crime and punishment. Voltaire writes that Simon Morin "was a deranged man who believed he saw visions, and even carried this folly so far as to imagine that he was sent from God, proclaiming that he was, in fact, Jesus Christ."

Sentenced to a lunatic asylum, the most remarkable thing happened: "There was at that time, confined in the same madhouse, another crazed man who called himself the Eternal Father Christ. Upon meeting him, Simon Morin was so struck with the folly of his companion, that his eyes were opened to the truth of his own condition. Having recovered his right senses, and having made known his penitence to the magistrates of the city, Simon Morin was granted release from his confinement."

Nor was this the only case of competing religious identities being used to break the logjam of a delusion. In the 1950s, at a mental institute in Maryland, two women, each claiming to be Mary, Mother of God, ran into each other on the hospital grounds. A tense but polite conversation occurred, after which one of the women—the older of the two—recanted. She must have been mistaken in her claims, she said. Perhaps she was the *other woman's* mother, the mother of the Mother of God. Having worked it out between them, that only one was the True Mary, and the other was her mother, the two remained on good terms. Soon after, the older woman shed that identity as well. She began to respond to treatment and was later discharged.

When Thomas uncovered these tales deep in the university archives, he hurried away, almost giddy, as though he'd stumbled upon something clandestine, pushing past other scholars and students buzzard-hunched over library tables, academics shovelling research into books, books that would never be read. (They are dancing for no one, these academics.)

The tale of Simon Morin in the 1660s and the two Marys of 1955 were notable in the redemptively shattering effect they had upon their subjects. But neither experiment—if you could call them that—was achieved in any systematic or scientific way. Thomas would change that. *Two identities cannot occupy the same space; one—or both—have to cede ground.* He could feel his skin tremble, a galvanic response, tangible, real, and measurable.

Sadly, there was a postscript to the tale of Simon Morin, one which threw the entire story into a more cautionary vein. But Thomas was too jubilant, too self-assured, too giddy, to take proper note of this warning, a warning that was reaching out to him from across four centuries, a warning he should have heeded. Simon Morin, you see, would relapse. This time, he would declare himself a prophet and would once again be arrested. Charged with blasphemy, there would be no reprieve. He was burned at the stake.

CHAPTER SEVENTEEN

Is IDENTITY IMMUTABLE? Or is it malleable? Is it transitory and temporary—something to be donned or discarded at whim—or is it woven into our DNA? Does it even exist? Perhaps identity is simply an agreed-upon fiction, a conglomerate of traits.

Thomas knew full well that the defining characteristic of our interconnected online age isn't anonymity but reinvention. You don't cloak who you are: you *change* who you are. In the either/or of binary equations, you can hide in plain sight, can dress yourself in layers: a dance of the seven veils in reverse. You can even claim the identity of someone else entirely. Your father's, say.

Two weeks, tops. That was how much time Thomas figured he would need. A provisional custody order (one month, on review) would be more than sufficient. *How much time do you need to jolt someone out of a falsely held identity?*

He was equally sure that the request would go through without a ripple. Why wouldn't it? It wasn't as though people were constantly stealing mental patients. Far from it. Hospitals were always looking for people to take custody of intractable cases—family, relatives, halfway homes, community groups. It was a matter of paperwork, of filling in the right forms, clicking on the right boxes. No one would step back to look at the larger picture. No one would ask why a patient was being released into the care of one Thomas Aaron Rosanoff.

He was nervous nonetheless. Everything depended on this . . . deception? No. This misdirection. It was sleight of hand, only that. And as Thomas had long known, it was always easier to ask for forgiveness after the fact than permission before it.

He came out of his downstairs bathroom drying his hands on a towel.

The magician was standing beside Thomas's desk, looking out the window to the church spire in the distance.

"You can use this bathroom," Thomas said. "There are fresh robes and towels in the linen closet. There's a pair of toothbrushes. Pick whichever one you like. Sebastian will be here soon. I bought some clothes as well, T-shirts, sweatpants. If they don't fit, let me know." He pulled up a chair. "Please, have a seat."

It was awkward, but it had to be done. He opened a portable blood collection unit—it looked like a bait case—and took out a rubber tourniquet and alcohol swab. "We need to make sure everything is okay before we start. So, if that's all right with you . . ."

The magician rolled up a sleeve of his frayed sweater. "Please. Be my guest." These were the first words Thomas had heard him speak, and the voice was unnaturally calm.

Thomas cleared his throat, pulled on a pair of latex gloves, tied the tourniquet, tapped out a vein. He could see the scars of older needle tracks along the magician's forearm but said nothing.

Blood filled the vial. Thomas withdrew the needle, labelled the sample, pressure-taped a tuft of cotton onto the magician's arm.

"You're good at this," said the magician. He spoke with so little inflection his words seemed almost disembodied. "I barely felt it."

"Thank you."

"Your apartment is quite nice as well. Ikea?"

"No, not Ikea." Thomas held up a pen in front of the magician's face. "Please follow the tip with your eyes." He moved it slowly across the magician's field of view, but the magician stared at Thomas instead.

"Please follow the—"

"I am."

"No, you're—"

"I'm watching the pen closely."

"You're not, actually. You're—"

"I can see it reflected in your eyes."

And that, perhaps, was the first moment in which Thomas realized things might not go quite according to plan. He tucked the pen into his jacket pocket.

"There's food in the fridge. I bought fish sticks and nonalcoholic wine. Seemed appropriate. You can help yourself to anything." He packed up the blood samples. "I'm going to run these down to the lab. Don't open the door to anyone. If the phone rings, let it go to voicemail."

When Thomas returned an hour later, he found the magician sitting in a plush robe, freshly showered and peering squinty-eyed into Thomas's microscope.

"Hey!" said Thomas. "Don't fool around with that. It's expensive. Anybody call?"

The magician shook his head without looking up. He flicked on the light under the microscope, adjusted the knob. There was no slide under the lens.

"That's odd," said Thomas. "The requisition must have gone through by now. Someone should have called."

At which point the doorbell rang. Thomas headed for the door, shouting at the magician over his shoulder, "Put that away, it's expensive."

A pair of frazzled hospital attendants greeted him. Hair askew, shirts untucked, they looked as though they'd been wrestling a bear.

"You Dr. Rosanoff?"

Thomas nodded.

One of the attendants shoved a clipboard at Thomas. "Sign here." He flipped a page. "Here. And here."

Thomas signed. It was his father's signature.

The other attendant handed Thomas a plastic bag filled with pills, and Thomas signed for those as well.

"He's down the hall, at the back door. That's as far as we got."

"Aren't you going to escort him in?" Thomas asked, genuinely puzzled.

The attendants gave Thomas a "you've got to be joking" look.

"You signed, we're done. He's all yours now."

And then, at full roar . . .

"Pharisees! Sons of whores!"

Thomas felt gut-punched. His knees gave out from under him. "No," he said. "No, wait!"

But they were gone. Thomas crept down the hallway to the stairs, peered around the corner—and there he was, wrists trussed in leather restraints, head back, voice booming to wake the dead. "Philistines! Fornicators! Sons of whores!"

Dr. Rosanoff's patient. The *real* Dr. Rosanoff. It was Thomas's father who'd had this man committed, so when a requisition was submitted under Dr. Rosanoff's name . . . The hallway began to tilt. Thomas felt nauseous, as though he were going to faint. *Oh God, oh God no.* One of his neighbours peered out from behind a chained front door.

"Babylon has fallen!" Eli roared. "The Kingdom of Heaven is at hand!"

"Oh no, oh God," said Thomas. "They sent me the wrong Jesus."

CHAPTER EIGHTEEN

The San Hendrin asylum, late afternoon.

A murmur of nurses. Crepe-soled shoes padding down the corridors. Mental patients, marooned in their own worlds, twisting their bodies in silent contortions.

Thomas, earlier, running back down the hallway into his apartment, pressing his credit card into the magician's hand. "Go! There's a store across the street. Go get cigarettes, now! Go, go!"

At the tempered glass of the San Hendrin reception desk, Thomas was rehearsing his alibi as he waited for the receptionist to return. But then he spotted the orderly he'd spoken with last time rolling a gurney down the corridor. An elderly lady, thin as famine, was draped under skeletal sheets.

What was the orderly's name again? Bill? Phil?

"Phil! Wait up!" Thomas hurried to catch him.

Thomas, earlier, desperate to stop his neighbours from calling 911, speaking to Eli in a frantic hush, "Listen. Calm down. I have cigarettes. They're on their way. But you have to stop yelling."

The orderly at San Hendrin wheeled the gurney around a corner. Thomas pursued.

Thomas, back in his apartment, sitting across from the smouldering, one-eyed mountain of a man that was Eli. Thomas, waiting for the magician to return, realizing he had handed over his credit card to a known confidence man. Thomas, wondering if he was ever going to see the magician again and what his next credit card statement might look like. Thomas, eyeing the restraints that held Eli's wrists to the belt around his waist, a permanent gunfighter's position. The magician, reappearing with an armful of cartons. "I wasn't sure which kinds he liked, so I asked for one of each." Eli, roaring at the magician: "DO I KNOW YOU?" Thomas explaining to the magician, "He thinks he knows everybody." Then, addressing Eli and realizing midway he doesn't actually know the magician's name, "Eli, this . . . this gentleman will help you light your cigarettes. You have to keep your restraints on, for now. I'll be back soon."

In the quiet corridors of San Hendrin: the rattle of wheels. The orderly was humming to himself as he rolled the elderly lady along.

"Wait up!"

"If it isn't 'Mr. Doctor,'" said the orderly, not breaking stride. "What brings you back? Need another member of our congregation?"

"Phil, listen. There's been a mix-up." Thomas had to scurry to keep pace; the orderly was moving faster than he thought. "It's a long story," said Thomas. "But I need to return one patient and sign out another. But before I speak with Admissions, I have a couple of questions, y'know, to make sure everything is done properly. It's basically a patient swap. Eli Wasser for Sebastian Lamiell."

"Patient swap? Never heard of such a thing," said the orderly. "So what's your question? And make it quick. I've got to get Joan of Arc here down to Psych."

"Joan of Arc? Really?" He looked at the elderly lady on the bed.

The orderly laughed. "Nah. Just run-of-the-mill dementia. Isn't that right, Alice?"

"It's lovely," she said, smiling.

They stopped in front of an elevator, but the orderly didn't push the button. He turned to Thomas. "So what exactly is the problem? You want to return Eli, and take temporary custody of that young priest. Not a big deal."

"It's not? Oh, thank God. You see——"

"Just submit your request for custody when you hand in your interim report on Eli."

"Report?"

"For the review committee."

"The review committee?"

"They meet every Wednesday, three o'clock. They'll go over the details with you in person."

Thomas, weakly: "In person?"

"Clinical reassessment. Standard procedure when a doctor returns a patient. You are a doctor, right?"

"Sort of."

"Sort of a doctor? Isn't that like being 'sort of' pregnant? Didn't think it was possible."

Oh, but it is. It is possible to be "sort of pregnant."

"There was no baby. Don't you see? I drew the line with a pen."

"I am," said Thomas, voice wavering, "a doctor. That is, I have——I have signing authority."

"Well, then. You've got nothing to worry about." He pressed the elevator button, and with a *ping!* disappeared inside with Alice. *Down the rabbit hole.* "And by the way," the orderly said as the doors closed. "It's Bill."

With that, Thomas was alone and on his own.

We like to speak of strange twists and marvellous coincidences, campfire stories of stepping off a ferry in a strange town and running into a friend we haven't seen in years, or of spreading out a blanket at a fireworks festival in a distant city only to realize we are sitting next to our neighbours from back home. But we never consider the *missed* encounters, the lost opportunities, the ones we were never even aware of. How many times have we passed a former lover or a childhood playmate on the street or in an airport without realizing? Statistically speaking, there must be far more of these missed encounters than there are fortuitous ones. (Perhaps today, while you were at the local Whole Foods, your old elementary school teacher was two aisles away, comparing prices of Müeslix and feeling wistful.)

And so it was, as Thomas walked, shell-shocked on shaky legs, out of the San Hendrin Mental Institute, he never knew that Amy left only moments earlier, and that she left in tears. Just as well they hadn't transferred Sebastian into his custody. Had Amy arrived to find her brother gone, what then? Thomas had until Amy's next visit to fix everything, though he didn't know this at the time. He knew only that he couldn't return Eli until he had cured Sebastian. And he couldn't cure Sebastian without the magician.

His apartment was about to get crowded with Christs.

CHAPTER NINETEEN

BERNIE LAUGHED. "SO IT'S easier to *take* a mental patient than return one?"

He was on speakerphone with Thomas, who was sitting in his Prius in the seminary parking lot.

"Apparently so."

"Don't worry about it," said Bernie. "It's probably for the better. You really can't run a proper test with only two subjects. You would need three anyway, at minimum."

Thomas hadn't told Bernie that one of the test subjects was Amy's brother; it would have compromised the objectivity of the experiment.

The last hour had been hectic. Thomas had scrambled back to the seminary, had sought out Father Patrice, had explained, in dulcet medical tones meant to reassure the elderly priest, that Thomas was there to help Sebastian, to guide him gently back to the flock. All he needed was a signature from Father Patrice, a formality, really, and Father Patrice had consented—with gratitude. He'd assumed he was signing off on in-house treatment, hadn't realized that it was a custody release form, or that Sebastian was being taken to a private residence for a treatment of unproven efficacy.

Thomas was worming further into the wet earth of duplicity, and he knew that those layers of subterfuge were becoming more and more suffocating, but if the experiment succeeded Amy's brother would be shaken out of his delusions once and for all. The other two Christs might be cured as well. Thomas would be celebrated, and even better, Amy would be grateful. He would win her back by saving her brother. *Cognitive therapy redefined!* And if he failed? Well, better to fall off that bridge when he came to it. . . .

"I have to admit, it's an interesting idea," said Bernie, Thomas's sole confidant. "Much better than sending Igor out for another round of brains. Our other experiment, the one you are always too busy to help with? Tracing thought patterns in brain cells? The tissue samples are decaying, something to do with the dye-to-PFA ratio. So it's a bit of a bust. This new idea of yours? This is even better than the God helmet. Have you told Cerletti?"

"Not the details, no. Or even the premise, really. If it doesn't work, I'd rather not draw attention."

"But it *will* work," said Bernie with a certain misplaced confidence. "Why wouldn't it? What could possibly go wrong?"

"What does that mean, exactly? Negative therapeutic reaction." "It means the therapy only made things worse."

"Nothing comes to mind," said Thomas.

It was a question that would stalk Thomas on the drive back to his apartment. *What could possibly go wrong?*

His unease followed him up the steps to his front door, a sense of undefined dread that preoccupied him to such a degree that he was only dimly aware of the sound coming from the kitchen when he entered his apartment. Thomas threw his keys in a ceramic bowl, removed his scarf in slow mummy-wrap turns, unbuttoned his overcoat. He now became more aware of a strange sound around the corner, *shhk, shhk, shhk*, like an envelope being opened repeatedly or a broom whisking the floor.

"Hello?" said Thomas.

The sound grew louder as he came closer.

Shhk, shhk, shhk . . .

A large knife was cutting through tomatoes. Eli, free of his restraints, was at the cutting board.

Thomas swallowed.

The magician was sitting at the marble-topped counter blithely flipping through Thomas's SDM:III manual, wholly unconcerned about the large, mentally unstable man with a knife standing across from him.

Thomas, trying desperately to remain calm: "Hey, guys."

The magician looked up from the book. "Hello, Thomas."

Shhk, shhk, shhk. Eli had moved on to cucumbers.

"So . . . Eli. How did you, um, get out of your restraints?"

"Know what you need?" said Eli, eyes wild with enthusiasm. "One of them Ginsu knives. That's what you need!"

"Eli, how did you—"

"Oh, those?" said the magician, referring to the restraints that now lay in a heap on the kitchen counter. "I took them off for him. They looked uncomfortable."

"Ever seen a Ginsu knife? Those things'll cut through anything! Frozen chickens. Regular chickens. Cantaloupes. Coconuts, even really hard coconuts. Steaks. Frozen steaks. Bones."

Eli continued his inventory even as Thomas spotted the plastic pill bottles lying on their sides. Empty.

"Eli. Did you take *all* your pills?"

"Pork chops. Frozen pork chops. Lamb chops. Frozen lamb chops. Metal tubings. The entire Yellow Pages. Anything! Leather boots. Copper wire."

Thomas, throat dry: "Listen to me, Eli. This is very, very important. Did you take all your pills?"

"Tin cans. Yams. Pineapples. Frozen pineapples. Particle boards. Two-by-fours."

"The pills?" said the magician. "We flushed those."

"Sheet metal. Sugarcane. Those hard nuts, you know, like walnuts but smaller. Action figures. Baseball bats. Iron rods."

Thomas looked at the magician. "You flushed his pills?"

"We decided he didn't need them anymore."

Eli dumped the sliced vegetables into a pot.

"But—he's on quetiapine. It's a dopamine inhibitor, 300 mg a day. Plus haloperidol. Plus a stabilizer. It's a pharmaceutical cocktail. He can't just *stop*. He'll crash and burn. It could trigger a full-blown psychotic episode, violent outbursts. *Shit*."

"Did you know," said the magician, referring to the SDM:III manual in front of him, "there are three hundred seventy-four different ways to be crazy? That's up from two hundred ninety-seven since the last edition."

Thomas felt numb, as though novocaine had been injected into his limbs. "The refills. When they dropped him off, they left a week's worth of refills."

He careened to the bathroom, flung open the medicine cabinet. Empty bottles rolled away. *Oh God, oh God.*

From the kitchen, he could hear Eli calling out. "Soup's on!"

Amy's brother arrived at his doorstep the next day.

CHAPTER TWENTY

THOMAS'S FIRST REAL CRUSH (aptly named, these youthful infatuations; they aren't at all pleasant) was on an older, wiser girl (Thomas was twelve, she was thirteen) and in his misplaced innocence he went to his grandfather for advice. Thomas's grandfather, dead these many years, had been a fleeting but formative figure in Thomas's youth. Crooked as a question mark, with suspenders and a concave chest, plagued by a bronchial cough, he shuffled through the family garden at Kingsley Hall, stopping only to hack mucus into the rose beds. ("Nutrients," as he put it.)

Manicured hedges formed a maze in the backyard—an easy maze, and one Thomas quickly memorized, so when he spotted his grandfather, stooped over, tuft of hair bobbing above the hedges, Thomas caught up easily enough. "Grandpa, wait!" And when Thomas explained his adolescent conundrum—How to make someone who doesn't like you, like you—his grandfather said, "Well, kid, somebody's got to tell you the truth about this stuff, so it might as well be me. And I can only pass along the advice I got from my own dad, dead these many years. That'd be your *great*-grandfather, biggest prick the world has ever seen. But he spoke the truth, such as he knew it, and here it is: Men give love in order to get sex. Women give sex in order to get love. Everything else is commentary."

(This incident, what Thomas had thought was a private moment, would later appear in Dr. Rosanoff's notebooks, sanitized slightly as: "Tommy walked through the gardens today, discussed the correlation between sex and love with his grandfather.")

By the time Thomas turned sixteen, he had outgrown the hedges, even as his grandfather had shrunken behind them, bent almost at a right angle as though he were constantly searching for something he'd lost. A few weeks before he died, Thomas's grandfather would give a final piece of advice, one that would stand Thomas in good stead lo these many years.

"At some point," he rasped, "every goddamn woman you ever get tangled up with is going to ask you the same damn question. It seems innocent enough, but trust me, it's a depth charge waiting to go off. She's going to look at you, probably when she's naked, and she's going to ask, 'Do you like me better with my clothes on or my clothes off?' Now understand, Tommy, there is no correct answer to this. Whatever you say will be wrong."

"So what do I do?"

"Trick is, you don't answer the question at all. Instead, you say, 'Just as long as I can see your eyes, that's all that matters.' Works like a charm. Hell, you'll probably get a blow job out of the deal."

It was the last conversation he remembered having with his grandfather. The next thing Thomas knew they were at the cemetery, taking slow solemn turns shovelling dirt onto Grandpappy's casket.

Memories of Amy: half dressed, half naked. Amy in a man's shirt, unbuttoned and open. The chubbiness of her thighs, the feathered down of her pubic region. Amy, hips at an angle, asking Tommy: "Do you like me better with my clothes on or my clothes off?"

He didn't miss a beat. "Honey, just as long as I can see your eyes, that's all that matters."

Amy, grinning. "Come here, you."

Thanks, Grandpa!

There was once a time, celebrated even now, when the story of "boy meets girl" would be followed by "boy courts girl," "boy buys girl flowers," "boy coaxes girl into bed." A time when you got to know each other first, and then you slept together. But that era has long since passed (it expired sometime in the mid-1980s) and exists today primarily in pop songs, paperbacks, and rom-com cinema. Today, sex is taken care of right at the outset, dispatched in a "let's get this over with" manner, so that, having cleared the air, you can then decide whether or not you actually like the person. Sex is the audition; the relationship (if any) comes later.

Thomas and Amy had followed this same pattern: their first semi-date had ended with them tumbling into each other's eyes, into each other's arms, and, soon after, into bed. True, Thomas held a distinct advantage over Amy: he had a full psychological profile and detailed brain scan of the object of his affection, whereas Amy didn't even know his real name. But his advantage didn't last.

As their clothes fell away, he'd asked her his question, had purred it into her ear: "How do you want it?"

To which Amy had pulled back. "How do I want what?"

Um . . . This had thrown him off his game. "You know, *it*."

"It?"

"Do you want it hard and fast?" he asked. "Or soft or strong?"

She laughed (snorted, really). "What, is that your *technique?*" she said. "Column A or Column B? Let me guess, no matter what I ask for, you're going to tease me." Then: "I don't like to be teased. You lie back. I'll take care of this." And before Thomas could stammer some sort of reply, she was already on top of him and he was inside of her and she was moving her hips, first in a rocking-horse fashion, then in grinding circles, then in slow figure eights—an infinity sign unrolling like a lariat—pushing deeper with every turn until the inevitable happened. Thomas gasped, bucked several times. "Shhh," she whispered.

Next time at bat, Thomas resisted the narrative, fought to regain the upper hand. He wrestled his way on top of her, only to have her flip him back over, part tango, part bullfight, until, weakened, panting, and with willpower sorely depleted, he allowed her to again climb astride. Amy leaned in, her hair falling over his face, and as she reached down to guide him in, she asked, half mocking, half serious, "How do you want it?"

Later, as she dismounted, chest sheened in sweat, she'd said, "Don't feel bad." (He didn't.) "It's always that way." (What way?) "I've always had trouble coming."

This was a devastating aside, and one that Thomas took as both a personal affront and a challenge. (A nifty trick, throwing down the gauntlet like that.) Thomas never worked harder than after Amy's admission. He tried all sorts of new positions, many of them cribbed from the *Kama Sutra*, some quite fanciful, others downright ridiculous, suitable more for balloon animals than the sexual arts. He researched new rhythms, flirted with tickling, tried more kissing, then less kissing, tried spanking, kneading, butterfly flutters, inner thigh pressure points, but it always ended the same—with Amy rolling him onto his back. Amy the cowgirl. Amy in charge. (He began to suspect it was all a hoax and that, counterintuitively, she was faking *not* having an orgasm to make him work harder. Several times over the days that followed, he would feel her contract around him like a fist flexing, only to be told, "Close, but no cigar.") He eventually did solve the Rubik's Cube of Amy's orgasms, more as a matter of sheer persistence than magical technique, but he never did manage to solve the Rubik's Cube of her sadness. It was always there. There was something profoundly sad about her, this girl who had been so desperate to find God.

"Tell me about your family."

"Not much to tell. Mom died when I was young. Dad works at Mattress Warehouse. My brother, Sebastian, is studying to be a priest."

"A priest? Wow. That's like meeting someone who makes fine whalebone corsets. Is there even a market for that anymore? Priests, I mean. I assume there is some niche fetish group keeping the whalebone corset business alive."

Memory is the hotel curtain that never completely closes. Memory always lets in just enough light to fill the room and ruin your sleep.

"So your brother wants to be a priest. Was he strict as a kid?"

"No. He was lovely. When Mom died, he watched out for me. He always watched out for me."

"Y'know, I still haven't met any of your family. We should get together, maybe have a—"

"Can we change the subject? Please."

Heart attacks hurt, but there are no pain receptors inside the brain. Memories cause mental anguish, but nothing physical. Thomas reminded himself of this daily, but it didn't seem to help. Every relationship he'd ever been in, no matter how fleeting, had always ended on his terms, some gently, some in tears, but always on his terms. Not so with Amy. Was it simply pride? Only that? This was, after all,

Thomas's first true heartbreak, and those are always the most devastating, the most intoxicating, the most compelling. (Everything we do is inevitably measured from that first heartbreak, the way epochs are marked. Before the Common Era and After.) So, too, would his life be forever divided into Before Amy and After. Every relationship that followed would be measured against her and would be found lacking. He knew that already. Some might be sweeter, most would be happier, but none would be Amy. He would look for her in the eyes that followed, would search for her reflection. Science requires standard units of measurement, whether metric or imperial, grams or ounces. For Thomas, life would now be measured in units of Amy.

She haunted not only his thoughts, but his senses, especially smell. It's the oldest of our senses, older than we are, older than mammals, older than primates. It existed in the earliest tadpole, is older than sight, older than taste, older even than touch. Our other senses are routed through the cerebrum, but our sense of smell bypasses the gatekeeper, feeds directly into our reptilian brain stem, into the deepest evolutionary layers of who we are. It is the sense most closely connected to memory. This is why a fragrance, a smell, a fleeting aroma, can flood the mind with associations. For Thomas, the minty smell of Crest toothpaste would hurl him back in time, would conjure up images of Amy, would bring him to his knees. At one point, he tried smearing tiger balm under his nose, but it didn't help.

Heartbreak is an ice cube caught in the throat. A tourniquet around the chest. You try to swallow, but you can't. You try to breathe, but aren't able to. People have died swallowing ice cubes the wrong way.

Heartbreak is a fractured bone, poorly set. A bad dream you wake into. A drug withdrawal. A waking case of the DTs. Thomas roamed the corridors of recollection on punitive missions, search and destroy—or was it search and restore? It was hard to tell at times.

Memories are like mythical monsters; you have to kill them three times before they stay down. And even then . . . The past collars us whether we acknowledge it or not; the only difference is the length of the leash. No matter how unfettered we feel, if we run far enough we will feel that leash tighten, yank us back. Thomas had once watched a dog in a park, tethered to a tree, turning in slowly constricting circles until it had to be rescued and unwound. At which point it started winding itself in anew. Heartbreak is a dog in a park on a tree.

The possibility that Amy would now only ever exist in the past tense: this is what he couldn't face, that any time he spent with her would be in retrospect, in the chemical traces that memories leave in the neural pathways of our brain. Her brother, then, was a lifeline, thinly drawn, toward a future with Amy.

Why did he love her so painfully, so completely, so inadequately? (The intensity of one's affections, after all, has little to do with the object of one's affection. Fixations are self-generated, like compound interest or the voices in your head.) A "splintered self" theory might say that he was searching for a missing fragment of his own psyche, that he saw something in her that he was lacking and was longing for. A certain sadness?

At some level Thomas still perceived himself, however imperfectly formed, as a healer. *She hates me and I don't know why*. How to heal one's self? Ah, but the premise was wrong. Amy didn't hate him. No. It was much worse than that. Ever since the Incident of the Feigned Pregnancy Test, after the initial anger subsided, Amy had been left with only a profound feeling of *indifference* toward Thomas. This was worse than hate: hate, after all, is predicated on passion. But indifference? One might manage to transform hate into love—certainly love was easily enough turned the other way—but indifference? That was a task of the first order, as close to impossible as any algorithm would allow. Which is to say, Thomas's quest—to cure her brother and win her back—was doomed from the start. As all heroic endeavours are.

Here was the hard kernel under the tooth: it was not that she had stopped loving him, but that she had, perhaps, never started. She never loved him, not in the way that he had loved her: painfully, completely, inadequately. She had loved that he loved her, that much was true, but Amy had always known that Thomas was only ever a way station en route to someone else, that One True Love waiting for her beyond words.

Should we tell him? Would it matter?

In the last few nights, Thomas had worked his way out from under the worst of his despair. He felt buoyant, upbeat, optimistic even. His heart had been broken, true. But he'd changed his brand of toothpaste and, even better, Thomas had a plan. And with a plan, anything is possible.

CHAPTER TWENTY-ONE

"Do I know you?!" This was the greeting Eli had shouted, spittle flying, when Sebastian arrived at Thomas's apartment.

"Don't mind him," Thomas said. "Come in."

The other Jesus—the magician—was on the far side of Thomas's spacious living room, once again peering through Thomas's microscope.

"Leave that alone," Thomas said. "It's expensive. And leave Sully alone as well." He could tell that someone had moved his pet skeleton. The Saint Patrick's Day hat was gone, and Sully was now facing the window, as though someone had been dancing with him, had spiralled him around loosely a few times, then left him there. Probably Eli.

"Just put your bags here, by the door," Thomas said, as Sebastian followed him in.

Someone had been snooping in Thomas's mail as well; the bills and flyers were spread across the kitchen counter. He spotted another postcard, written in the same boxy capital letters as before, like a culprit trying to hide their handwriting in a ransom note: REMEMBER ME?

And below that, underlined forcibly: THINK. Thomas threw it into the recycling along with the flyers.

"Gentlemen, gather round. And leave that microscope alone! It's not a toy."

The three men crowded around the marble-topped counter. "There are two floors," Thomas explained. "This is the main floor. There's a balcony on the second—Eli, you can smoke there if you need to—but otherwise, I would like the three of you to stay down here. We'll put Eli on the couch, Sebastian in the guest room—that's at the end of the hall—and we'll put"—he still didn't know the magician's name—"you in the pantry. It sounds cramped, but it's not. It's more of a walk-in storage unit, almost as big as the guest room. If any of you aren't happy with your sleeping arrangements, let me know. We can move them around. I have an extra futon and some blankets as well."

"I admire your domicile," said Eli, nodding his approval. "Very chic. Ikea?"

"No, not Ikea."

"Where do *you* sleep?"

"My bedroom? It's upstairs." *With a lock on the door in case any of you crazy fuckers tries to kill me in my sleep.*

"Not where. What on? D'ya sleep on a plank or a cot? Cardboard?"

"A mattress. A regular mattress."

"King-sized?"

"Queen."

"Well, it'll have to do. I'll take it."

"What? No."

"You said—"

"I meant amongst yourselves. If you aren't happy with the sleeping arrangements, you can sort things out *amongst yourselves*."

"Let's put it to a vote."

"I am *not* getting voted out of my bed, okay?" He could feel a migraine coming on. "I'm going upstairs."

"Hypocrite," Eli said, under his breath.

CHAPTER TWENTY-TWO

THE SCHOOL'S NEURAL-IMAGING LAB was located deep in the catacombs, across from the biometrics department. Bernie was at home, but on call. He was always on call.

Half awake and fumbling for his glasses, he answered his phone without checking the number. Someone this late? He didn't need to check. It could only be Thomas. Bernie breathed onto his lenses, tried to clean them on his undershirt, to no avail. "Did Cerletti sign off on this?"

He could hear the grin in Thomas's voice. "He hasn't *not* signed off on it."

Unlike the lab's older PET machines with their IV units of the sort they'd tested Amy on, the school's MRIs required two passcards and a key.

"There's a log as well," Bernie pointed out. "Every time one of the MRIs is fired up, there's a record. Cerletti will know."

"Yeah, but how often do they check the log? Never. So who's going to know?" Bernie's many part-time jobs at the university included on-call night supervisor at the neural imaging department. If someone booked an MRI or a SPECT scan after hours, Bernie signed them in. "And if anyone does notice," Thomas said, "who are they going to report it to? You."

"I don't know. This seems . . ."

"Listen. Cerletti approved this project. He doesn't know the exact details, but he gave his blessings."

"For *therapy*. Not for brain scans."

"Look. I've got three guys who think they're Jesus. Their problems are either physiological or cognitive. If I'm going to begin therapy, I first have to eliminate the possibility of any physical causes: brain damage, lesions, fossilized tumours, depleted forebrain activity—the usual fault lines that might cause a brain to misfire."

Bernie was beginning to waver. "It's late. The buses aren't running."

"One step ahead of you, buddy. I've already sent a cab to pick you up. It's on its way."

He knew Bernie would give in, just as he knew Bernie would be alone on a Saturday night. Thomas piled his three Christs into his Prius and set off to meet Bernie at the imaging lab. As they glided down empty lanes, past parking garages and shuttered storefronts, he explained the basics of brain scans to them—emphasizing that it was a way of illuminating their inner powers.

"Sounds diversionary," said Eli. "I'm in!"

He used the word like a compliment. Good things were *diversionary*, bad things *trepidary*. "What kind of wattage are they drawing?" he asked.

"Not really sure," Thomas said, as he made the turn from Massachusetts Avenue onto Everett. A nondescript red building slipped into view.

"I used to work in the railyards, at the switch house, monitoring the relays," Eli said. "Back in the day."

"I thought you were a carpenter," Thomas joked. "Back in the day."

But Eli missed the humour. "I worked electrical at the railyards, was never in carpentry. I did the wiring. Fuse boxes and such."

"He means your father," said the magician, leaning up from the backseat. "It's an allusion."

"Illusion?" Eli was more confused than ever. "My father was a farmhand. Don't know where you're getting your information."

He knows, thought Thomas. *At some level, he knows. When his guard is down, he is fully aware of who he is and where he came from.* It seemed to Thomas that there were layers of reality involved, and that Eli's competing identities were not as segregated as they seemed, but seeped into each other. If so, how does one go about disentangling the two?

Eli had calmed down a great deal since that first day. He was still prone to fits of declamatory rage, but when Thomas read through Eli's medical records from San Hendrin, it became clear that for all his bile and bluster, the only person Eli ever really hurt was himself. The magician seemed to have a soothing effect on him, which was surprising considering they were both occupying the same psychological space, both claiming the same name.

Mr. Wasser has shown marked improvement in temperament. This is what Thomas wrote in his journal. He then added: *You would almost think that being cuffed and left alone in a room was bad for one's mental health.* But, realizing that he needed to adopt a more scientific tone— these journals were, after all, being written for posterity—Thomas crossed out those comments and wrote instead: *Test subject E. Wasser has experienced negative therapeutic results in regard to his restraints. These restraints, therefore, have been removed.*

Eli was still an intimidating figure with a booming Old Testament demeanour. When Bernie met them at the side door of the Neurobiology Imaging Lab, Eli roared, "I know you!"

"Don't worry," Thomas said. "He does that to everyone."

"I know you!" Eli repeated, eyes frenzied.

Bernie was shaken by Eli's accusation and remained rattled even as the MRI hummed to life, even as the test subjects were laid out, one by one, on the cold comfort of a medical slab, even as the halo headrests were swivelled into place, even as the machine rotated, layering their brains in colour-coded imagery.

"Remain perfectly still," Thomas advised. "It's going to get loud. Lots of clanging and banging, but don't move. No pens in your pockets or plates in your heads, right? Great." Then, to Bernie: "Let's set the crosshairs on the lateral ventricles. Should get good fluid density there."

When Eli balked at following Sebastian into the MRI, Bernie explained, "There's nothing to worry about. The scan tracks oxygenated blood flow to specific regions. It uses magnetic resonance. We're basically reading echoes."

"Echoes?" asked Eli as he lay down.

"In the form of radio waves. Creates a three-dimensional image." Bernie leaned across, adjusted the settings. "Allows us to see inside a living brain."

"Blasphemy!" Eli shouted as his head was being strapped down. "We're not bats, you know!"

"Please," said Bernie. "Don't move."

Eli eventually complied, eyes closed, whispering repetitively, "The time will come, the time will come."

Bernie had to ask. "What time?"

"When we will envy the dead. We, the wounded, the damaged, the unrepairable. Our time will come."

It was a phrase that would stay with Thomas over the next three weeks: *We, the wounded, the damaged, the unrepairable.*

"Please," said Bernie. "Try to relax."

"Don't you need a license to operate one of these?" the magician asked when it was his turn.

"What's to know?" said Thomas as he helped Eli off the table. "You enter the information, press a button, machine does the rest. The hard part is reading the results. Fortunately, we have one of the best in the biz with us tonight. Bernie here is an old hand at this."

Bernie had indeed assisted on hundreds of experimental scans, had watched the professors tease meaning out of the topography of the mind. He was something of a protégé.

Each scan took less than twenty minutes, but the prep time between stretched the procedure well into the night. When it was done, Thomas and his three test subjects sat in a dimly lit room, under the buzz of fluorescent tubes, while Bernie correlated the results, uploading each one into separate files. Eli was soon stretched out over three chairs, snoring, a chest-rattling catarrhal sound more alley cat than lion. Sebastian, pale and weak, rocked back and forth, eyes closed, mumbling catechisms to himself. The magician sat waiting patiently with a bemused look on his face, like someone who knows how a trick is done.

It was the confessional hour of night, somewhere between darkness and dawn (although, in the windowless rooms of the catacombs, it would always be night). While they waited for Bernie to wrap things up, the magician moved his seat next to Thomas's.

"What are you looking for?" he asked.

Thomas blinked. "With the brain scans?"

"With everything. With us."

"Honestly? I think you're broken. I think you're broken and I want to help. Not only you, but Eli as well, and Sebastian. Especially

Sebastian. Three people. Same name, same claims, same identity. Something is seriously wrong here, and the problem is either in the way your brains are wired or in the way you think. It's either physiological or it's cognitive. That's the question."

"Not spiritual?"

"Spiritual?" said Thomas. "Listen. If I were to scan your brain while you were praying, I could pinpoint the neurochemical pathways your prayer follows. I can draw you a map to God. I can hook you up to an EEG, chart your brain waves, or run a CAT scan. And if I were to inject radioactive tracers into the bloodstream of, say, a Tibetan monk while he's chanting or Franciscan nuns while they're reciting the rosaries, and run a SPECT scan, I can show you the human soul lit up like a Christmas tree."

"You've seen it, then? The human soul."

"In a manner of speaking, yes."

Here, then, was the Soliloquy of Thomas the Lesser, patron saint of the empirical, advocate of the neurochemical gospel, champion of the synapse (that microscopic gap between neurons, that thin rill where the arc light of mind occurs):

"Searching for magic?" Thomas asked. "You don't need to look far. You certainly don't need to turn to the stars or the heavens. The human brain weighs three pounds. It's the size of a small cantaloupe, uses less power than a refrigerator light, and yet a cubic millimetre of it contains more than a million synapses. Where we once mapped unknown continents, we are now mapping the human mind. Things we once thought of as abstract entities have been pinpointed with uncanny accuracy. Joy, memory, fear, regret—these are nestled in real places, in specific clusters of cells. The greatest explorations of our age are inside our own heads. Who cares what a lot of dead stars and cold planets provide? The mind is far more complex. A gelatinous organic computer, throbbing with life, with electricity, there are as many neurons in the human brain as there are stars in the Milky Way. If you're going to look for God, start there." He tapped his temple. "This loose coil of wet rope contains everything humankind is capable of: cathedrals and symphonies, gas chambers and slave ships, Monet and Mozart. There's more than enough wonder inside us. We don't need to insert an imaginary being into the equation; the math works quite well without it."

And therein ended the soliloquy. Thomas came out of it as if from a dream. Somewhere, he could hear choral music and the sound of voices singing. Where was this music coming from, down here in the catacombs?

"You want to meet God?" Thomas said. "I can send an electrical current through your left temporal lobe and you will meet God. The devil, too."

"The devil?"

"He dwells in the lower reaches, next to our childhood fears and primal anxieties."

"And joy? What of joy?"

"Simple. Joy lives in the medial forebrain. Euphoria as well. I can pinpoint altruism in the basal ganglia, empathy in the midbrain. I can show you where a sense of pessimism is rooted, where optimism is bred, where our intuitions and 'hunches' are generated. I can even bore a tiny hole in your skull, insert a syringe, and suction out your identity along with your hippocampus. I can erase your autobiography."

"Really? You can contain us in a syringe?"

"Who are we, if not our memories? Erase that and you erase the self. And what is memory anyway? Just protein synthesis and synapse connectivity. And the act of forgetting? The art of letting go? I can isolate that in a petri dish as well, in a single squirt of calcineurin enzyme."

"You want to reduce us to a series of chemical reactions."

"You say that like it's a bad thing. Want to know why you can't stick to that diet, get yourself to the gym, why you keep making the wrong choices in life? Blame your anterior cingulate cortex, that's where impulse control is handled—or mishandled. Got a bad feeling about something? I can pin that down as well. Bite your nails, afraid of dogs? Our compulsive habits are tangled up in the clotted seaweed of the basal ganglia. Phobias are lodged in the almond-shaped amygdala. Emotional trauma is seared into the somatosensory cortex. Everything we do can be localized and quantified, all of it. Looking forward to something? Anticipation is just the cells in the brain's reward centre preemptively secreting dopamine."

"And doubt?"

"Doubt, denial? Those are in the lower neural substrates of our prefrontal cortex. The seat of consciousness? That's your thalamus sorting through incoming information, making sense of the senses."

"And what of guilt?"

"That's the central nervous system firing distress signals back and forth within the amygdala. Creates a clammy sensation on the skin, the feeling of trying to recoil inward from ourselves. The physical manifestation of a guilty conscience. And feelings of remorse? Those are just memories that have begun to ferment. Remorse lives in the brain's insula."

"Trying to explain human emotions and ideas by referring to their molecular foundations is like trying to explain a cathedral by holding up a brick."

"Listen. Rational thought dwells in our frontal lobes, emotions live in the limbic system. The two are braided together. Fear, bliss, worry, dread: these all have specific neural correlates. Imagination lives in the hippocampus. Feelings of social obligation—what you might call a conscience—are situated in the orbitofrontal cortex, just above our eye sockets, nestled in our frontal lobes."

"And love?" asked the magician.

Thomas hesitated. "Well, that's a little different. Love is what we would classify as a 'polygenic phenomenon.' It's diffuse. It spreads throughout the brain, hard to locate in any one area."

"Love, hope, and charity. These three abide, but the greatest of these is love." The magician was quoting Saint Paul.

Thomas was unimpressed. "Paul was an epileptic who suffered from hysterically induced blindness. As for love, it depends on what type of love you're talking about. The love of a parent for a child? Of a couple married for many years? Are we talking companionship? Or raw passion? Hormonal love? Intellectual love? The love of a good meal?"

The magician smiled. "It sounds like a modern version of phrenology, of reading the bumps on people's heads."

"I suppose it is, in a way, but this time it's *scientific*."

"Phrenologists were scientific, too."

"Yes," said Thomas, "but now we know better." Then, looking around: "Do you hear that? The music. Is there a radio playing somewhere?"

But the magician didn't hear anything, and before Thomas could wander off to investigate, Bernie had reappeared, looking tired but triumphant.

"All clear," he said. "The verdict is in."

Eli woke with a start, momentarily disoriented. Sebastian opened his eyes as well, and the magician leaned forward, intently focused.

"I'll have to go over it again more closely," Bernie said, "but everything looks normal. Near as I can tell, there's nothing wrong with your brains."

The three Christs seemed relieved. Thomas felt elated. *It's cognitive, then.*

We know people can be talked *into* madness—brainwashed by cults, hectored by abusive spouses into emotional collapse, raised in toxic communities, breastfed on poisoned ideologies—so why can't we undo it the same way? Why can't we talk ourselves *out* of madness?

This is what Thomas would set out to prove, this was the single insight he would kindle and fan, the church door to which he would nail his thesis: *We can talk our way out of madness.*

CHAPTER TWENTY-THREE

IDENTITY THERAPY: SESSION ONE. *The following is a transcript of a session conducted by THOMAS ALEXANDER ROSANOFF (recorded on digital audio, supplemented with notes) with the following test subjects: ELI WASSER, SEBASTIAN LAMIELL & JOHN DOE (aka THE MAGICIAN).*

Subjects are seated in a semicircle at the residence of T. Rosanoff. On the table in front of them are the following items: a portable blood collection unit; a Bible; a revised SDM:III manual; notepads and paper; and the medical files of Eli Wasser and Sebastian Lamiell, as provided by the San Hendrin mental facility.

THOMAS: Good afternoon, gentlemen. I would like to start by introducing myself. I mean, we've already met, but—anyway. My name is Thomas. I'm a doctoral candidate at the Hawthorne Institute of Brain Sciences. It's affiliated with Harvard Medical. I study experimental neurology, with a specific interest in developing restorative treatments based primarily on physiological diagnoses.

Subjects: no response.

THOMAS: Brains. I study brains. The biological foundations of behaviour, beliefs. What can go wrong, and how to fix it. That sort of thing.

ELI: Like with rats?

THOMAS: Not with rats, no.

ELI: With mice?

THOMAS: No, not with mice, either. I mean, I did work with mice as an undergrad, but that was a long time ago and my research now is primarily—

ELI: With rats?

THOMAS: No, not with rats. For want of a better word, I study the human psyche.

THE MAGICIAN: (*cutting in*) The psyche?

THOMAS: Yes.

THE MAGICIAN: Not the soul?

THOMAS: Same thing. Now, before we get started, there are a few items we need to—

THE MAGICIAN: (*softly, almost to himself*) Thomas…Thomas… Do you have a last name, Thomas?

THOMAS: We will need to run regular blood tests, make sure everyone stays healthy. There are some standard psychological profiles I need to compile, questionnaires I'd like you to fill out, a Multiphasic Personality Inventory, or MPI, plus a thematic ap-perception test and so on. To get a baseline, nothing too complex. Mainly, I want us to talk. I want to find out more about you, who you are, what you believe. And (*turning to the magician*) to answer your question, my family name—it's Rosanoff.

THE MAGICIAN: Rosanoff?

THOMAS: That's right. Now then, before we—

THE MAGICIAN: Rosanoff? Like the Boy in the Box?

THOMAS: Yes. Well. The reason I brought the three of you here today—

THE MAGICIAN: I heard you went mad. I heard you killed yourself.

ELI: Is that true? You killed yourself?

THOMAS: Okay. First off, there was no box. I was there, I should know. And secondly, do I look like I killed myself?

They lean in, consider Thomas carefully.

THOMAS: It's a rhetorical question, for chrissake. Of course I didn't kill myself!

THE MAGICIAN: So you are Tommy? The boy in that . . . experiment?

THOMAS: My eternal albatross, yes.

THE MAGICIAN: Strange childhood.

THOMAS: No, actually. It was perfectly normal, boring even. It was like any other childhood, except for the mirrors.

THE MAGICIAN: The mirrors?

THOMAS: One-way mirrors, in every room. Not as invasive as it sounds. A little weird, granted, but not invasive. (*laughs*) I was always turning on a light and surprising myself.

THE MAGICIAN: Mirrors?

THOMAS: Mirrors and music. They would play different types of music while I was doing different tasks. My childhood had a soundtrack. Does that answer your question? Now, why don't we go around the table and you can each tell us a little bit about yourself. Sebastian?

Sebastian: eyes down, no reply.

THOMAS: Sebastian? We can't move on until you say something.

SEBASTIAN: (*whispering*) Not Sebastian . . . I am Jesus. Jesus of Nazareth.

THOMAS: I see. (*turning to Eli*) And you?

ELI: I am the Son of God! Lord of the Dance! King of the Jews! Christ the Redeemer! Lion of Judea, returned from Heaven! Born anew! . . . But you can call me Jesus.

THOMAS: Okaaaay. (*turning to the magician*) And . . . ?

THE MAGICIAN: What he said.

THOMAS: Well, now. You see, I'm confused. It's like—"Would the real Messiah please stand up?"

All three stand.

THOMAS: Kidding! I was kidding—listen. (*Thomas opens the New Testament to a bookmarked page*) Matthew 7:15. "Beware false prophets. They come in sheep's clothing, but inwardly are as hungry and ravenous as wolves."

He turns the Bible, slides it across to the others so they can read it for themselves.

THOMAS: "Beware false prophets." All three of you claim to be Jesus. But there can only be one Messiah, one Christ. So, either one of you is right or all of you are wrong.

THE MAGICIAN: You're the man with the microscope. What do you think?

THOMAS: What do *I* think? I don't think any of you are Jesus. I think it's a story you tell yourselves to help you cope with the pain and disappointments of life. And I think, at some level, you know this.

Eli slams his fists against the tabletop.

ELI: Blasphemy! (*looking upward*) Father in Heaven, smite him down! Smite him down now!

Long pause.

ELI: (*arms crossed, sullen*) He's busy. (*Eli thrusts an accusatory finger at Thomas.*) But it's coming!

The magician passes the Bible back to Thomas, open to a new page.

THE MAGICIAN: John 10:20.

THOMAS: (*reading*) "Of Jesus, many said of him: He has madness within. Why should we listen to him?"

THE MAGICIAN: And here as well (*he flips through the pages*) in Mark. See? His own family thought he was mad.

THOMAS: His. You said *his* family. Not yours.

THE MAGICIAN: The royal "we." His own family wanted him committed. Even they thought Jesus was mentally ill. Was he a prophet or a madman? His own family couldn't tell, even with all the miracles he was performing—healing the sick, turning water into wine—they still weren't sure.

ELI: Smoke break?

THOMAS: No. You can smoke later—but only on the balcony. (*turning his attention back to the magician*) Not to question your sources, but as I understand it, the Gospel of Mark is also the origin of snake handlers and talking in tongues. So there you go.

THE MAGICIAN: You didn't answer my question. How are we to tell a prophet from a madman?

THOMAS: Well, I hate to break this to you, but the Church of England decided this matter back in 1604, a little doctrine known as "the cessation of miracles." Haven't you heard? The age of the prophets is over. Any mystics or miracle workers you encounter now are either charlatans or deluded. So, to answer your question, any prophet today is, by definition, false. (*turning his attention to Sebastian*) Now. Mr. Lamiell . . .

ELI: Smoke break?

THOMAS: No. Moving on . . .

Thomas opens Sebastian's file.

THOMAS: Sebastian Henri Lamiell. Age twenty-eight. Admitted to the San Hendrin psychiatric facility. Affective schizophrenia disorder. Akinesia tendencies. Auditory hallucinations. Intrusive thoughts. Suicidal tendencies. An undue preoccupation with spiritual matters. Obsessive-compulsive religious behaviours. Currently taking antipsychotic medication. Is this correct?

Sebastian: no response. He stares down at the tabletop. His facial muscles twitch. His tongue darts out between his lips.

THOMAS: (*closing the file*) Sebastian, let me come clean. I know your sister. And what you're doing is killing her. It's breaking her heart. . . .

Sebastian: no reaction. Thomas waits, but there is no response. He turns to Eli's file instead.

THOMAS: Mr. Wasser, according to the police report, you were picked up in Boston Common dancing. Naked.

ELI: Not dancing.

THOMAS: It says dancing.

ELI: Not dancing.

THOMAS: But it says dancing. Right here. Look. "Eli Wasser. Age fifty-seven. Indecent exposure, public nuisance, resisting arrest. Suspect was seen dancing in the nude." You were dancing, Eli, without any clothes on.

ELI: Not dancing. Whirling.

THOMAS: Whirling?

ELI: Like David. At the temple.

THOMAS: Okay. So, why were you . . . whirling, in the park, naked?

ELI: (*leans in, whispers*) Angels. I was calling them down from on high to take me to a better place. They were coming to rescue me. But the others—they conspired against me.

THOMAS: The others? Who?

ELI: Who? You're asking me *who?* Dammit, man! Do I have to spell it out for you? The CIA. The FBI. The scribes. The voices on the TV. The Samaritans, the good ones and the bad, all of 'em! They've been co-opted. They're secretly working for the Pharisees. Only thing is, they're in disguise.

THOMAS: Disguise?

ELI: Flesh masks, which are provided by the Sadducees, who are really—ha!—agents of the Pharaoh. Don't you get it? We must have chaos within us to give birth to a dancing star!

THOMAS: Um . . .

THE MAGICIAN: Makes sense to me.

Sebastian nods. It makes sense to him, too.

ELI: Y'see, the Sadducees and the Pharisees, they're in cahoots, the whole lot of 'em. Frauds! They can look or not look, they can send messages through the telephone wires or rend their robes, doesn't matter, because they are insignificant next to me. I refuse to be tricked into dancing for the Pharaoh and his Jezebel whores, not when the Sadducees and their surrogates are still roaming the woods with the sins of the father burning their flesh. That's why tinfoil is only shiny on one side! Think about it.

Eli sits back, convinced he has won whatever argument he thinks they were having.

The magician is staring at Eli, at Eli's blind eye.

THE MAGICIAN: I have a question for Eli.

THOMAS: (*to Eli*) Is that okay? Can he ask you a question?

ELI: As long as it's not about my eye. Is it about my eye?

THE MAGICIAN: It's about your eye.

THOMAS: (*cutting in*) As I understand it, Mr. Wasser attempted to, um, to remove his own . . . I'm not sure why, exactly. Was it an "eye for an eye" sort of thing?

ELI: It was Matty's fault. He told me to.

THOMAS: Matty? Who's Matty?

ELI: Matt. I call him Matty. His name's Matthew. He's in the Bible. (*turns the pages*) Here.

THOMAS: (*reading*) Matthew 5:29. "If your right eye offends thee, pluck it out and cast it away." . . . But—but he was speaking metaphorically, surely.

ELI: Can never be too sure. (*looking around the room as though searching for invisible foes*) Fornicators! Sons of whores! They're listening. They're in the air ducts and the wall sockets. I can hear you! I CAN HEAR YOU! (*suddenly stopping*) Smoke break?

THOMAS: (*sighs*) Fine.

Twenty minutes later.

THOMAS: You are Jesus Christ, correct?

Eli nods.

THOMAS: (*referring to Eli's file*) But it says here, you're from Connecticut. My understanding is that Jesus was born in Bethlehem.

ELI: That's right. Connecticut. In the Holy Land.

THOMAS: Connecticut isn't in the Holy Land.

ELI: Yes it is.

THOMAS: No. It isn't.

ELI: It is.

THOMAS: It's not. It's really not.

ELI: That's just your opinion.

THOMAS: No, it's not an opinion. It's a fact. Connecticut is not in the Holy Land.

ELI: Ha! I can prove it. The Son of God is from the Holy Land, yes? I am the Son of God. I was born in Connecticut. Therefore—ha!—Connecticut is in the Holy Land! Check yer Bible.

He crosses his arms, triumphant.

THOMAS: Listen to me, Eli. Connecticut is not in the Bible.

ELI: Yes it is.

THOMAS: No it's not. If you can find Connecticut in the Bible, *I'll* dance naked in the park. But I gotta say, the case you're making—that you're the Messiah—it's not holding up.

Thomas turns his attention to the magician.

THOMAS: Now. Our third and final Jesus . . .

THE MAGICIAN: I have a question. (*He flips over the heavy SDM:III manual.*) It says here, on the back cover, "This comprehensive manual is known as the gospel of mental health professionals."

THOMAS: And?

THE MAGICIAN: Your father wrote this manual.

THOMAS: He oversaw the project, yes.

THE MAGICIAN: Your father wrote your Bible?

THOMAS: Well, so did yours. Now then, Mr. . . ? (*He stares at the magician.*) You're not going to give me your name, are you?

THE MAGICIAN: You have my name.

THOMAS: Your real name.

THE MAGICIAN: You have my real name.

THOMAS: If not your name, your age, then? Thirty-eight? Thirty-nine?

THE MAGICIAN: Something like that. I've lost count.

THOMAS: And you're Christ?

THE MAGICIAN: I am.

THOMAS: So these other two, are they Christ as well?

THE MAGICIAN: They believe they are.

THOMAS: But are they?

THE MAGICIAN: It's better you ask them that question directly.

THOMAS: I did.

THE MAGICIAN: Then you have your answer.

THOMAS: I'm confused. You're in your late thirties, Sebastian is in his twenties, Eli is in his fifties. But as I understand it, Jesus died when he was thirty-three.

THE MAGICIAN: Reports of my death were greatly exaggerated.

THOMAS: I see. (*referring to the Bible in front of them*) But it says here that you died and ascended to Heaven. You left. It's one of the few things that all four gospels agree on.

THE MAGICIAN: You shouldn't believe everything you read in books.

—END OF TRANSCRIPT—

CHAPTER TWENTY-FOUR

THOMAS TURNED OFF THE recorder, looked at the magician.

"Okay. Here's what I know. You're homeless, living on the street. And you play three-card monte down at the station."

"What you say is not false. But it is misinformed. Am I without employment? Yes. But consider the lilies. *Solomon in his finest robes was never so beautifully arrayed as the lilies of the field. Yet they neither toil nor worry*. Wasn't Christ himself often without a home? *The Son of God has nowhere to rest his weary head*. Do I play cards? Yes. Do I perform miracles? When I want to. Am I the eternal spirit reborn? Without a doubt. I have existed since the first moment. I existed when the world was first called into being."

"You were there, at the birth of creation?"

"I was there on the first day, yes. In the beginning was the Word, and the Word was with God. Through him, all things were made. And through me, all things are made."

Eli was becoming agitated. "He's crazy. I'm God. Not him. He's trying to trick us!" His voice grew louder, more insistent. "I am the Lord of Creation! I made the world and everything in it!"

"Did you make me?" Thomas asked.

"Are you in the world?"

"Yes."

"Then OF COURSE I FUCKING MADE YOU!"

The magician leaned forward, held Eli's fists between his hands until they opened up. "It's okay, it's okay," said the magician.

But Eli remained agitated. "I made the world, goddammit! I made the sun and the moon, I made TVs and baboons. I made upside-down trees and fuse boxes, I made stars and cellophane. I even made Ginsu knives!" Voice dropping: "I made those on the second day of creation."

Sebastian spoke, his voice so soft they almost missed it.

"We are all of us empty," he said.

Thomas wasn't sure he'd heard correctly. "Empty?"

"Tin men. Small gods. Our chests have been scooped out. They have been replaced with clockwork hearts and old rags."

Sebastian didn't say anything else. Instead, he collapsed back into himself.

"Tin!?" Eli roared. "I am NOT made of tin! I am Christ Everlasting, and I come to rain fire, not as a lamb—but a lion!" He was so angry he was shaking. "I'm God, for Christ's sake!"

"Of course you are. No one is saying otherwise," said the magician.

"*I* am," said Thomas, exasperated. "I'm saying otherwise. We're not here to act as each other's enablers. Listen. There can't be two Christs—*three* Christs, sorry. I forgot about Sebastian. " He addressed the magician. "You claim that you're Jesus."

"I don't 'make the claim.' I *am* Jesus."

"What about Eli? Is he lying?"

"No."

"So you think Eli is Jesus as well?"

"I do."

"Ha!" said Eli. "See? He admits it! I *am* God."

"God?" said Thomas. "By what proof?"

"By his own word," said the magician. "His testimony is proof. His words are proof."

"That's not proof!" said Thomas. "A double-blind, variable-controlled trial—that's proof. A *feeling* is not proof."

Sebastian, in a whisper: "A feeling is proof that you feel."

Eli leapt at this. "See? Even he agrees with me! Why are *you* so dense?"

Thomas, still exasperated: "That's a tautology. It's like— It's like saying a thought is a proof of what you think. Or a belief is proof of what you believe."

"Exactly!" said Eli.

"I think he's getting it," said the magician. "Look at it this way, Thomas. Belief is what we *assume* to be true, yes? We don't need to daily test that the sun rises in the east or that water runs downhill or that objects fall when you drop them. We start with that assumption. Well, I start with an assumption of God."

"But you also claim to *be* God. So . . . so, you *believe* in yourself?"

"Of course," said the magician. "Doesn't everyone?"

"Unpopped!" Eli pointed a crooked finger at Thomas's chest. "That's what you are! Your heart, it's like a bag of unpopped popcorn. You're the hard nuggets at the bottom of the bag that only heated up but didn't burst!"

Thomas pushed back his chair, sighed. "Let's try this again." He turned to the magician. "You believe that you are Jesus Christ. Correct?"

"No."

"No? You don't believe you're Jesus?"

"I do not."

"But you just said—"

"I don't 'believe.' I *know*. I am Jesus of Nazareth, son of Joseph and Mary. That is a fact, not an opinion. A fact is what's true, whether we believe it or not. Rain falls downward and steam rises upward, regardless of whether you believe in gravity or chemistry. And I am Jesus Christ, Son of God, whether you believe in me or not. It's simply a fact."

"And you know the difference between facts and beliefs?"

"I do. Let me show you."

The magician swept his hand across the tabletop, leaving three creased playing cards facedown, weathered and well worn, corners dog-eared and bent.

Thomas looked at these three cards, then up at the magician. "Let me guess. Find the lady?"

"Not the lady, the heart." He flipped over the middle card. It was the ace of hearts.

"Please follow this card," he said. "With your eyes."

The magician flipped the card back, and it began: a fluid dance, palms moving, over, under, around, again and again, faster and faster until the cards became a blur, and then . . . his hand faltered. One of the cards rose, ever so slightly, and there it was: the ace of hearts. It happened in a blink, and the magician quickly slapped the card down again, but it was too late. Thomas had seen it.

"Well?" asked the magician.

Thomas leaned forward, laid a finger on the middle card.

"You seem very sure," said the magician.

"I am."

"What shall we wager, then? Your pride? Sebastian's soul? A cigar for Eli?"

"Yes!" Eli hollered. "A cigar for me! A good one, too. A Cuban. And I get to smoke it at the kitchen table, don't have to go outside. Can't believe God has to go outside when he wants to smoke."

"Fair enough," said Thomas. "A cigar for Eli. And if I win?"

"If you win," said the magician, "I will proclaim that I am not Christ and nor is Eli, or Sebastian."

Thomas smiled. *One Jesus down, two to go.* "I accept." He extended his hand to the magician and they shook on it. "But I'm afraid this is a bet you're going to lose," said Thomas. "I saw the card. It lifted up, just a little, but enough for me to see."

"So you *believe* that this card is the ace of hearts?"

"I saw it."

"Well," said the magician. "There's what we believe and there's what we know." He leaned back. "Please. Be my guest."

Thomas flipped the card over. It was the eight of spades. He flipped over the next card and the next. All three were the eight of spades.

"Ah," said Thomas, smile tightening. "The parable of the playing cards. I'm assuming you palmed the ace somehow, hid it up your sleeve or something?"

But then Thomas noticed Sebastian looking past him, staring over Thomas's shoulder . . . in awe. Thomas followed his gaze, turned to see—

The ace of hearts.

Everywhere.

There were a dozen or more. Sticking out of the books on Thomas's shelf, tucked into picture frames, hidden in potted plants. There was even one inside the SDM:III manual in front of Thomas, and one in the Bible as well, like bookmarks.

Thomas felt his chest contract. *He must have hidden them during the break, back when we were waiting for Eli to finish his first cigarette.* But did the magician even leave the table? Thomas wasn't sure, couldn't remember. *He must have tucked them in when I wasn't looking. But how?* (That's the way it begins, with troublesome doubts.)

Sebastian's eyes grew wide with wonder.

"Nice trick," said Thomas. "Well executed." But the doubts remained, like a cat underfoot.

Eli whispered, "I believe you owe me a cigar."

Thomas nodded. "I believe I do."

CHAPTER TWENTY-FIVE

THE HOMELESS SHELTER WAS more crowded than ever. A tattered exodus, fleeing the devil in Tent City, had fanned out across Boston and many of them had ended up here, tended to by a small band of volunteers and one very tired nun.

"Look what the cat dragged in."

Thomas gave her a pat on the shoulder. "You say that every time."

"It's true every time."

"Repeating something doesn't make it true, Frances. You should know that. And anyway, when a cat presents a dead mouse to someone as a gift, it's supposed to be a sign of love."

"Sure it is. So what brings you down here?" They were in her office, a glorified storage room crowded with boxes. Thomas cleared a space for himself across from her desk (he assumed there was a desk under there somewhere) as Frances spooned some Nescafé into a styrofoam cup. She added hot water from an electric kettle, plopped in a lump of chalky powder, stirred it together.

"Coffee?" she asked.

He peered into her cup. "I don't think it is, actually."

"Suit yourself. And before I forget, if I give you a list of medicines, do you think you could get them for me?"

"What, like some common pusher?"

"Consider them samples," she said. "Our stocks are running low. We need expectorants, antibiotics. We can always use bandages and gauze, too. The university will have more than they can use."

"I'll see what I can do." It wasn't the first time he'd plundered the school's stockrooms for Frances. "And if you need antipsychotic medications, too, let me know. We have all kinds of trial prescriptions—"

"Antibiotics, not antipsychotics."

"Okay, but if you change your mind, the offer stands."

"You have access to general stock as well?"

"I do."

"Can you get me inhalers, laxatives, maybe some Maalox? A new thermoscan if you can snag one. And condoms. Lots of condoms."

"I'd have to dig into my personal stash for that last one, but sure, I'll see what I can do." Thomas slipped his hand into his overcoat pocket, retrieved his phone. "I have a question."

"This isn't about a girl again, is it? You really should consider getting advice on your love life from someone who hasn't taken a vow of celibacy."

"Not a girl. A magician." He held up his phone. "Do you know this man?"

She looked closely. "I do. He lives down the street, across from the church. Comes in from time to time. Asks for wine—and bread."

Thomas laughed.

"We serve him grape juice instead. He said that's okay, it'll transubstantiate when he drinks it. He's very gracious. Helps out with the other patrons sometimes. Hasn't been in lately."

"You don't know his name, his background?"

"Not really. He's clearly educated, though. Articulate. Not sure what demons he's wrestling with." She swirled her cup, finished it off, down to the dregs. "Why do you ask?"

"He's living with me."

"With you?"

"As a houseguest. I'm trying to help him shed his delusions. Spirituality, God, all that nonsense."

"Nonsense?"

"I didn't mean it that way." (What other way could he mean it?) "What I'm trying to say is, he's tormented and he needs help."

"We're all tormented, Tommy. It's just a matter of degree. He believes he's Jesus. Well, there's Jesus in all of us, isn't there?"

"But people with confused identities, insidious delusions, can't function in society, their lives don't mesh with reality. They're alienated. And I'm trying to"—he almost said "save"—"help them. Without surgery, without pharmaceuticals."

"Well, that's a start." She placed her empty cup to one side. "Can I tell you a story? A parable of sorts."

"Sure, I always enjoy a good parable. They're like Aesop's fables, but without that annoying explicit moral tacked on at the end. So long as it's not the one about the Prodigal Son. I'm sick of that one. Heard it so many times, I know it by heart. Stupid kid never should have come home in the first place." *Some might say your entire childhood was a parable, Tommy.* It was something Frances had said to him years before, in passing, but it still stung: the idea that his life was only ever meant as a lesson for others, that his entire existence was a morality tale.

"Here goes," she said. And she told him the story of the shoe on the roof.

"It happened at the Harborview hospital in Seattle. I knew one of the doctors," she said. "He was there when they retrieved the shoe. He's still rattled by what happened. Science can only take us so far, Tommy. There will always be something just out of reach. Something elusive. We might as well call it God."

"That's it?" said Thomas. "A single shoe? You're up against the entire weight of the scientific method, and all you can throw at it is a shoe?"

"How do you explain the shoe on the roof, then?"

"I don't have to. It's what we call an 'anomalous experience.'"

"Tommy, *everything we do* is an anomalous experience. *Being alive* is an anomalous experience. That's the problem with science; it always falls silent right when the questions start getting interesting."

"Science isn't simply the search for answers, Frances. But for better questions. Listen, the day you can put a human soul on a scale and measure it is the day I say, 'By Jove, these Bronze Age myths might be on to something!' But in the meantime, I'll stick to those pesky little things called facts. And anyway, God is dead. Didn't you get the memo?"

"I've read that obituary before," she said. "He's not dead, he's sleeping."

"Hell of a slumber." Thomas placed his smartphone on the desk in front of him with the image of the magician still frozen on the screen. "Why would you dedicate your life to Bronze Age myths in the first place? *Just So Stories* told by semi-literate people who thought the world was flat and slavery was the natural order of things. You know he never condemned slavery, not once, not even in the Sermon on the Mount? Your man was perfectly happy to give the earth to the meek and blessings to the poor, but he didn't once condemn slavery."

"You'd almost think he was a product of his times."

"Ah, but your man was supposed to transcend time!"

"And you," she said, "should have been a lawyer."

He grinned. "I'll take that as a compliment."

"Take it however you like. Just make sure you pick up the supplies I asked for. And as for him"—she nodded toward the image of the magician on Thomas's phone—"I'd be careful if I were you. It's dangerous fooling around with people's identities like that, even if they are delusional."

"Noted." He tucked his phone back into his overcoat. "Let me ask you something else. You and my dad, you two ever . . . you know."

"I'm a nun."

"Still a woman."

"A woman who's a nun."

"You haven't answered my question," he said.

A phone call rescued Frances. She shoved aside a pile of papers as she disentangled the cord of a clunky, old-fashioned receiver.

Do they even make those anymore?

Frances held up a finger for silence.

"Hello," she said, "*Sister* Frances here." She emphasized the "Sister" for Thomas's sake.

But as she listened to the voice on the other end, her face went pale.

Shallow breaths. Lips, dry. Bad news.

She let the receiver fall away from her but didn't hang up. She looked at Thomas. "It's about Charlie. You remember Charlie?"

"The old guy? The one with the ants?"

"They found his body in Tent City. They're calling it an overdose. There's a detective on the phone, and she wants to talk to you."

Music, faintly rising. Choral voices and a question: "Thomassss, re-member me?"

"Tommy?"

Frances seemed far away.

"Tommy, she wants to talk to you."

In a vivid haze, he took the phone, his hand moving as though under-water, grasping the receiver, bringing it to his ear. When he spoke, his voice sounded strange and detached. "Good evening," he said. "This is Thomas Rosanoff speaking." He couldn't shake the feeling that somehow, unwittingly or otherwise, he was the cause of Char-lie's demise.

The phone call was a formality, the detective explained, so they could close the file. Thomas's name was listed as the consulting phy-sician on a prescription made out to the deceased.

"But I only ever changed his bedpan, helped with his dressings. . . . Where? Here, at the shelter. I was—I was helping out. I can't write prescriptions. Not yet. I'm only a— *Dr.* Rosanoff? That's my father. He must have been doing outreach with the homeless community, providing antipsychotic drugs. . . . Charlie was mentally ill, so if he was ever admitted to Massachusetts General then I suppose my father might have prescribed something. I really don't know. . . ."

Thomas handed the phone back to Frances, still reeling from the news of Charlie's death. As Frances spoke into the phone, he felt himself falling farther and farther away.

"Sister Frances here. . . . That's right, we're strictly a recovery centre. . . . Nursing, immediate concerns rather than long-term prog-nosis. . . . Oh, the usual. Pink eye, lice, bedsores, assorted wounds. . . . Ointments and creams, mainly. . . ."

Had Thomas only known.

He was a lot closer to the scene of the crime than he realized. Beside Charlie's body, the police had found a postcard, and on the postcard was a question—a question aimed at Tommy. No address, only a question. But the detective never mentioned it and Thomas never asked, and the postcard was never delivered.

CHAPTER TWENTY-SIX

ON THE SECOND-FLOOR REFERENCE room of the R. J. McMurphy Library, Thomas pulled out the largest biblical atlas he could find.

"Comprehensive, see? It says so right here: *International Geographical Society Comprehensive Atlas of Biblical Times*."

The three men squeezed around him. They were dressed in identical white bathrobes, which—Thomas had to admit—did give them a certain prophetic air. Thomas had purchased the robes for them to wear around the house, but they wore them everywhere, cinched at the waist like overcoats. They'd caused a murmur of attention when they marched into the reference room, but Thomas didn't care. They could wear whatever they wanted. It was what was inside their heads that needed to be addressed.

Thomas peeled back the oversized pages of the atlas.

"Here. A map of the Holy Land." He ran a finger down the page. "Jericho . . . Jerusalem . . . The Dead Sea. . . . No Connecticut."

Eli refused to give in. "This proves nothing."

"What? This proves everything!"

"It absolutely does not."

"It absolutely does too!"

Across the atrium from them, a security guard was hounding a wino out of the building—*"C'mon. Out you go."* *"I got rights!"* *"You've been harassing people. You have to leave."*—when the dishevelled man spotted Thomas and the others.

"Jeezly God!" he yelled, eyes wild and jubilant.

He squirmed free of the guard and hoofed it straight for Thomas and the others. Jaundiced eyes, matted hair, a voice so loud it drew the attention of people at other tables.

"Oh, no you don't!" said the security guard. He tried to steer the wino back toward the elevators, but the man slipped past, grabbed Eli's hand, shook it ferociously.

"It *is* you!" he chortled, mouth like a toothless comb. The man's nose was flattened, his jaw misshapen. *He needs reconstructive surgery,* thought Thomas. *That, and a good orthodontist.*

"I seen you, and I said to myself, sure as shit that's Eli!"

Thomas noticed an expression of anguish flit across Eli's face, there and then gone, as the security guard wedged himself between them, sought a handhold on the wino's stained jacket.

"They said you was dead, Eli! You rose again from the looks of it, eh?" Leaning closer, he said, "No hard feelings, eh, Eli?" He was referring to his broken facial features. "The jaw. The nose. Ribs and everything. No hard feelings, eh? That's the way it goes, right?"

Thomas felt his stomach clench. *Patient is not considered a danger to others, only to himself:* This is what Thomas had written in Eli's files. Eli, released from his restraints, allowed to wield a kitchen knife.

By now the security guard had grappled his way into a semblance of control and was frog-marching the man to the nearest elevator. As he was dragged off, the wino hollered back to Eli, "They was askin' about you down in the Peg! They said you went crazy! Got locked up! Crazy? I says, 'Crazier is more like it,' eh, Eli?"

Eli hadn't said a word throughout this entire encounter, and in the vacuum of silence that followed, Thomas watched him, waited for a reaction. But there was none.

Finally, Thomas said, "You know that man?"

Eli nodded.

"The Peg? What is——?"

"Clothes Peg Alley," said the magician. "It's what we call the abandoned tenements across from Tent City." Tent City was transitory; the Peg was more permanent.

Thomas had heard of it. "That's where the squatters are, right?" He'd seen it on the news.

"Not squatters," said the magician. "Residents."

"It's where I used to live," Eli said, voice hollow and hoarse. "Before the scribes and the Pharisees got ahold of me. Before things . . . happened."

Sebastian spoke, his voice like the flutter of a wing. "You were wrong, Mr. Rosanoff."

Thomas looked at him. It was always surprising when Sebastian said anything. "What do you mean, wrong?"

"What you said. About Eli." Sebastian was staring at the tabletop, avoiding eye contact. "You said Eli was homeless, but he's not. He has a home."

CHAPTER TWENTY-SEVEN

AN EARLY-EVENING INTERLUDE (or, reflections in a minor key): We often stumble through life cast as minor characters in other people's stories (just as they exist as minor characters in ours). Given that it is the fate of many of us to be the background players in narratives larger than our own, let us consider one such secondary presence: a professor with a distinct widow's peak, a lesser Caesar, an Ichabod figure walking alone under snowy streetlamps. It's the first snow of the season: a faint dusting, soft as flour sifting down, but a chilly reminder nonetheless. Autumn was ending, summer was a long way gone, and winter was creeping in on cat's feet.

When we are young, we live our lives in a kinetic whirlwind, a constantly unfolding *now*, an all-embracing present tense. But as we get older, we find ourselves adrift in a seaweed of "should've dones" and "might have beens," where the future shrinks even as the past grows ever distant. This was where Anton Cerletti dwelled, lost between vanishing points.

His past was fading away, was losing its details, its textures, its taste. It was changing from a photograph to a daguerreotype, from a daguerreotype to a smudged charcoal outline. Not memories but the *memory* of memories. What is it like to go through life as a secondary character, as a supporting role in someone else's biography? It's like writing a diary in vanishing ink. It's like looking the wrong way through a pinhole camera. It is like walking on a winter street alone, with no one watching.

And what is it that Professor Cerletti sees when he peers through the pinhole? What is it he sees as he trudges onward? A life lost along the way. Opportunities squandered, possibilities denied, colleagues who fell away, one by one, until only a single name remained: Dr. Thomas Rosanoff. *We never took Tom seriously. How could we? He came from such thin stock, was so puffed up and self-important, even as a student. A rube with few social graces, yet he made up for it with his un-wavering, self-preening confidence.* That he would become the golden boy of their cohort? It was to laugh.

And what does Professor Cerletti glimpse as he moves soundlessly through the snow, skirting the edge of the down below, that realm of shopping-cart travellers and itinerant panhandlers? Cerletti has out-walked the snow, has gone much farther than he realized, somnolent as a sleepwalker in a self-induced fugue, when he sees, under the win-ter glow of the streetlamps, someone else, another figure, vaguely fa-miliar, hurrying across the cobblestones in front of him. Or perhaps it was his own shadowy projection, a trick of the light. After all, light plays far more tricks on us than the darkness ever will.

CHAPTER TWENTY-EIGHT

THE RAGTAG ASSORTMENT OF lean-tos and shanties looked almost biblical. Canvas tarps draped over tent poles, giving the appearance of nomadic encampments. The snows of last night had melted into mud, leaving a sharper chill hanging in the air and with it the wet scent of smoke and ash, and something reminiscent of sandalwood. Had a camel caravan loped past, Thomas wouldn't have been the least bit surprised. Bodies moved down narrow pathways: underage runaways and beauty queen addicts, the sad and the lonely, the downcast and the dispossessed, an Ellis Island's worth of lost souls. *All those trajectories, ending here in Tent City.*

Thomas should have been nervous, but he was too fascinated to be afraid. It was like walking through an open-air laboratory, a nature preserve of mental disorders: here a paranoid schizophrenic, there the walking embodiment of masochistic personality disorder, here a dominating delusional psychosis shouting madness at passersby, there a body dysmorphic disorder smeared in lipstick. You could stroll through Tent City with the SDM:III manual and check items off the list as you saw them. *Cerletti should've had us take our practicums down here, rather than at the hospital.*

Eli shepherded Thomas and the others past mounds of smouldering refuse and small gardens that had stubbornly taken root—tangles of tomatoes, leafy beds of lettuce—then across a muddy field littered with glints of glass and the occasional unravelled condom.

A pair of abandoned tenements—former vanguards of the Roxbury projects, windows broken, bricks scorched—formed a narrow canyon, and running down the length of it were the overlapping corrugated rooftops of Clothes Peg Alley.

They had come to the Peg to reclaim Eli's belongings. The men were dressed in bathrobes, except for Thomas, of course, who had led them across the tracks below Roxbury Crossing like a mallard with her ducklings. Once they entered Tent City, though, Eli had taken over and was moving through with great purpose.

"When they arrested me," Eli shouted over his shoulder, "the police wouldn't let me go home to get my stuff. They dumped me into the lion's den, said, 'What home do you have to go back to anyway? Give us an address, give us an address.' Well, I could damn well draw them a map, but I couldn't give them an address, now, could I?" Then, under his breath: "Fuckers."

The police, Thomas noted. *Not Sadducees. Not the Pharaoh. The police.* Madness might kick down the front door, but reality has a habit of escaping through the side window.

Eli held up his hand and they stopped in front of a collection of planks and particleboard that was held together mainly with chicken wire and wishful thinking. A shopping cart was parked out front, stuffed like a horn of plenty: broken radios and one-eyed dolls, lampshades and rags, egg cartons and reams of copper wiring.

"Do I know you?!" Eli bellowed at the man who was peering at him from inside the tumbledown shack.

"Eli," the man pleaded. "You were dead, is what I heard. Others said they put you away, for good, but I figured no, sir, you'd never let 'em take you alive."

"Where," said Eli, "is the rest of my stuff?"

The squatter rubbed the back of his neck. "Your stuff? Most of it got tossed. Some of it's still there in the cart."

Sebastian was rocking back and forth on his heels, saying, "*A home to the desolate, succour for the sickly, manna for the ill at heart.* Psalms, that's in Psalms. God will give a home to the desolate, succour for the sickly, manna for the ill at heart. . . ."

Eli rummaged through his cart. "Where's my teleporter?"

"Teleporter?" said Thomas.

"For the angels," he explained. "Weren't you paying attention? The Pharisees, remember? If you dance the angels down, you have to use a teleporter to get back up. Everybody knows that. It's common sense." He shook his head at Thomas's appalling lack of knowledge. "What are they teachin' you at school?"

Thomas turned to the magician for help, but the magician was staring past Eli's jerry-rigged shack to a row of card tables that had been set up in the muck at the end of the lane. Two young men in puffy jackets and baseball caps—they dress by rote, these men—held stacks of dollar bills sorted by denomination between their fingers. They were peddling their wares to the residents of Clothes Peg Alley with the alacrity of auctioneers. Crystal meth and ecstasy. Plastic vials of illicit OxyContin. Nickel bags and angel dust. A veritable cornucopia of self-medication.

Eli looked at the dealers in the alley. "They're back," he said, flatly. "When?"

The other man shifted and twitched, scratched at his jaw. "Dunno. About a week, maybe more."

Thomas felt his scientific detachment falter; he hadn't planned on crossing paths with criminals. "Maybe we should go," he said. "Eli, why don't you grab your stuff and we'll—"

But the magician was already striding toward the dealers' tables, anger in every step.

"Thieves!" he yelled as he pushed his way through the jumble of bodies surrounding the tables. "Thieves in my Father's house!"

The taller of the two dealers—a pockmarked fellow named Gustus; gold teeth and a thin grin—looked up from the transaction he was completing (crystal meth doled out to a woman with sores on her face). "What the fuck?" he said.

"In the name of the Father, I cast you out!"

Gold Tooth laughed, nudged his partner. "Hey, Des, check it out. Crazy fucker thinks he's—"

But before he could finish his sentence, the magician was on him. He flipped the first table over, scattering baggies and vials and loose coins in the air—they seemed to hang there a moment before plunging down to the muddy ground—and then the next table and the next, and now, Thomas really was scared.

The commotion was instant. Voices clamouring. Bodies scrambling. Gustus and Desmond on their feet, ready to kill before the second table hit the ground. "What are you, a fuckin' *bat?*" But then they spotted Eli, arms crossed, standing behind the magician, and their confidence faltered.

It was as though they'd seen a ghost, holy or otherwise. Eli didn't say a word. Didn't need to.

"Hey, Eli. Didn't see you there at first," said Gold Tooth. "We thought you were—"

"Out!" screamed the magician. "You have turned this City of God into a den of thieves! Out!"

The two dealers hesitated, then hurriedly gathered the nickel bags and crumpled bills from the mud while Eli loomed above them. (If Thomas could have slowed the footage down and studied the micro-expressions on the dealers' faces when they looked at Eli, he would have seen something not unlike fear. Fear—and respect. And oh how often are those two aligned.)

Eli walked back to his particleboard-and-chicken-wire shack. The magician followed, breathing hard, still angry. Then Sebastian, then Thomas. The crowds parted before them.

The squatter watched Eli coming toward him, but Eli said nothing. He reached into the shopping cart and wrested loose a wooden sign. It read: HOME SWEET HOME.

Eli turned to Thomas. "We can go now."

CHAPTER TWENTY-NINE

IN THE EMPTY QUIET of a stained glass interior, the three Christs sat on a pew in their bathrobes, heads tilted, staring at the crucifix above the altar.

"They never get my eyes right," said the magician.

"Or my nose," said Eli.

Elderly parishioners were petitioning the saints, on their knees, hands clasped on rosaries. Yearning voices. Abject desires. Too much God? Or not enough?

Thomas stepped out from inside the confessional.

"So what did'ja tell him?" Eli asked, voice too loud for their surroundings. "The Sadducees have these places bugged, so you gotta be careful! And the Pharaoh has agents everywhere, even here. Specially here."

"I didn't confess," said Thomas as he buttoned up his overcoat. "I had a question."

Is what I'm doing ethical? Is it right?

"And?" asked the magician.

"No one answered."

No one at all.

The magician looked over at the confessional; the curtain was partly open. "The booth was empty," he said.

"Exactly," said Thomas.

On the drive back from Tent City, they'd stopped here unexpectedly, with Thomas pulling into the parking lot at the last moment. "Here we are," he said, eyeing Sebastian in the rearview mirror. "Our Lady of Constant Sorrow. I used to come here with Amy, your sister. She dragged me here every Sunday like clockwork."

Sebastian didn't answer.

And now they were inside, and Thomas was looking at these small gods on the pew before him. "How can you all be Jesus?" he asked. "I need an answer."

"How can water be ice and steam and liquid?" the magician replied. "Same substance, different forms."

Thomas thought about the anger that had shown itself in the magician when he overturned the tables in Clothes Peg Alley. He wasn't playing a role; he was truly in the grips of righteous rage. How do you tease out the delusions from the underlying character? How much of it is entwined, and what is lost if you extinguish the delusion? Much like cutting out a potentially cancerous growth, the question becomes, How much of the healthy tissue around it are you willing to sacrifice?

Back outside, a cold wind was sending the last of the leaves scuttling along the sidewalks. Thomas pointed to the street corner where the magician had once kept vigil. "Your old spot," he said. "Why were you there anyway, day after day, across from the church? Was it a protest?"

"Not a protest. A reminder."

"A reminder?"

"That I'm still here."

"Do you think that's why Eli blinded his eye, was dancing naked under the stars? Was he trying to remind the world that he was here?"

"Perhaps."

Eli was tromping ahead of them, kicking his way through the fallen leaves with the deliberate gait of a schoolboy. When a man in a suit bustled by, Eli asked him for spare change.

"Get lost."

"I already am," Eli replied.

And as they made their way through the crumbling leaves, the magician said something that would stay with Thomas long after everything went wrong, long after it all fell apart. "Do you know what Eli's problem is?" he said. "No one cares about him. Only God."

And if you remove that?

CHAPTER THIRTY

Dusk settled, almost tactile. As soft as dust and nearly as imperceptible. They arrived at Saint Mathurin's Seminary at that time of day filmmakers call "the magic hour," when the sun has slipped below the horizon, but is still refracted across the sky. A time of indirect warmth, of diffuse blues, of light without shadows.

From where they stood, the seminary looked like an advent calendar, lit from within, some windows shut, some open and empty, others glowing yellow. The one-a-day chocolate countdown to Christmas. (As a child, Thomas never went to church, but Frances brought him an advent calendar every year—which he immediately looted like some sort of fevered second-storey man, leaving behind nothing but gouged windows and torn cardboard. "Pace yourself," Frances would always advise. But he never did. Advent calendars were supposed to teach children the virtue of patience; instead, they taught the exact opposite.)

The seminary grounds were quiet. Thomas parked his Prius and, with his three Messiahs, he walked up a small hill beside the main building to where the advent lights were reflected in a pond, brackish and awaiting winter.

Eli and the magician stayed back while Thomas walked along the water's edge with Sebastian. Wisps of cold mist. Cat tails and lily pads, curling at the corners.

"This is where they pulled you out, isn't it?" Thomas asked. "This is the pond where it happened. I've read your file, Sebastian. In the days before your breakdown, you weren't eating, you weren't sleeping, were studying all day, praying all night. That's when it happened, isn't it? That was when God first spoke to you."

A small breeze wrinkled the surface of the water.

Sebastian stopped and closed his eyes. "A dove descended from Heaven. It said, 'You are my own dear Son. And I am pleased with you.'" When he opened his eyes, they were wet with pain.

"They had to repaint your dormitory room after you left. Did you know that? 'God is love and love is God.' That's what you wrote, isn't it? Again and again, on the walls of your room? You wrote a commandment, 'Love God,' a thousand times in your own blood, until you passed out, had to be rushed to the emergency room." Thomas had seen the scars that criss-crossed Sebastian's forearms. "You weren't trying to kill yourself, were you, Sebastian? You were trying to say something, trying to write it in your own flesh, a message, a distress signal."

Sebastian stared at the water. "Thou shalt love the Lord God with all thy heart and all thy soul, with all thy strength and all thy mind." His eyes grew wetter, but they never spilled over. "I have done that," he said. "I have kept the faith."

"Sebastian, what you wrote on those walls, that directive: *Love God*, that's from the Epistles of Saint John, right? But here's the thing: I looked it up, and I read the rest of the passage. There's more to it than that. Here." Thomas pulled out a slip of paper from his wallet. "The entire passage goes: *Love God, but first, love one another. If*

*you cannot love your brother, your family—whom you can see—how can
you possibly love God, whom you cannot see?"*

He waited for Sebastian to say something, but he didn't.

"For Amy's sake, for your family, for those who love you, I would
ask that you reconsider your beliefs."

The magic hour was ending and the darkness was upon them. The
lights of Saint Mathurin's had grown deeper, and the wind was picking up. Across the pond, Eli and the magician had become silhouettes.

Thomas turned to go, then stopped. Listened.

"Can you hear that?"

Sebastian looked at him. "Hear what?"

"Just there . . . under the wind."

"The silence?"

"You can't hear silence."

"Yes you can," Sebastian said, more to himself than to Thomas.
"You just have to listen really closely."

Thomas turned his head. "It's gone. The music. Must have been
from inside. Choir practice or something." Then: "You can go back
to San Hendrin anytime you want to, you know that, right?"

Sebastian nodded.

"Why stay with me, then?"

"I felt—I felt maybe you were the one who could do it."

"Do what?"

"Untangle me."

Eli was now hollering from the other side of the pond. "Pharisees!
On their way! Take heed!"

A groundskeeper was walking up the hill toward them in a slow
but determined stride. The white bathrobes of the three prophets
were highly visible in the gathering darkness. "Gentlemen," he said.

"We were leaving," said Thomas, coming down to meet him.

"Do I know you?!" Eli roared, startling the other man. *Fight, flee, or submit.* The groundskeeper's amygdala was quickly flipping through its options. He decided to stand firm.

"This is private property," he declared.

"Private?" yelled Eli. "I am the Lord Jesus Christ. I own these buildings in their entirety and all the lands that surround them!"

The groundskeeper reached for his cellphone.

"There's no need," said Thomas. "We're leaving, all of us." He looked at Eli. "Now."

Eli growled, but relented, and they walked back to the car like an abridged set of apostles. *Who's leading whom?*

On the drive home, Eli shouted from the back seat, "I could have smote him! If I wanted to."

I'm sure you could have.

A night sky, implacably black and bereft of stars. Thomas thought about the old wino at the library with the broken nose and the misaligned jaw, and of the pair of drug dealers they'd encountered earlier that day in the alley and how fearful they had been of Eli. *I'm sure you could have.*

Something else as well, a murky message bubbling up from below, something one of the Tent City dealers had said: *"What are you, a fuckin' bat?"* What a strange thing to say. He must have meant "rat." Must have misspoken, or perhaps Thomas had misheard him. (This was in fact an urgent warning, if Thomas had only recognized it. Instead, it fell away, leaving only a nagging trace behind. *Why would he say bat?*)

Thomas took the long way home, over the Alford Street bridge and then down along Inner Belt Road. Streetlights moved past as though on a conveyer belt.

Sebastian was in the passenger seat beside Thomas, staring at himself in the window. The magician was awake, but Eli had fallen asleep in the back and was snoring—loudly.

"Well," said Thomas. "At least he's not smoking his cigar." Eli had tried to light it up on the way to the seminary and had been shouted down.

The Prius was eerily silent as Thomas took the exit onto 3rd Avenue, across the tracks and past Mattress Warehouse. He watched for a reaction, but Sebastian didn't say anything. Instead, he continued to stare both at and through his own reflection.

"Doesn't your dad work here?"

There was no reply, but as they drove through the sparse neighbourhoods and industrial parklands beyond, Sebastian finally spoke, softly. "Have you ever noticed? God only matters when he's silent. Why is that?"

"Sorry?"

"When you talk to God, you're praying, and that's perfectly acceptable. But if God ever answers you, they say you're crazy. They tie you down and feed you with tubes. They take away your visions with medications and—other means."

Sebastian, strapped onto a table, mouth-guard in place. Sebastian, eyes filled with fear as a nurse applies gel to his temples, and a doctor presses a pair of handheld electrodes to either side. "Clear!" With today's muscle relaxants and analgesics, he doesn't convulse violently. He twitches instead like a muscle spasm, like a frog in a high school experiment.

"God only matters when he's silent. Why is that?"

The magician leaned up from the back seat. "God chose you, Sebastian. He chose you for a reason."

"No, he didn't," said Thomas. "Stop saying that. It's not helping."

"Now then, Thomas," said the magician. "I don't mean to play the braggart, but I am the Son of God, and I know of what I speak. O ye of little faith."

"Gimme your hand. C'mon."

The magician extended his palm to Thomas as he drove.

"See?" said Thomas. "Nothing. Show me the holes. Let me poke my fingers through them, then maybe I'll believe you." And then, realizing they might actually try this: "But don't go sticking nails through your hands! It'll take more than that . . . believe me."

"A sign?" said the magician.

"Sure. A sign from God. That'll do it."

And—*bam!*—the Prius blew a tire.

Thomas swerved, fighting to keep it on the road before bringing the vehicle to a jerking halt.

"Goddammit!"

Eli lurched awake. "Wazzit?"

Thomas slammed the door behind him and stomped around back, muttering dark invectives under his breath. He popped the trunk, rolled out the spare. No jack. *Shit.* He'd taken it out when he'd had the car in for servicing, had forgotten to put it back. *Jesus H. Christ.*

The others had piled out now and were standing on the deserted sidewalk. The magician was watching Thomas with an amused look on his face.

"Don't," said Thomas. "Not a word."

When he realized there was no jack, Eli squatted down and tried to lift the car by sheer force, grunting like a discount-bin Hercules.

"You'll throw your back out! Stop it!" Thomas checked his phone. Limited service.

Then, coming through the empty streets, a chugging minivan approached, slowing to a crawl as it drew nearer. Thomas stepped into the headlights, flagged the vehicle down.

Inside: a carload of nuns. In full habit.

They smiled at Thomas, faces brimming with benevolence.

Thomas walked back around the car with the borrowed jack in hand, glared at the magician as he passed. "This. Proves. Nothing."

As Thomas cranked the car off the ground, spun the lug nuts clear, and replaced the flat tire with the spare, the sisters of mercy chatted with Eli and the magician. (Sebastian held back, eyes down but listening.) They asked Eli about the bathrobes they were wearing, were dumbfounded when he cheerfully informed them who he was—and then introduced the other two in similar terms.

"They're with me!" Thomas yelled over his shoulder, as he wrenched the last lug nut back into place. "It's a form of therapy."

"For who?" one of the nuns asked.

And thus ended the road trip.

CHAPTER THIRTY-ONE

IT WAS HARD WORK, saving people from themselves, and Thomas stumbled into his apartment exhausted. The others followed, weary as well and besieged with yawns.

Past the messy, blanket-strewn sofa and up the stairs, Thomas entered his bedroom, flopped down face-first onto his mattress. Kicked off his shoes, was soon asleep.

He probably should have locked his bedroom door.

An hour (a minute? a lifetime?) later, his thickly lathered slumber ended with the creak of a door. Light fanned across his room. A hand shook him by the shoulder.

"Thomas, wake up."

But he ignored this, hugged his pillow more resolutely.

Another nudge. It was the magician, insistent. "Thomas, wake up. We've found it."

"Go 'way."

"We found Connecticut in the Bible."

Thomas buried his face deeper into the pillow. "No you didn't." Then, to himself: "Crazy bastards."

The magician shoved him again. Harder this time.

"We did. We found it."

When Thomas came stomping down the stairs, groggy and annoyed, Eli and Sebastian were huddled around the kitchen table like a pair of World War I generals examining a battlefield map. Except it wasn't a map they had in front of them, it was a Bible, open to the first page.

"Here," said Eli. "Ha!"

Thomas squinted. Blinked a few times, eyes still foggy. " 'Published by New Testament Books, printed and bound in Bridgeport, Connecticut.' Oh for chrissake. That doesn't count. I'm going back to bed."

"Hypocrite! Fabricator!"

Then, quietly, forcefully, Sebastian spoke. "You made a promise."

CHAPTER THIRTY-TWO

CONTOURED WITH PONDS AND walking paths, with summer-sweet shrubs and overhangs of weeping willow, the public gardens across from Boston Common offers a reprieve in the heart of the city. Beech trees and elm. Maidenhair and silver bell. This is where autumn first appears in the city, the ornamental maples blazing early, reflecting in dapple-dab, Monet-like arrangements on the waters of the lagoon. It's where winter first breathes as well. A park for Sunday strollers and families, elderly couples, walking in step, and sigh-heaving office clerks on their lunch breaks. At night the shadows deepen and the bright greenery of day becomes freighted with darkness and an almost tangible sense of dread. This is the id of the city when the sun goes down.

"Get naked!" said Eli. His breath came out as steam.

Thomas ignored him, tromped on ahead, hugging his overcoat for warmth. The three Christs fell in line behind him, walking in single file.

Thomas stopped, looked around. Seemed secluded enough.

"Fine," he said. He pulled off his overcoat and sweater, threw them on a pile with his jeans and shoes. Sighed. Stepped out of his boxers. Kept his socks on.

And he danced.

Bare-assed and shivering, turning circles, he made a failed attempt at performing the twist and something that looked like an Irish jig, threw in some boogaloo and a bit of Running Man and then—the sudden blast of a spotlight. The whoop of a siren. A voice on a megaphone.

"Shit!" yelled Thomas.

Eli and the others fled and Thomas followed. The siren was louder now and getting closer quickly, with the red-and-blue lights of the patrol car throwing shadows wildly across the grass. Thomas, lungs burning, still naked and clutching his pile of clothes to his chest, ran.

Ahead of him, Eli and the others crashed into the underbrush, through brambles and branches so thick they were almost cross-hatched.

"Wait!" said Thomas. "Wait, you bastards!"

Sock feet on bare pebbles. "Ow, ow, ow, ow, ow, ow!"

He caught up to them in a clearing. Everyone was breathing hard in ragged gasps, trying to be quiet. Thomas pulled his clothes back on, peered through the foliage to see if the police were still there.

"I think they're gone," he said.

And immediately the spotlight was upon them. The branches lit up as though caught in a flare's glare over no-man's-land. *Shit, shit, shit.*

Thomas pulled on his shoes and ran, laces loose, through the thornbushes as the siren grew more strident. He lost track of the others, came to a pond, crouched down under scant cover. *Trapped!* He could hear the patrol car roll to a stop behind him. Could hear the doors open, could see the first bobbing beams of the flashlights sweeping the edge of the area he was hiding in.

On the other side of the pond, across the water from Thomas, the three Christs stood safe—and dry. They were waving for him to join them. Ripples were spreading across the surface of the water. *How did they get there? They must have walked. Impossible. And yet . . .*

"Hurry!" Eli shouted.

The flashlights were closing in.

What if . . . ?

Thomas Rosanoff made the leap of faith. He ran out onto the water—and immediately plunged in. He came up, soaked and sputtering, choking.

"The rocks, the rocks. Use the rocks!"

Thomas floundered onto his feet, shin deep, saw a series of stone pilings that formed stepping-stones along one side of the pond. He pulled himself onto them, slipping and sliding across the water as the flashlights hit him. He reached the other side. Ran like hell.

CHAPTER THIRTY-THREE

WHEN THOMAS CAME DOWN in his bathrobe, hair still damp from the shower, Eli and the magician broke into applause.

"Well done!"

"That was some fine dancing!" said Eli. "Very diversionary!"

Sebastian hesitated, then joined in as well, clapping with a halting rhythm, rocking back and forth.

"Well, I hope you assholes are satisfied. I was almost arrested."

Eli remained magnanimous in victory. "I just wanna say, to everyone involved, that this evening went splendidly in every way. This is the first time in a long while, longer than when I was born or when I created the world, that I can count three friends among my acquaintances." (That was the problem with being the world's saviour. When you're busy saving everyone else, who will save you?)

Thomas: mutter, mutter. "Glad you're happy. . . . Connecticut in the Bible. . . . Use the rocks, use the rocks. . . ." He picked up his phone, scrolled through nearby restaurants. "I'm starving." At which point he spotted his box of microscope slides on the kitchen counter, shoved in every which way, blatantly out of order. "Jesus Christ."

All three looked up on hearing their name.

"Not *you*." Thomas made a sound somewhere between a sigh and a snarl. "Stop messing around with these, okay? They're expensive." He tried to straighten the slides, gave up. "So what do you guys want? Chinese? Italian?"

They considered the question.

"Well?"

"Loaves. Fish," said the magician.

"Fish," said Sebastian.

"Loaves," said Eli.

"Fish and loaves," said the magician.

Thomas looked at them. "So. Pizza and anchovies?"

They nodded. Sure. Close enough.

"Fish and loaves it is."

Thomas ordered two extra-large pizzas, one with anchovies and one with feta and olives. He could almost hear Bernie asking, *"Who the hell puts olives on a pizza?"* And he thought how exhilarating it was to have escaped a police dragnet. (It was actually a single patrol car with two officers, but that is not how Thomas would tell it. Over the years, he would layer the story with more and more embellishments until eventually he was fleeing across open water as bullets flew past him.) Memory, after all, is a reconstruction, and even the simplest of events becomes papier-mâchéd with myth as the years go by. It was a process as old as time. It was how gods were made. Thomas found it vaguely disconcerting, the malleability of memory: Was Amy herself even real anymore, or was she slipping into myth as well? He remembered Amy in a snowstorm, winter melting on her lashes, was startled to realize that it couldn't have been Amy, had to have been Wendy. Yet he could recall Amy there, vividly. Could remember her turning toward him, folding herself into his embrace.

Remember me. It was a message he longed to send.

The latest anonymous postcard was waiting for Thomas when he and his three Messiahs had returned from their road trip to the Saint Mathurin seminary. *"Remember me."* No question mark this time: a small shift, but a significant one, and one Thomas should have paid more attention to. With that single change in punctuation, the message had shifted from a question to a command; it went from pleading for attention to demanding it. *Remember me.* Everything turned on this: a single question mark, or a lack thereof. Yet Thomas missed the implications of this. He was distracted by life (as we all are).

Thomas finished drying his hair, threw the towel over the back of a chair. The magician was standing in front of the main bookshelf: floor-to-ceiling with science and psychiatry.

Pulling out a hardcover of *The Good Son*, the magician studied the cover. "First edition. Must be rare. May I?"

Thomas shrugged. He didn't care.

The magician flipped through the pages as though looking for a pressed leaf or a ticket stub, something tucked between the pages, forgotten. "I've read this," he said. "Your story. In bits and pieces over the years."

"And?"

He looked up at Thomas. "That wasn't a childhood. That was a hostage-taking."

"It wasn't that bad," said Thomas.

"We have a lot in common, you and I."

A street-corner magician and a Harvard medical man? "How so?"

"We both have public biographies. Our lives are, quite literally, open books."

"I suppose." *Except yours is delusional and mine actually happened.*

Back in the kitchen, Sebastian and Eli were setting the table for pizza. They were being very thorough: forks, knives, butter knives, soup spoons, pickle stabbers, fondue forks, salad tongs. Sebastian was lining each one up with absolute precision. Eli was complaining that Sebastian wasn't doing it right.

The magician had a question for Thomas. "Why is Sebastian so important to you? Why does it matter what he believes?"

"Sebastian has a mental illness. He needs help."

"What some might call a mental illness, others might consider a spiritual test. A crisis, perhaps. Or an awakening of angels."

"Angels? Really, now you're talking angels?"

"We all carry angels inside us. And demons. They usually slumber undisturbed but they *can* awaken, and they do. We go through life catching colds and missing buses. An unexpected encounter, a leaf falling at a certain angle, a puddle avoided, a parking ticket issued, and either one might appear—the angel or the other."

"People don't have spiritual crises anymore," said Thomas. "They have chemical imbalances. Every emotion, every phobic fixation, every memory leaves a chemical trail in the brain. *Neurons that fire together, wire together*. That's a central maxim of neuroscience. Repetition strengthens belief, and beliefs strengthen neural connections. Yell at a child long enough and you will alter not only her sense of self, but the actual physical properties of her brain. Sebastian is caught in a feedback loop, both chemical and cognitive, each bolstering the other."

The magician thought about this for a moment. "Do you know what I think Sebastian's problem is?"

"I would love to hear your diagnosis. Possessed by evil spirits, perhaps? Shaved his beard on the Sabbath? Had the unabashed effrontery to wear mixed fabrics in the presence of a menstruating woman?"

"I don't think he has an illness. I think he has a sob, caught in his throat."

"A sob?"

"Like a fish bone. I think Sebastian is just very, very sad. And being sad, that's not a mental disorder, is it?"

"Listen. Sebastian's problem isn't that his life has no meaning. It's the exact opposite. We're not talking clinical depression, we're talking schizophrenia. And with schizophrenia *everything* has meaning. Hyperconnectivity. You see patterns and portents, omens and hidden messages in every detail, no matter how fleeting. It can heighten creativity, but it can also lead to paranoia and panic, seeing cabals and conspiracies where there are none. Eli being a case in point."

"Eli is only trying to—"

"What do we know about Jesus of Nazareth? He was a healer. A doctor, I suppose. But we also know he heard voices, had visions, was deeply delusional. He believed he was on a divine mission from God. Textbook schizophrenia. Today, we'd put him on 400 mg of Seroquel and be spared the Crusades, the Inquisition, and the Mormon Tabernacle Choir."

"Thomas, I assure you, when I was preaching the Gospel in Galilee—"

"Enough, okay? Enough." Thomas steadied his gaze on the magician. "Who are you? Really."

"You know who I am."

Thomas smiled. "That's the thing about delusional disorders. Such conviction! They believe it so deeply, and after awhile, others start to believe it too, and they follow them into their madness. Do you know why we always find God on a mountaintop?"

"Closer to heaven?"

"Oxygen depletion. Shimmering lights, the dizzying floating sensation, the fear and awe, the sensed presence: mountain climbers experience these same symptoms at high altitudes. The scientific definition of God? A delusion of the mind."

"And the mind?"

"A delusion of the brain."

"I see. Elephants all the way down."

"Listen. Mind is a by-product of the brain. Mind is what the brain *does*. The brain itself is simply organic circuitry, electrical currents firing inside a jelly bowl. Revelations are the brain talking to itself. A neurobiological process, nothing more. So when Sebastian hears voices, it's his own tortured mind he's hearing. Like I said, he's caught in a feedback loop."

"And God? Where does He fit into this?"

"He doesn't. As I said, the equations work perfectly fine without that variable. It is, quite literary, all in your head. It's in here." He tapped his temple.

The magician slid the hardcover back into the shelf, turned to face Thomas. "Perhaps. But what kind of God would it be who only pushed the world from the outside?"

Thomas sighed. "Don't you find it odd that the more we know about the world, the fewer miracles there are? Miracles used to happen all the time. Now? Not so much. Rainbows were once a magical covenant with God; now they're just light refracting through the atmosphere after a rain. Religion used to explain everything, now it explains very little. Haven't you noticed that God's realm keeps getting smaller and smaller, until now it only covers those narrow gaps that we haven't yet filled in? Is that what we're left with? A god of the gaps? And if that's the case, what's the point?"

"Maybe," said the magician, "God *is* the gap."

Talk him out of his madness? Thomas couldn't even talk him out of religious superstitions.

"Tell me about your father," said the magician.

"My dad? Well, he's not as accomplished as yours," Thomas said. He was about to make another sortie against the magician's defences when the apartment buzzer sounded.

"Get the door!" Eli hollered. "It's pizza time!"

"This isn't over," said Thomas, holding up a cautionary finger at the magician.

He walked through the kitchen, grabbing his wallet and cinching his bathrobe. He opened the door and . . . standing there before him was not a pizza deliveryman, but an Easter Island figure, risen up: Thomas's father. Dr. Rosanoff was holding a folder from the San Hendrin mental facility, and he didn't look happy.

"Tommy," he said. "We need to talk."

PART THREE

THE CESSATION
OF MIRACLES

CHAPTER THIRTY-FOUR

MEMORIES OF AMY.

The blue of the veins on the back of her wrists, the connect-the-dot constellation of freckles along her collarbone, the way she sneezed when she stepped into bright light, those stubborn traces of paint under her nails, the manner in which her hair never seemed to hold a scrunchy for longer than 16.4 minutes (he timed it), her snorting laugh, her laughing snorts, the way she insisted on pronouncing "extraordinary" as though it were two distinct words (even though he'd corrected her, repeatedly).

Thomas had found her on the rooftop of her building once, telescope angled haphazardly at the moon. "I'm not really sure how to use this," she admitted. "It was a gift from my brother. It used to be his. He was president of our school's astrology club. I know, major dork, right?"

"Your brother? The one you told me about? The priest?"

"That was before he joined the seminary."

"I thought telescopes didn't work in the city. I thought the glare of streetlights and buildings washed out the stars."

"That's not true. You just need to know where to look," she said.

"And do you know where to look?"

"Nope."

She'd given up on the stars at this point and was examining the moon through her lens the way one might examine pores in a vanity mirror.

It reminded Thomas of his own Ladner XII microscope, a gift from his father, and it seemed to him, as he watched Amy fiddle with the focus of her brother's telescope, that the only way to look at the world was to either come closer or step back, zoom in or zoom out. Anything else and you would be lost forever in the middle ground, caught between vanishing points, the first unimaginably large, the other unimaginably small.

Amy on the roof: peering at the moon with the same seriousness with which she had once searched for perfect blue.

"Anyone sees you out here," Thomas warned, "they're going to think you're some kind of pervert, spying on people."

She pulled back her hair with her hand (the scrunchy had already come out) and gave him a sly, sidelong glance. "Why should I worry? You're the one they'll grab. You already have the name and everything. *Peeping Thomas.*"

"Condemned on the basis of my name alone!" he cried. "Story of my life." And then: "So how about it? Wanna peek in some bedroom windows?"

"No!" she said. "Well, maybe."

They never did peer into anyone's bedroom, but they did screw ferociously on the tar-paper rooftop, Amy bending at the waist, hands against the door like she was being arrested, Thomas with his head craned back, eyes blurring, a full moon looking down on them like a polished lens.

That was gone now.

Amy had slipped away to the far side (of love, the moon, everything) and Thomas was alone, down here on earth, squinting up at her through the wrong end of the telescope.

In the days After Amy, Bernie had asked, "What is love anyway?"

They'd been walking across the squat stolidity of the Harvard Bridge, darkness pressing in and the Charles River sliding silently below. The bridge was anchored at either end by a cluster of lights; it seemed to be floating both on and above the water.

Thomas was moping and Bernie, in his way, was trying to comfort him. "Think of it in terms of drive reduction," said Bernie. "What are our primary drives? Hunger, thirst, sex. These are basic human urges. And how do we defuse them? We eat, we drink, get drunk, sleep with strangers. So think of love as—as the emotional correlate of this. Falling in love is an exercise in drive reduction."

"That's the dumbest thing I've ever—"

"Or look at it as a mathematical formula. Romantic love is simply: p x d + pa. Proximity *times* duration *plus* physical attraction. With Amy gone, proximity and time have been removed from the equation. So drive reduction is no longer necessary. The various factors cancel out. See? Problem solved."

"You can stop comforting me anytime," said Thomas.

They came to a small, balcony-like abutment that jutted out from the side of the bridge. It was apparently meant to act as a scenic viewing platform of sorts.

"Ah yes," said Bernie. "These extra two feet really open up the view, in the same way that jumping gets you closer to the sun."

Thomas looked at the river flowing below, felt that familiar vertigo appeal of high places as the mind tries to close the gap, tries to reconcile a skewed sense of perspective. Part of him wanted to step over the edge, part of him wanted to step back.

"I was thinking of asking Wendy out," said Bernie. "You remember Wendy?"

"Who? Oh, right. How is she?" Thomas was barely listening. He was watching the river sliding past. "Go for it, Bernie. Wendy's great."

"Alas, she's with somebody else. She wanted me to tell you that she's happy now. She wanted me to use those exact words: *she's very happy without you.*"

Thomas laughed. "I'm sure she did and I'm sure she is. Too bad for you, though."

"See? I can't even *get* to heartbreak."

"How's your gut?" Thomas asked.

"Not so good." He laid his hands on his stomach. Bernie had been haunting the upscale oyster bars on the pier recently in an attempt at meeting women, even though oysters didn't agree with him. "I figured any woman who's up for eating oysters has a sense of adventure." And Bernie was only too happy to be somebody's bad decision.

"Fair enough," said Thomas. "How's it working out?"

"Not so good," he said. "Their sense of adventure seems to end with the oysters. I've eaten buckets of bivalves." And it showed. He was looking sickly.

"You have been a bit clammy lately. Good to see some of the colour has come back to your cheeks. That colour, unfortunately, is green, but still—it's a start."

Bernie stared at the waters below. "*The dark night of the soul is upon us,*" he said, and when this elicited nothing more than a puzzled look from Thomas, he added, "Saint John of the Cross. No? And here I thought you knew everything."

"Everything? I don't even know anything." Thomas had been drinking.

"Saint John of the Cross," said Bernie. "Spanish mystic in the 1500s. Tormented by feelings of anguish. He was caught in an existential crisis, what we would call clinical depression today. *'If by chance you see him I love the most, tell him I am sick, tell him that I suffer.'*"

"I always forget that you're a former Catholic."

"Not former, lapsed. There's no such thing as a *former* Catholic. It's like herpes. The best you can hope for is remission."

This was in the early days of the heartbreak, before Thomas had discovered the truth about Amy's brother, before he'd witnessed Sebastian's tormented anguish firsthand, before he'd been forced to face his own dark night of the soul.

"I saw your dad today," Bernie said. "Down by the station." He'd never felt comfortable around Thomas's father. To Bernie, Dr. Rosanoff always seemed like a grand marshall waiting for a parade to muster behind him. "I didn't talk to him. He seemed to be in a hurry." Bernie had in fact ducked into a doorway to avoid him.

But Thomas was no longer listening. He was looking down at the water, trying to imagine what it would feel like to step into nothingness.

He would see Frances the following day, would phone Bernie the following morning. "Do you still have those tapes? Of Amy on the first day?"

CHAPTER THIRTY-FIVE

TO SPEAK OF THE DEVIL *is to call him forth*: a common bit of folklore, largely self-fulfilling. Make a mocking comment about a coworker, turn around and you'll find him standing right there, aghast. Awkward, certainly. But unnerving? Not really. This is an example of confirmation bias: we don't remember the many times we badmouthed someone and they *didn't* appear, when we thought of an old friend and they *didn't* show up, when we spoke of the devil and nothing happened.

And yet—*speak of the devil!*—the magician had just mentioned Thomas's father, and Thomas had just recalled that strange comment Bernie had made earlier, of spotting Dr. Rosanoff in the down-below streets of Boston (*What would Dad be doing down there? Some sort of outreach program with the residents in Tent City?*) when the buzzer in Thomas's apartment rang. *That'll be the pizza.*

Thomas grabbed his wallet, cinched his robe closed, and opened the door, not to pizza but to his father glowering down at him. The deliveryman arrived soon after, leading to a clumsy "you hold this while I pay that" moment. (It didn't help that Eli had roared, "Do I know you?!" at the poor sap delivering the pizza. He'd scrambled away as soon as he was paid.)

The three Christs were now crowded around the kitchen counter, pulling apart pie-chart segments drooping with mozzarella, while Thomas and his father sat across from each other in Thomas's open-concept Finnish-inflicted living space. The silence had weight. Thomas's father was going through the transcripts and notes that Thomas had hastily assembled for him.

"Um, it's—it's still a bit rough," Thomas said, trying to decipher his father's stony expression. "I mean, I haven't had a chance to prepare a proper abstract or anything. . . ."

Dr. Rosanoff looked up from the files. "Eli is *my* patient. Mine. Do you understand that?"

"I do, and I know I shouldn't have done what I did, but—he's doing really well. He's off his meds. I haven't run a white-cell count yet or checked for any—"

"Don't bother. He's fine."

"Are you sure? With quetiapine, there's always the risk of—"

"He was never on any medications. The code on his chart, here, in the bottom corner. He's been getting placebos."

"He wasn't on quetiapine?"

"Did he look sedated?"

At the kitchen counter, Eli was attacking a slice of pizza in the manner of a wolf ripping apart a woodland carcass.

"But—why was he on placebos?"

"I've been running tests for one of the pharmaceuticals. Third-generation antipsychotic medications, mainly. Risperidone derivatives. D-cycloserines. . . . A waste of time, if you ask me, but they needed someone to sign off on the MRIs and SPECT scans, to check for brain damage, diminished cognitive abilities. Eli is in the control group."

"So he's not getting any treatment for his—"

"He's in the control group."

"But—"

"*I said*, He's in the control group." Dr. Rosanoff levelled his gaze at Thomas. "Mr. Wasser was naked and covered in his own feces when they picked him up. He had bruises over his entire body, was crawling with lice. We washed him, fed him, gave him comfort and a roof over his head."

And restraints on his wrists. Thomas tried to speak, but the words got caught inside of him. He looked again at Eli and the other two as they ate and laughed and bickered over the pizza. They were blithely unaware of what was occurring.

"The terrible truth is this," said Dr. Rosanoff. "In today's world, the prescription now drives the diagnosis—not the other way around. Pharmaceutical companies craft a pill and then go looking for a disorder it will cure. The SDM manual was meant to add scientific rigour to our field. Instead, it's become a drug dealer's cheat sheet. Want to know which pharmaceutical stock to invest in? Ask yourself which mental illness is currently in vogue. They come and go, you know. There are trends in mental illness, as there are in anything else. For a while it was low self-esteem; before that it was repressed memories magically revealed through hypnosis, even though there is absolutely no neurological mechanism in the human brain that can 'hide' traumatic memories. The easiest thing in the world is for a therapist to plant a false memory. Remember those incestuous Satanic cults? No? Well, that was before your time. But a lot of dads and daycare workers were sent to jail before psychologists realized, Oops! We might have been a little overzealous in our rush to diagnose. I remember one summer when every second celebrity was announcing—proudly— that they had 'bipolar multiple-personality disorder,' which doesn't even exist. Another summer it was adult attention-deficit disorder. Lately, it's been post-traumatic stress disorder. That used to refer specifically to people who have faced violent life-threatening situations, such as combat or horrific natural disasters. But not anymore. You witnessed a car accident? Your prof was mean to you? Congratulations! You've got PTSD! But don't worry, we've got a pill for that. The latest fad? Trigger warnings. Listen, son, *life* is one big trigger warning. Trust me, in twenty years the hysteria about trigger warnings will be looked upon in the same way we now look upon past-life regressions and mood rings. You ever notice how whatever mental disorder is currently in fashion suddenly becomes endemic? Funny, that. You'd almost think it was the power of suggestion at work."

"I never looked at it that way, but—"

"Thomas, the bare fact that mental illnesses are subject to trends should be a huge red flag. The SDM was supposed to reduce these sorts of culturally influenced aspects. It was supposed to add stringent scientific criteria. Instead, it's been hijacked. We are treating the symptoms, not the cause, not the underlying *character* of our patients. How do you end up sleeping in a gutter, soaked in your own urine? I'll tell you how: a series of bad decisions, each one inevitably aided and abetted by a society that holds up victimhood as the highest ideal. Pharmacology has replaced lobotomies, Thomas. Do the drugs work? Of course they do. So does a blow to the head."

Thus ended the Soliloquy of Thomas the Elder, patron saint of hard choices, practitioner of the Gordian blow, master commander of harsh succour.

Thomas's father opened Sebastian's file, flipped through the pages. "Look at this. It's one antipsychotic medication after another. Luvox, Celexa, Lamictal, Effexor, Depakote, Haldol, Serzone, Zoloft,

Remeron, Wellbutrin, Cytomel, Dexedrine, Parnate, Thorazine. The list goes on and on. He's probably got more pharmaceuticals in his bloodstream than platelets, and what has it done for him? Nothing." Dr. Rosanoff slid the file to one side, stared at his son. "What exactly are you trying to do here?"

"Well, it's—it's basically a cognitive approach. We're dealing with messianic psychoses, but more than that we're dealing with wrong *thoughts*. The way they see themselves in the world."

"How do they rank on the Stanford-Binet Scale?"

"Mental abilities? Fine. Intelligence is fine. Abstract, quantitative, verbal reasoning, short-term memory, it's all fine."

"So you think their problem is cognitive? In the *ideas* they hold."

The three Christs were crowded around the kitchen counter, fighting over the last of the pizza. They were far enough away that they couldn't hear, but Thomas dropped his voice anyway. "They claim the same identity. My goal is to confront them with this fact. It's— It's like how two objects cannot occupy the same space at the same time. I think this applies to identity as well."

"I see."

"What I want to do," said Thomas, "is engage their practical intelligence, their common sense. I want to give them a clear choice—madness or reality—and then have them resolve this conflict in favour of reality." It sounded less convincing the more he explained it. "I mean, we know people can be talked *into* madness, so I thought, maybe, you know . . ." His voice trailed off.

The pause that followed was beyond pregnant. Dr. Rosanoff looked to the Christs in the kitchen, then turned his head, slowly, like a gun on a turret, back toward his son.

"So, um, what do you think?" Thomas asked.

"What do I think?" Dr. Rosanoff chose his words carefully, giving equal weight, equal importance to each one. "I think it's brilliant."

"It is?" Thomas felt a wave of relief wash across him.

"This is the stuff careers are made of, Tommy."

"Really?"

"Absolutely. Skinner had his mice. Harlow had his monkeys. We've got Messiahs. However, this experiment, as it's set up now, too many variables. We'll need more controls, stricter protocols, a location better suited for this sort of thing." He stood up, beamed. "Thomas," he said, "you're going home."

CHAPTER THIRTY-SIX

AMY IN THE PAST TENSE, languid under loosely thrown sheets. Amy, snorting with laughter. "The Boy in the Box! That was you? And I thought *my* childhood was messed up!"

"I know, right? I was the only kid whose playmates had to sign a waiver."

"A waiver?"

"More of a nondisclosure agreement. I only found out about it years later." It had been at a conference in Chicago. A pair of psychiatrists whose daughter had played with Tommy as a child told him about it. *"We didn't mind. It was a thrill to be part of the experiment!"* (And by experiment, they meant, of course, Thomas's childhood.)

Amy rolled over, placed her hands on either side of Thomas's head, peered into his eyes as though checking for hidden messages. "You seem suspiciously well adjusted," she said, "considering everything you went through."

"You seem almost disappointed," he said. "And anyway, have you ever met anyone well adjusted who wasn't *suspiciously* so? I had a happy childhood, if you ignored the mirrors."

She reached out, stroked his hair. "When I was a little girl, I had an imaginary playmate. Her name was Ellie and she lived in the cupboard."

"I never had imaginary playmates. I had mirrors."

"No friends?"

"Oh, I had lots of friends. Transitory, mainly, but aren't all friends transitory? I remember this one girl—I want to say Sally, but it must have been something else. Samantha, maybe?—the daughter of a Methodist minister. Her mother worked at the university, I think. She was my first kiss."

"Oh my!" Amy, scooching in closer, eyes shining. "Tell me more. Were there fireworks?"

"In a manner of speaking, yes. Sally, or Sam, cornered me in the activity room—it was this Montessori-type area with various workstations—and she said to me, face flushed, 'Wanna see something?' I said, 'Sure.' And she began unbuttoning her shirt. Alas, before she could take it all the way off, the doors flew open and in roars my dad and her mom saying 'Tommy! Julia!'—that was her name: Julia—'Who wants lemonade? Let's have some lemonade!' I didn't realize, of course, that every step of her would-be elementary school seduction was being monitored." He laughed. "I can imagine the scene on the other side of the mirror, headphones being flung aside, clipboards scattering, papers flying as they raced for the door."

"So when did she kiss you?"

"Ah, but you're assuming *she* kissed *me*. Maybe I took the initiative. Maybe I swept her into my arms like a junior Fabio, planted a smooch on her with confidence and aplomb."

"Get real. She kissed you. Am I right?"

Sigh. "Yes. You're right. It was before her mom dragged her out of the room. Julia gave me a kiss, right on the lips. A goodbye kiss, as it turned out. She never came back."

"No wonder! The girl was clearly a vixen."

"I think the correct term is *precocious*."

Amy sat up. "Shall I put on a shirt and then slowly unbutton it for you?"

"What? And despoil the memory of . . . of . . ."

"Julia."

"You'd have me tarnish her legacy in such a tawdry fashion? I think not!"

"I don't even remember my first kiss," Amy said, with a touch of regret. "Must have been at summer camp. There was a lot of kissing going on at those camps. I don't remember the first one, though."

"It was with me, remember? That's what you told me, anyway."

"Oh, right. Yes, of course. You were my first."

"Damn straight."

And they curled into each other's arms, lost in their own pasts. He said, "I remember my artwork disappearing. Paintings and drawings. They would go away, then reappear the next day. I didn't realize they were making copies. My drawings still show up in textbooks and childhood development seminars."

"I didn't know you were an artist," she said.

"We're all artists, Amy. It's just that most of us grow out of it." At which point she rabbit-punched him in the ribs. *Oof!*

"Are you saying my artwork is a sign of stunted development?"

"Well, if the shoe fits—" At which point she punched him again. What he wanted to say, what he should have said, was this: *From the manner in which my paintings disappeared and reappeared, I always thought art was a form of magic, that it was outside the rules of our nor-*

229

mal world. But he was afraid she would punch him again, especially for the use of the word "normal." (She wouldn't have. If he had said that, she would have kissed him, would have kissed him right on the mouth.)

Unstated things: Amy never asked Thomas about his mom, and he never asked about hers. The agreement was tacit, but clear. (And what would they have discovered even if they had discussed it? Two different types of cancer, variations on a theme: one ovarian, the other breast, both terminally female. A magic act of its own: the vanishing mom.)

She had more access to his past than he had to hers. Advantage: Amy. Thomas's childhood, after all, was in the public domain. Dr. Rosanoff's "Seven Stages of Development"—sensory motor, concrete operational, socially reflective, and so on—was still considered the template for childhood studies, though it was in fact the template of *a* childhood: Thomas's. Everything from early-adolescent egocentrism, as marked by imaginary audiences and persecution fables, to semenarche: it was all there, his entire story told in that extended narrative form known as "the longitudinal study" (*def*: a scientific survey following the same subject over the span of many years). *The Good Son* was considered the gold standard of longitudinal studies. In Thomas's case, the imaginary audience of his adolescent years wasn't imaginary in the least. It dwelled on the other side of the glass, hiding behind his reflection. Had Amy ever read The Book of Thomas, she might have known this. But she never did, and he never asked her to. Advantage: squandered.

Amy in the past tense, slipping further and further away.

CHAPTER THIRTY-SEVEN

KINGSLEY HALL WAS A sampler plate of architectural styles. Originally a staid Protestant manor with mansard roof and suitably dour windows, the original building had all but disappeared under a succession of cupolas, towers, and added wings. Ornate panels of stained glass were set above the windows and, although designed to be airy and bright, the Rosanoff home, silhouetted upon its hill, would always be more Bates Motel than Mansfield Park.

Thomas had only vague memories of life before the manor: his mom and dad in a small apartment, his mother laughing as his father play-wrestled with him on the couch. *"Gonna getch'a, gonna getch'a!"* He knew his mother primarily through photographs, a series of freeze-frame moments, smiling at the camera as she fed him with his Winnie the Pooh spoon. He remembered his mother's loud unabashed guffaw and the smell of something faint and fragrant— probably fabric softener, yet it lingered still. He remembered running down the hallway, squealing, as his mother counted down in the kitchen. *"Ready or not . . ."*

Hide-and-seek in the cramped bedroom, scrambling under the hamper, changing his mind, hiding behind the drapes instead as his mother's voice came closer and closer until . . . *"Aha!"*—with a sudden fling of the curtains, his mother disappeared into bright sunlight. He could remember everything about that moment except her face. That was supplied by photo albums. And then one morning, Thomas woke up in a bigger bed in a larger house.

Childhood, Thomas realized now, was like living inside a Grimm's fairy tale. The milestones and key moments melt away, and you find yourself falling asleep and then waking up in a different place. Sometimes you fall asleep in the backseat of a car on the drive home and then wake up in your room, tucked under your Thomas the Tank Engine blankets. Sometimes you fall asleep in your stroller and then wake to find yourself at the supermarket. Fall asleep again and you wake up at a coffee shop as your mother visits with her friends, and sometimes you fall asleep to the sound of your mother laughing and you wake up to silence. A hospital room, a doctor speaking in hushed tones, your father holding your mother, your mother holding you. . . . And then you fall asleep again, and you wake up and she's gone, and if you run down the hallway to the hamper, she's not there. Years can go by between memories. According to the Rosanoff Stages of Development, Thomas's mother passed away during Thomas's "pre-concrete early operational stage," when one's sense of self is only half formed and still emergent. (It was the worst time to lose a parent, or the best, depending on your point of view.)

Gothic gingerbread and curled cornices. Wrought-iron gates and latticework verandas. As the convoy of sedans pulled into the circle driveway, Thomas felt a familiar mix of nostalgia and nausea overtake him, what some might call dread (of an unspecified nature; *see*: SDM:III, Chapter 21). Oak trees and elm. Ivy draped across the windows like hair across an eye. A front stairway of the sweeping variety. The three Christs had been chauffeured to the Rosanoff home in separate vehicles (to avoid "cross-contamination," as his father put it, referring to the collusive corroboration that often happens among mental patients when psychiatrists are not on hand to monitor and guide them).

Dr. Rosanoff was waiting to greet them. "Gentlemen," he said. "Follow me."

He led Thomas and the others up the stairway, past looming pillars and dark trim. It was all very familiar: the gravitas of the front doors swinging open like a piece of stagecraft, that final step into the rounded foyer—a foyer larger than his first-year dorm room, he realized—where the evening light filtered in from above through stained glass of a nonreligious nature, and suddenly he was home again.

"Welcome to Kingsley Hall," said Dr. Rosanoff.

Beyond the foyer, a long corridor stretched out in front of them like a first-year art school study in perspective. The three Messiahs looked around, ill at ease. They seemed smaller somehow, less godlike. Eli was clutching his HOME SWEET HOME sign to his chest.

"It's a name that came with the building, I'm afraid," Dr. Rosanoff explained. "It was originally dubbed 'Kingsley Manor,' but I changed that to 'Hall.' Less pretentious, more down-to-earth. I have a housekeeper and a cook. They will provide you with meals. If you have any dietary restrictions—commandments to avoid shellfish, say—please let them know. As for your day-to-day concerns . . . Ah, here they are now."

A pair of orderlies, unintentional twins with close-cropped heads and starched white uniforms, came down the hallway toward them. Their gait was less "medical staff" than nightclub bouncer, but Dr. Rosanoff assured everyone that they were fully qualified. "They're here to help," he said, though he didn't say who they were here to help—or how.

Eli attempted to roar his usual greeting, *"Do I know you?!"* but the question got lost somewhere inside his chest.

The magician bowed slightly, almost gallantly, and said, "It is a pleasure to meet you," but they were immune to his charms.

"Come with us," they said. "We have blood work to do."

"And lemonade!" shouted Dr. Rosanoff after them. "Make sure our guests are comfortable! Thomas, you come with me."

Thomas and his father walked down the hallway into the converging lines of perspective.

"You're concerned about something. I can sense it."

"It's just—this is a private residence." The patients had been staying at Thomas's apartment, true, but that hadn't been set up as a laboratory. This seemed different somehow.

"Kingsley Hall is a registered psychiatric treatment facility. Limited in scope, of course, but fully registered."

"I grew up in a psychiatric facility?"

"Technically speaking, yes."

They came to a small, unassuming side door. Dr. Rosanoff turned the key and they slipped in, behind the walls of the manor. They'd entered a narrow maze, a parallel world. Thomas and his father turned down one corner, then another, passing what appeared to be windows but were actually the obverse sides of one-way mirrors that looked into various rooms. A playroom, filled with oversized blocks. A library of children's books, the walls brightly painted. A music room, more subdued, with an upright piano and cartoon treble clefs adorning the wallpaper. Each one, frozen in time. They looked like dioramas.

"We'll put Eli in the library," said Dr. Rosanoff. "Sebastian in the music room. And—I'll have some beds brought in for them—we'll put our third guest in here."

They stopped in front of a boy's bedroom, circa 1992. A time capsule complete with a racing car bed and spaceship blankets. The walls were painted soft blue, with stars.

"Your old room," said Dr. Rosanoff. "Brings back memories, no?"

Thomas peered across oceans, across decades, to the bedroom on the other side of the glass. He could hear the muffled sound of music even though he knew none was playing. As a child, he'd had the run of the main floor, and the garden and the yard beyond, but his bedroom was windowless, almost soundproof. Only the sirens got through. At night, when he lay in bed, Thomas could hear the faint sound of ambulances and police vehicles in the city below, and he would feel comforted by it. A siren is not a sad sound. It meant help was on its way. Right now, somebody somewhere is falling down the stairs, drowning in a bathtub, clutching at their chest, stepping off a balcony. A siren means someone cares. It's a lack of sirens that's unsettling.

"We'll separate our test subjects," said Dr. Rosanoff. "Set up three discrete case studies. We'll need to manage their interactions with each other carefully, make sure the confrontational aspects are arranged in an appropriate fashion—anything less would be unethical. And of course, we'll have to watch out for the cohort effect."

"But," said Thomas, "isn't that exactly what we're doing here? Using the cohort effect to help them." He looked over at his father. "I don't think feelings of solidarity among patients are necessarily a bad thing."

"Yes, but it has to be done in a properly controlled manner. We'll set up spreadsheets for data analysis, cross-reference their responses."

"But—but we won't be observing them in a naturalistic environment. It seems sort of . . . contrived."

"Not contrived, *controlled*. We are removing any outside variables that might undermine the data."

"We're manipulating events."

"That's what an experiment is, Tommy. It's life, but controlled."

"But—I didn't think of this as an experiment. I thought of it as therapy."

"Same thing. Come along, there's a lot to do."

Thomas stayed back, looked through the mirror into his old room. He could hear children laughing, music building, a voice asking, *"We'll still be friends, right?"*

Tommy, as a child: staring at himself in the mirror, shifting back and forth on his feet ever so slightly, mesmerized. His father would write: *"Possible narcissistic tendencies?"* But Tommy wasn't looking *at* himself, he was looking through himself, or trying to. He thought he could see movement on the other side of the mirror. *Was someone there?*

He still didn't know the answer to that.

CHAPTER THIRTY-EIGHT

Sister Frances Bedford pulled slowly on the suture. It caught on the flesh for a moment, then came out, leaving a pink seam above the woman's mouth. These were emergency room stitchings, quickly done and without the aid of self-dissolving threads. Triage always leaves a scar.

"Pass me a bit of gauze and some rubbing alcohol."

Thomas rummaged around in the tray, grabbed a handful of moist towelettes. "Close enough?" he asked.

She nodded. "Hang in there, Helen. Almost done."

The woman's face had been split from lip to nose. It was healing, more or less, but still . . .

"Shouldn't she have gone to a hospital to have those taken out?"

"With no medical coverage?" asked Frances. "To sit for six hours, clogging up an already overextended community health centre when we can do it ourselves right here?"

"I'm assuming those questions are rhetorical."

As Frances cleaned up, Thomas checked Helen's blood pressure—arms so thin, the band went around twice and almost ran out of Velcro. He listened to her chest. A rattle in her upper airways, but not pneumonic. Not yet, anyway. "Expectorant and antibiotics ought to do the trick."

"Thank you, Doctor," she croaked.

"Oh, I'm not a doctor," he said.

"No?"

"I'm just helping out."

"So, you're more of an avid hobbyist?" she said in a quavering voice.

"Something like that."

They came to the next cot: an emaciated woman, looking older than her age, sleeping fitfully. She was hooked up to a portable oxygen tank. Shallow breathing, pallid complexion.

"Obstructive pulmonary?" Thomas asked.

Frances nodded. "Chronic."

After they'd checked the woman's vitals, Frances wheeled the cart back to her office as Thomas explained his latest venture.

"Three of them under one roof? Interesting idea," she said. "Not sure if it'll work."

"My dad's convinced it will."

"Your father's involved?"

"He's kind of taken over. Moved the entire operation to Kingsley Hall, so that Sebastian and the others can be observed as unobtrusively as possible. The patients"—he almost said "test subjects"—"are settling in nicely, though. Their beds arrived this morning. Well, cots, really. We start in earnest tomorrow morning."

Her desk was buried beneath the usual drunken stacks of paperwork. "Coffee?" she asked.

"Good Lord, no."

Frances turned her attention to the cold Nescafé in her cup. "Can

you microwave styrofoam? If it's on low? Probably not. Anyway..."
She plugged in her kettle, waited for it to boil. "What are you going
to do if none of your subjects concedes defeat? How long will you let
this go on for?"

"Good question. If we get stuck, maybe you could come down,
pick Him out for us. It's more your area of expertise anyway. It would
be like a police lineup. Spot the Messiah. 'That's him! That's the guy
who ruined my perfectly good water, turned it into wine!'"

Frances had the uncomfortable habit of staring into Thomas's eyes
when she asked a hard question. She did that now, as though studying
his face for poker tells, looking for telltale slips of the mien. "How
does it feel," she asked, "being back in that house again? Stressful?"

"More surreal than stressful. Like I've returned to the scene of a
crime. Which is silly, because it's just a home. My home." *And yet ...*

"Don't be too hard on your father," she said. "He took your
mother's death badly. It was how he handled his grief: he was going
to raise a son without sadness." She poured the water into her cup
without waiting for it to boil, stirred in some more powder. "It always
bothered your father that he finally made it big with— What was the
title again? Not *The Good Son*. The other one."

"My dad wrote a lot of books."

"You know the one. The pop psychology book."

"*Be OK, Do OK?*"

Dr. Rosanoff's earlier work had been promoted in the hyperbolic
manner of book publicists everywhere as "a transformative new plan
to alter human behaviour!" and it lived on even now in drugstore
pocketbook format. Thomas liked *Be OK, Do OK!* the most of all his
father's books if for no other reason than that he wasn't in it.

"That's right," said Frances. "'Change your actions, change your

Self'—with a capital 'S,' as I recall. How we could stop smoking, find love, empower our inner child, and so forth, through the power of behavioural modification. What was it he said? 'Give me a dozen healthy infants with the right conditioning, and I can turn them into whatever you like: a doctor, lawyer, beggar, thief.' He wrote that book on a card table in a one-bedroom apartment by the campus while you crawled over him like a pet ferret."

"I can imagine."

"It broke his heart how your mother wasn't there to enjoy the success that followed, after all those years of scrimping. I'm not so sure, though. I think their days together in that crappy little apartment on Parker Street were the happiest of her life." Frances sipped her coffee, winced at the taste. "Do you remember that apartment?"

"I do. Snippets, mainly. I remember the bathtub had daisy stickers on the bottom and rust rings around the drain. I remember playing hide-and-seek with my mom. Wrestling with my dad. I think I had a hamster at one point. It's all sort of vague and cloudy."

"I used to babysit you. Do you remember that? No? Just as well. I wasn't one for changing diapers. It's a good thing Freud's been debunked. You'd have had some serious anal-retentive issues by now with the saggy diapers you had to drag around while I was allegedly taking care of you."

"Frances, did my mother ever take me to church?"

"Probably. I know she wanted to have you baptized at one point. That was a bone of contention with your father, I can assure you." She looked at Thomas, tilted her head as though trying to bring him into focus. "Why?"

"Nothing. It's just—I've got this piece of music stuck in my brain.

Religious music of some sort. A choral arrangement, weirdly familiar. I thought maybe it was a memory of my mother."

"You're hearing music?"

He nodded. *Music—and voices.*

She stared, unblinking, into Thomas's eyes. "Are we talking full-
blown auditory hallucinations?"

"What? No. More like a tune I can't get out of my head." Then,
quickly changing the topic, "I'll let you know how it goes with my
three Messiahs."

"*My* Messiahs? Interesting choice of words."

"A figure of speech."

She pushed her chair back. "I have to say, there's something disconcerting about the program you've set up. We're all of us crazy
in some way, Tommy. We all have our delusions about who we are.
We're all living under assumed identities. These three patients you
described, they took on these identities for a reason. Assuming the
role of a suffering saviour: it's part of who they are. Ripping that
away from them might do more harm than you realize. Patients are
more than a sum of their symptoms."

"Meaning?"

"Our problems are as much cultural as they are chemical. The
question is not only *who* you are, but *where* you are and *when* you are.
Soil and seed, Tommy. Soil and seed. You want to understand why a
plant grew the way it did? You need to understand the seed *and* the
soil it grew in." She sighed. "Working here, I often feel overwhelmed.
Look around, Thomas. I know that what I do is a stopgap measure,
cleaning wounds and combing out nits. The bedsores are the least of
the problems these people face. So much of the anguish I see here
comes out of loneliness, out of feelings of isolation. And labelling

mental disorders doesn't fix any of that. It can even make it worse. We end up treating the label, not the person. There are immediate health concerns, of course—the bedsores I mentioned, substance abuse, bronchial infections—but what these people really need are better life skills, vocational training, coping strategies. They need a sense of purpose. Isn't that what we're all striving for? A slightly better version of ourselves? Maybe that's the best any of us can hope for. That, and the basic human need to love and be loved. There's no pill on earth that can replace that."

Thus ended the Soliloquy of Frances Mary Bedford, patron saint of lost causes, caretaker of the wounded heart, cartographer of the stopgap soul.

Thomas laughed out loud. "That's such a nun answer! 'To love and be loved.' Listen. There are four lobes and a billion synaptic connections in the brain, and none of them are labelled 'meaning of life,' or 'God' for that matter. Is that why you joined the Holy Order of . . ."

"The Carmelites."

"Is that why you joined, to traffic in homilies? At least my mom came to her senses. But you kept going. Why?"

"Why? I was greedy, I guess."

"Greedy?"

"I couldn't see myself getting married, limiting myself to only one person. I wanted to embrace as much of humanity as I could."

"Ah! You were promiscuous."

"Spiritually, I suppose I was. Rivers will always find the sea, Tommy. They aren't looking for the sea: it just happens. It's inevitable. It's the interplay of gravity, geography, and time, but the fact remains: if there is a sea out there, a river will find it. Put a droplet of water anywhere on this world and it will eventually reach the sea."

"You and your metaphors," he complained.

"You and your numbers," she replied.

Frances smiled at him with a faint glint of malice (always unnerving when it comes from a nun). "Speaking of bedpans . . ."

"Oh for chrissake." But there was no point arguing with her. He rose to his feet, reluctant and truculent and grumbling in opposition. "You're a mean old woman," he said. "Anyone ever tell you that?"

"Only you, all the time."

And so he went, herded along by Sister Frances, to do good in as begrudging a manner as possible.

CHAPTER THIRTY-NINE

IN THE GUEST ROOM at Kingsley Hall, Thomas lay awake under the covers staring at the ceiling. The faint sound of church melodies bled in from a far-off room. He was now *actively ignoring* the music, if such a thing is possible. Tomorrow morning, they would start with Session One. (He'd tried to explain to his father that he and the Messiahs had already had three full sessions, but Dr. Rosanoff reset the clock to zero anyway. *"A fresh start, a clean slate."*) As Thomas stared at the ceiling, details emerged like messages in a Magic 8-ball. Memories of mice and mazes and earlier experiments.

"Think of it as culling the herd," said Bernie. He was talking about the mice. "If we can't do something as simple as this, how can we ever hope to become doctors?"

"I don't think mice travel in herds," said Thomas.

"Flocks?"

"That would be pigeons."

"Packs?"

"That would be rats." Thomas thought for a moment. "We have a murder of crows, a bevy of swans. Why not 'a field of mice'?"

"Not to be confused with field mice," said Bernie.

This was in their undergraduate days, the first time they'd ever worked together, back when Thomas was still seeing Wendy. The experiment was an attempt to locate empathy in the brain. "We'll be studying the effects of mirror neurons," their supervisor explained. "We want to know if stress is contagious. Is trauma transmittable? We know about the effects of second-hand smoke. We're looking for the effects of second-hand stress."

Bernie and Thomas would separate litters of mice into pairs. They would then "stress" one mouse and leave the other alone. Stressing a mouse could be done through mild electrical shocks to the feet (0.05 milliamps every thirty seconds for two seconds, say) or by taking them "swimming" (that is, putting them in a vat to tread water for five minutes). The stressed mouse would then be united with its "buddy" (an actual term, that) to see if the traumatic effects in one mouse would register in the other, either physically or in terms of behaviour.

And how would you evaluate behaviour? By reviewing thirty-minute videos of the mice after they were reunited. With 140 pairs, that came to seventy hours of mice videos, all of which had to be reviewed *in real time*—one couldn't fast-forward in case one missed some crucially important mouse action. *Seventy hours* of mice videos, and you had to pay close attention as well, clicking keyboard codes for each behaviour as it came up: sniff, walk, climb, fight, sleep. Oh, the glamorous life of an undergrad!

"We'll be looking for structural changes in the hypothalamus as well," their supervisor explained. "We want to find out if being around a stressed mouse will affect the brain structures of the non-stressed buddy."

It was a way of looking at the ripple effect of trauma on others, on the siblings and friends of abused children, for example.

And how would they check the hypothalamus?

"First, you'll need to give them an anesthetic, to put them to sleep. You then insert a needle between the ribs, into the left ventricle. You'll draw out the blood and then rinse their system with saline. After that you'll inject PFA."

"PFA?"

"Paraformaldehyde. If you try to scoop out a brain without preserving it beforehand, it will fall apart like oatmeal."

"Scoop it out?"

"Exactly. You need to harvest the brains. What you'll do is cut through the skin on the top of the head and then peel it back with tweezers to expose the skull—mouse skulls are thin, so be careful. You remove the brains and incubate them overnight in sucrose. The next day, you'll freeze them in liquid nitrogen and then take thin slices, 30 microns thick. We have brain atlases for you to consult." He referred to heavy books, opened like Gutenberg Bibles. "They show every layer of brain possible, so when you reach the cross-section of the hypothalamus, save those slices. You'll need to lay those on the slides and stain them, to look for structural changes. We'll be keeping an eye out for landmarks, white matter tracks, ventricles and so on, as we slice."

"Surely we don't slice the brains by hand?" said Thomas. "I'm not good with scalpels."

"We have a precision slicer, a cryostat. It's like something you'd use in a deli. Except instead of salami, you'll be, y'know, slicing mouse brains. The good news is, you'll be working with designer mice."

"Designer?"

"Genetically modified. They're called 'tomato mice,' because their brains have been specially bred to appear bright red under a laser microscope. Makes analysis a lot easier. Patent pending."

Thomas felt queasy and they hadn't even started yet.

It was hard to know which was worse—the hours watching mouse surveillance videos, clicking on a keyboard and feeling like the world's saddest voyeur, or harvesting the final product. It was trickier than it looked, killing something. Thomas often punched his needle clean through the heart and ended up spurting blood onto his gloves.

"I really hope God isn't a mouse," he said, after the fifth or sixth botched execution.

He eventually got the hang of it, and it became easier and easier as time went on, though no less monotonous.

"Do you find it ironic," Bernie asked, "that an experiment on the origins of empathy involves the wholesale slaughter of helpless mice?"

"A mouse apocalypse," said Thomas.

"For the greater good," said Bernie.

"Culling the herd," Thomas repeated.

"Exactly. We'll be fine, so long as we don't get too attached to any of them." He picked up the next allotted mouse, held it in his palms. "I named this little guy Squiggles!"

Bernie was joking, of course, but Thomas blanched nonetheless.

"What's wrong?"

"It's nothing, it's just— Squiggles was the name of my hamster."

"Oh shit, sorry."

"Don't worry about it. Really."

"These brains have to incubate for twenty-four hours anyway," said Bernie. "So, let's go get a drink."

And that was how Thomas and Bernie became friends.

Later, having dispatched the last of the mice, and having lined up the relevant slices onto the lab's high-precision confocal microscopes, and having peered at the lunar landscape of the enlarged brain tissues, rendered in stark relief on the microscope's monitors, having prodded and poked, and teased out the secrets of their micron-thin samples, and having tentatively concluded that empathy may indeed affect the physical structures of the brain, Bernie and Thomas now sat at their lab counter happily eating Japanese noodles out of soggy-cornered takeout boxes. The gruesome nature of their completed task hadn't dimmed their appetites.

Thomas dug into his yakisoba, slopping it partly into his mouth, partly down his chin. "You suck at chopsticks," said Bernie.

"I suck at a lot of things."

This surprised Bernie. His impression of Thomas was of someone who skimmed lightly across the surface of the world, as though gravity didn't apply to him.

"If you can't handle chopsticks," said Bernie, "how are you going to handle a scalpel?"

Thomas opened a can of beer to a satisfying *fizzzz*. "As long as I don't have to finesse takeout noodles with a scalpel, I'm good."

Something else Bernie said pulled at Thomas's memory, like a child tugging on a sleeve: "I had lunch with Professor Cerletti today. He wanted to bask in my gratitude."

Bernie was on a bursary for academically accomplished students who might not have the financial wherewithal to attend Harvard unaided. Which is to say, Bernie had a scholarship. (Thomas, meanwhile, had his name—or rather, his father's name.) Professor Cerletti had championed Bernie's enrollment from the start, something he liked to remind Bernie of regularly. Hence the lunches and royal audiences.

"Know what Cerletti ordered?" asked Bernie.

"Fresh blood?"

"Brains. Seriously! Calf brains on a plate. It was like watching someone stuff steak tartare into their face, with his mouth all gummy, lips wet. And the whole time he's eating, he's asking me what I thought my role was in the laboratory of the human mind. That's what he said, 'the laboratory of the human mind.'"

"What did you tell him?"

"*The pursuit of truth!* or some such nonsense. And then he wipes his mouth with a napkin and says, 'No. We deal in refuse, Bernie. Not truth. Our job is to sift through the wet leaves and mulch of evolution. And as we root about in the cellars of the psyche, is it any wonder we might find . . . unpleasant things?'"

"Middens," said Thomas. "That's what they call ancient latrines. The archaeologists who work on them specialize in fossilized shit. Except, of course, it's no longer shit. It's now an artifact, an historic inheritance, a relic, a treasure trove of knowledge. Diet, grains, ancient migrations, medical conditions, even life span. It's all there. If we are archaeologists of the mind, that's where we ply our trade as well."

Bernie raised a toast. "Here's to us! The miners of mulch, excavators of fossilized feces. I am so glad I gave up my job as a movie star for this! Question: If you discovered that Saint Francis of Assisi— you know the guy, the one draped with loving creatures, with bluebirds perched on his shoulders, fawns eating from his palm—if you found out that he secretly hated animals, that he flicked the bluebirds from his shoulder whenever he had the chance and dropkicked furry woodland creatures when no one was looking, would it matter?"

"Would what matter?"

"Proposition: Who we are in private is different than who we are in public. Agreed or disagreed?"

"Agreed."

"So, which is more real: the private us or the public us?"

"Public."

This tripped Bernie up. Everyone always said private.

"A person isn't a person except in relation to someone else," said Thomas. "The real test isn't, How do we act when no one is around? It's, How do we act when we *know* we're being watched? That's the real test of socialization. Hell, our entire society depends on it." He pointed the chopsticks in Bernie's direction. "We are not our raging ids."

Bernie could feel the pain from here. *The Boy in the Box*. Still there, after all these years. And as the night wound down and their thoughts turned inward, Bernie raised another toast: "To our ineluctable march into insignificance, to that last step into nothingness."

"Hear! Hear!" said Thomas (drunkenly).

"Y'ever think," said Bernie (philosophically), "that life is merely a series of smaller and smaller capitulations, practice runs for that final surrender at the end?"

"I suppose."

"Know what I think?" said Bernie. "I think every obituary ever written should simply read: *That was it?*"

"You really know how to lighten the mood."

Bernie raised yet another toast, sloshing his beer in salute. "The greatest of tragedies can exist right beside us and we might never know!"

"What's that from?" Thomas asked.

"It's something Cerletti said. He's an odd duck, that one."

"My dad knew him from way back when. I ever tell you that? They were graduate students together. Were fairly close at one point, I think. Y'know, Cerletti asked me the exact same question. Wanted to know what I was hoping to find, poking around in the brain." It was at a dinner with the dean. She was holding forth on her favorite subject: herself. (She found herself endlessly fascinating. If only others shared that fascination!) And as Thomas's father was topping up the sherry, Cerletti had leaned across and asked Thomas the same question he'd posed to Bernie, apropos of nothing. *"What are you looking for?"*

"What did you tell him?" Bernie asked.

"I said, 'I want to map out the final continent, I want to unlock the secrets of the last great mystery, I want to pin down God once and for all.'"

"Really?"

Thomas grinned. "Not quite. I said, 'The pursuit of truth!' Or some such nonsense."

They raised a toast to God.

"For a nonexistent being, he's certainly caused a lot of trouble," said Bernie.

"Amen to that," said Thomas.

And now, lying awake in the guest room of Kingsley Hall, unable to sleep and thinking of mice and hamsters, long forgotten, Thomas recalled a woman he'd caught sight of the other day. He was crossing the street and when she saw him, she looked away, instantly embarrassed. One of his soccer moms, no doubt, yet he was damned if he could remember her or her name. (It had taken him almost a week to remember Bernie's first name after they'd met, and months more to learn his last name. *Donovan? Flanagan?*) Thomas had self-diagnosed this as a mild form of prosopagnosia, "face blindness," a glitch in the fusiform facial recognition area of his brain, the one that assigns identities to names and facial features. But Wendy had said it had nothing to do with his brain. "You just don't care. You can't be bothered to remember people." A cruel assessment, perhaps, but not entirely untrue.

And now the postcards were piling up in his apartment: REMEMBER ME. REMEMBER ME. And a voice from *long away* and *far ago* was asking: *"We'll still be friends, right?"*

Thomas stared at the ceiling. He stared at the ceiling until the music faded and the memories disappeared like faces into a fog.

CHAPTER FORTY

DR. ROSANOFF WAS ABOUT to open the door when he stopped, stepped back, and looked at his son with a warm smile. "You've never been in here before, have you?"

Thomas shook his head, felt his mouth go dry. He knew the room existed, but had never known exactly where.

They were standing at the far end of his father's capacious study. Tall windows. An expansive view of the river, misted in the distance. Oak trees and the rooftops of lesser manors. The cobblestones of Beacon Hill. A cityscape rendered in diminishing gradations of grey. Traffic, sorting itself out on the esplanade below, the red brake lights wet in the early evening, flowing into lanes like corpuscles in a vein. And out on the river, sculling boats: thin elongated teardrops, sliding soundlessly under Longfellow Bridge, leaving concentric circles and slowly spreading lines of water in their wake. *Going forward, looking backward*. The art of rowing.

Dr. Rosanoff's desk was a swath of polished mahogany, the blotter as big as a billboard. A decorative globe, an inkwell, bookshelves with standard-issue leather-bound volumes, glass-framed doctoral pomp and sundry academic honours: the accoutrements of a learned man.

Thomas had only ever been in his father's study a handful of times and, even then, he was usually too wonderstruck to have noticed the doorway at the far end. If he had noticed, he would have assumed that it led to an antechamber of some sort, perhaps to a restroom or a storage closet.

The room behind that door had indeed been an antechamber of sorts, used by the various lords of Kingsley Hall over the years as a cloakroom, a smoking parlour (poorly ventilated), a walk-in wine cellar (albeit one located on the third floor), even as a janitorial storage space by one of the less refined owners who'd disdained the airs of the nouveau riche. Under Dr. Rosanoff's directives, the room had been repurposed for more scientific pursuits.

"After you."

It was a dim space, crowded with shapes: squares and looming obelisks hiding under draped cloths. Cords snaked across the floor. A fluorescent light flickered on in the sickly green of shifting spectrums.

Dr. Rosanoff pulled one of the shrouds away, revealing a row of rounded TV monitors and a flat-topped reel-to-reel tape deck. He pulled aside another drop cloth in a slow-motion conjuring that revealed toggles and switchboards, with an intercom and a built-in microphone, all in the same shade of putty-grey plastic. Cutting-edge technology in its day, now a museum of the near past. Thomas's father flicked a switch and the unit hummed to life. Murky images swam onto the TV screens.

"I had it tested a few years ago. *Psychology Today* was doing a feature story, a look back at the great experiments of the twentieth century." He flicked another switch, and another. "It should all be up and running."

The TV monitors peered into the various rooms in the house,

black-and-white images of Sebastian sitting on a piano bench, rocking back and forth, of Eli pacing like a captive bear in the library room, of the magician standing perfectly still in the middle of Thomas's childhood bedroom, staring directly into the camera.

"The main observations were via the one-way mirrors. Graduate students, psychology classes. But we also recorded the more important bits, for posterity."

Dr. Rosanoff rolled his chair up to a bank of TV monitors. On one screen, Thomas could see the two orderlies standing guard in the central hallway. He could see the large kitchen where the housekeeper and her staff were preparing a meal. The stairwells and the corridors. The sunroom and dining hall. He could see himself as well, reflected in the curve of the TV screens.

"Y'ever play with yourself, Tommy?"

It was his grandfather's voice, still resonant after all these years.

Thomas, walking along the garden hedges. His grandfather, more stooped than ever, "Y'know. You ever diddle your willy?"

Thomas had balked, immediately embarrassed. "What? No!" This was a lie. An emphatic lie, but a lie nonetheless. (And a lie is no less a lie for being emphatic.)

"Well, if you do, make sure it's under your covers with the lights out, okay? And not in front of a mirror. Never in front of a mirror."

Why on earth would anyone do *that* in front of a mirror? And why on earth would Grandpa say such a thing? (Thomas now understood exactly why.)

Another voice, closer at hand, nearer in time.

His father had asked him a question, and it pulled Thomas back to the present. Dr. Rosanoff repeated his query, tapping a finger on Sebastian's TV monitor. "He's on Risperidone. Correct?"

"He is, yes."

"Blood pressure?"

"A little low."

Dr. Rosanoff leaned closer, watched as Sebastian rocked back and forth on the piano bench. "There! Did you see that?" Thomas's father moved a toggle, zoomed in with a series of jerking lurches. The image of Sebastian's face filled the frame, grew so large it began to break up. "See? There it is. Again."

Thomas moved closer, not sure what he was looking for. On the screen, Sebastian's mouth twitched, and then—so quickly, Thomas almost missed it—his tongue darted out. Once. Twice.

"There!" said Dr. Rosanoff, triumphant. "Flycatcher's tongue. Not a good sign. An early indication of tardive dyskinesia. The facial tics, the involuntary spasms, the way he moves back and forth. That's not the illness you're seeing. That's the drugs. We got to him just in time." Dr. Rosanoff rolled himself back, made a note of it in the log-book. "First thing we do is pull him off his meds."

"But—if he crashes?"

"He crashes. The shock might do him some good. Might shake things up a bit." He swivelled around to look at Thomas. "I've reviewed your transcripts. The idea was good, but it's not working. The entire process seems to have stalled. They aren't confronting each other or their delusions. Why do you think that is?"

"Well, they did confront each other at the start," Thomas said. "But as the sessions went on, they seemed to have focused on me instead. They sort of ganged up on me. I was becoming worried that they might have been reinforcing each other's delusions."

"You're right to be concerned. It's a common problem with group therapy, patients banding together to form a 'solidarity of madness.'

Understandable, I suppose. Harsh truths are often unpalatable. Fantasies are so much more alluring. Our role is to act as envoys, Tommy. Envoys from the real world. Here, have a seat."

Thomas rolled a chair up to the monitors. He found it distracting seeing his three Christs boxed in like a life-sized game of *Clue*. (*Mr. Green, in the conservatory, with a dagger.*)

"They've each adopted a different strategy," said Dr. Rosanoff. "Have you noticed that?"

"I have. They're using denial, withdrawal, and avoidance. Eli denies there are any contradictions in what he believes. Sebastian won't engage. And the magician sidesteps the conflict, turns it back on itself."

"The magician? Why don't you use his real name?"

"He won't tell me his real name."

"No identification?"

"None on him."

"That's peculiar. Even the most down-and-out hobos in Tent City have some sort of ID on them, even if it's an expired out-of-state driver's license."

"I've asked. He won't tell me, he says, 'You know my name.'"

"He's playing games. If he won't give you a name, assign him one. You've referred to him as John Doe in the transcripts. Call him that to his face. For someone with such an inflated sense of self, having a boilerplate name slapped onto him will get under his skin. Call him John Doe till he gives up his real name. Referring to him as 'the magician' only elevates his status at the expense of your authority. Having a secret name gives a person power; naming them diminishes that power. It undercuts any phony mystique they may try to claim." Dr. Rosanoff tapped the TV screen that displayed the magician. "Our friend here. What exactly are we dealing with?"

"Um, not entirely sure. I mean, I have an idea. Probably a schizophrenic delusional disorder—we have active-phase symptoms—but overall, his behaviour is fairly coherent."

Dr. Rosanoff swivelled his attention onto Thomas. "Living in an alley, sleeping in your own filth, eating out of a garbage can. That's coherent, is it?"

"Well, no, but . . . We found traces of naloxone in his blood."

"Is that so?" A smile twitched on his father's lips. "The thread begins to unravel. Do you know what 'schizophrenic' means, Thomas? From a purely medical point of view? It means 'Fucked if I know. Give 'em a pill.' " He looked back at the monitor where the magician remained, not moving, staring up at them. "Do you want to know what I think? I think he's trying to play us. I don't think he's delusional, I think he's manipulative. My preliminary diagnosis, based on your notes and my observations? Possible antisocial personality disorder."

"Really? That seems a bit . . . extreme. I mean, we haven't seen any evidence of a lack of empathy toward others. Quite the opposite."

"Extreme? Or decisive? And anyway, I said *possible*. We'll see if his apparent displays of empathy are real. As for Sebastian, I'd say we're dealing with a dependent personality disorder: passive, reactive, unable to care for himself. With Eli, we have a classic case of persecution complex accompanied by paranoid delusions. But those are only the outer trappings of what's going on below the surface. Ask yourself, What is their cardinal trait? Their defining characteristic?"

"Faith?"

"*Esteem*. Elevated, inflated, unearned, unwarranted, pathological levels of self-esteem. We aren't dealing with a physical illness here. We're dealing with false beliefs, and it's our job to hammer these beliefs down by any means necessary, to confront these delusions head-on. They need to work their way back to reality. It's our responsibility to make sure they don't falter or fall."

"But if we push them too hard . . ."

"They'll leave? I don't think so. We won't let them."

"I don't think we'd have much choice in the matter," said Thomas. "The magician is free to go anytime he likes, and Eli and Sebastian can always request a return to San Hendrin if they find the therapy too stressful."

"True, true. The regulations regarding nonvoluntary commitment are stringent. We can't hold them indefinitely. Unless . . ." Dr. Rosanoff smiled, a satisfied turn of the lips. "Unless they might be considered a danger to themselves or to others. If that were the case, I could arrange emergency medical custody, renewable on review, of course. Consider our friend Eli: destructive tendencies, a history of violence, tried to remove his own eye, for God's sake. And Sebastian? A pattern of self-harm, several attempts at suicide—none successfully. Poor bastard, he's even a failure at that. And as for our last fellow, the magician? Delusions of grandeur, highly manipulative, oppositional. As I said, he may have an antisocial personality disorder. Run him through Hare's Psychopathy Checklist. You may be surprised at what you find: glibness, superficial charm, a grandiose sense of self-worth, pathological dishonesty."

"But—"

"On Axis V of the SDM, where would you place him?"

"The magician?" asked Thomas. "Zero: not enough data for an assessment."

"No. We place him at a one."

"One? On a scale of one hundred?" Thomas was taken aback. He knew what that diagnosis meant. It meant the patient was an imminent danger to himself and others.

"A score of one hundred would be optimum," said Dr. Rosanoff. "You and I would score in that range. Fifty is iffy. But if we place him at a one, it gives us a certain . . . leeway."

"But an assessment like that, it's committable."

"Exactly. Remember, what we're doing here is for their own good. We're trying to help them. Don't ever forget that. If someone were drowning, wouldn't you do anything to save them, even if they were flailing about, even if they were scratching and clawing and pushing you away?"

"I—I suppose."

Dr. Rosanoff rose to his full Easter Island height. "Come with me, Tommy. I want to show you something."

Leaving the confines of the control room, they returned to the expansive views and warm leather of Dr. Rosanoff's study. *Professor Plum, in the library, with a crucifix.* Dr. Rosanoff opened his laptop, brought up Thomas's file on the third Jesus, aka "John Doe," aka "the magician."

"Let's say we add a notation of SPD to his file: 'Severe Personality Disorder.' Seems reasonable enough, yes? But after that, all it takes is a single letter, one stroke of the keyboard, a 'D' in front of it and suddenly we have a classification of DSPD: 'Dangerous and Severe Personality Disorder.' That's all it takes. That single letter gives us the authority—and, I daresay, the duty—to take whatever measures are necessary to treat him. This can include a recommendation for indefinite confinement."

"But he isn't dangerous."

"A manipulative patient with psychopathic tendencies and oppo-sitional beliefs? That's not dangerous? Danger comes in many fla-vours, Thomas. It only takes one letter. . . ." His hand hovered over the keyboard, above the D. "But let's hold off on that for now, shall we?"

He smiled and stepped back: from the brink, from the keyboard, from his son. He smiled, but the threat was implicit.

"Our guests are waiting," he said. "Shall we?"

CHAPTER FORTY-ONE

IDENTITY THERAPY: SESSION ONE. *The following is a transcript of a group session conducted at the Kingsley Hall medical facility by DR. THOMAS ROSANOFF on test subjects ELI WASSER (57), SEBASTIAN LAMIELL (28) & JOHN DOE (age uncertain), with Thomas Rosanoff observing. Test subjects are seated around a large table. Water has been provided. John Doe is holding a copy of Dr. Rosanoff's book* Be OK, Do OK!

(Not noted in the transcript? The fact that Dr. Rosanoff's two burly orderlies stood next to him, on either side, arms crossed, unsmiling.)

DR. ROSANOFF: Let me start by saying: I don't care.

The three Jesuses shift in their seats, not sure how to respond.

DR. ROSANOFF: Your uncle fingered you behind the woodshed when you were four? Your parents never bought you that toy fire engine you wanted when you were five? You were toilet-trained too soon? Or too late? Your mother breastfed you too long, or not long enough? She was cold and aloof, or she smothered you with love? Your father was violent? Your father was passive? Whatever it was: I. Don't. Care. I accept no alibis, no excuses. We must not blame others. Everything we do in life is a choice, and you have chosen madness. We need to be clear on this from the start: You do not hear voices, you *choose* to hear voices.

The three Jesuses say nothing.

DR. ROSANOFF: So. Here are the ground rules. There are really only two: First, we must accept responsibility for our actions and the consequences of our behaviour, and—just as importantly— we must understand that retreating into silence will not be tolerated. Choosing not to speak is a sign of weakness, a sign of avoidance. If you three gentlemen truly are God incarnate, you are not weak. Agreed?

He waits for a response.

DR. ROSANOFF: Agreed?

Mumbled replies of assent from the three men.

DR. ROSANOFF: Thank you. (*turning his gaze to Sebastian*) Mr. Lamiell, you have put your family through utter hell. You have caused untold pain and suffering through your actions, and you have tormented them with your madness. Your father and sister are in anguish—because of you. How do you respond? No comment? Nothing to say for yourself? Empathy isn't in your emotional repertoire, is it, Sebastian? Self-pity, yes. Self-centred delusions, clearly. But empathy, for your family, your loved ones?

No response. Dr. Rosanoff next turns his gaze on Eli.

DR. ROSANOFF: And you, Mr. Wasser? No thundering invective? No lightning bolts from Heaven? You say you're God, but you can't even strike me blind or cause a few locusts to fall from the sky. I say you are a fraud. Prove me wrong. If you can.

Nothing happens. The doctor now turns his attention to the magician.

DR. ROSANOFF: As for you, Mr. Doe, you seem awfully quiet. Nothing to add to this?

Unlike the other two, John Doe (aka the magician) meets Dr. Rosanoff's gaze headlong. When he speaks, his voice does not waver.

JOHN DOE: Get thee behind me, Satan.

DR. ROSANOFF: Ah. You see me as an antagonist. That's understandable. I'm not here to coddle you. I'm here to challenge your beliefs. In this room, we do not ask why. We ask *what*. We ask what you're doing that's self-defeating, and what you can do to change this. (*addressing all three patients*) Gentlemen, I've seen the tests that young Thomas ran on you, the brain scans and medical assessments. (*He flips through the report Thomas has prepared.*) Galvanic skin responses, muscle contractions above 2.0 volts, all within standard range. Sebastian here was on the higher end of the anxiety scale, Mr. Doe on the lower, but all three results were normal. EEG readings, same thing. MRIs as well. Your temporal lobes and auditory cortices are in proper working order. No signs of congenital defects, no damage to the impulse control regions, no thinning of the brain's cerebral cortex, no history or evidence of epilepsy or injury. No aneurisms, no structural abnormalities. Everything looks perfectly fine, which is to be expected. Brain trauma causing behavioural changes is exceedingly rare. So let's be clear. You are not sick, gentlemen. You are crazy. And there is a difference between the two. Sickness is *physical*. Crazy is how you act. Crazy is within your control. Eli, you look distressed! You shouldn't be. This is good news! This is *very* good news. A brain trauma or a tumour can be almost insurmountable, can take years to overcome. But crazy is a matter of choice. Stop acting crazy and you will stop *being* crazy.

SEBASTIAN: (*softly*) Judge not, lest ye be judged.

DR. ROSANOFF: What was that?

Sebastian repeats his comment.

DR. ROSANOFF: An excellent point, and I commend you for contributing to this discussion. But I must respectfully disagree. To become healthy we must change, and to change we must be willing to judge—and be judged. That's how reality works. (*He pushes his chair back.*) We have become a nation of enablers. Adopting the mantle of victim is now actively encouraged. It's become a coveted role. There was a time when being a victim was something to overcome. Now it's something to aspire to, something to revel in. Gentlemen, when I look around this table I see three strong individuals. Individuals who are more than capable of becoming healthy members of society, individuals who can change the way they look at the world, who can stop wallowing in madness and self-pity. I see three individuals who might yet become whole again.

SEBASTIAN: Four.

DR. ROSANOFF: I beg your pardon?

SEBASTIAN: (*avoiding Dr. Rosanoff's gaze*) You said that you saw three individuals in front of you. But there are four of us.

He is referring to Thomas.

DR. ROSANOFF: Young Thomas is not being treated. I was referring to the three of you, each claiming to be the same person.

ELI: (*under his breath*) Blasphemy.

DR. ROSANOFF: What did you say?

ELI: Nothin'.

DR. ROSANOFF: (*turning his attention back to Mr. Doe*) You've been holding a copy of one of my books this entire time. Is there something you would like to say?

JOHN DOE: There is, yes. Something I'd like to read to the group. May I?

DR. ROSANOFF: Certainly. That book was written for a popular audience, so it's meant to be accessible to readers such as yourself. But the fundamentals behind it remain as strong now as they did when first published. Please. Go ahead.

John Doe (aka the magician) opens the pocketbook to a folded page and reads.

JOHN DOE: "Many accomplished and well-adjusted figures in history have entertained eccentric or even strange beliefs. Holding strange beliefs in and of itself is not an indicator of mental illness."

Long pause.

DR. ROSANOFF: Your point being?

THOMAS: (*interjecting*) Um, Dr. Rosanoff? If I may—I think what Mr. Doe is suggesting is that *ideas*, on their own, although they might be eccentric, are not necessarily indicative of a disease. They might simply be a way of looking at the world that is—

DR. ROSANOFF: (*impatiently*) Of course it's not a disease. I never said it was. There is no such thing as a mental *disease*, because the mind is not an organ. There is indeed brain disease. That's physical. But there is no *mind* disease. As for Mr. Lamiell,

Wasser, and Doe, we aren't trying to cure a disease. We are trying to change behaviour.

John Doe raises his hand.

DR. ROSANOFF: Mr. Doe, you don't need to raise your hand to speak.

JOHN DOE: Do you know what I think?

DR. ROSANOFF: I would be delighted if you could elucidate the issue for us.

JOHN DOE: I think society needs people like us to define what normal is. The mad serve a useful role—always have. If madness didn't exist, we would need to invent it. (*pause*) Some might say we have.

DR. ROSANOFF: So you admit you're mad?

JOHN DOE: Well, it's either you or me. We can't both be right. Can we?

Loud noise.

—END OF TRANSCRIPT—

CHAPTER FORTY-TWO

"LOUD NOISE," OF COURSE, could mean anything: a crack of thunder, a sudden burst of laughter. In this case, the transcript was referring to the sound of breaking glass.

Dr. Rosanoff told the orderlies, "Stay here with our guests. I'll see what's going on."

He strode down the hallway with Thomas hurrying behind him. The Kingsley Hall staff had gathered by the front door, looking anxious.

"Security is on its way," one of the valets assured them.

A stained glass panel framing the main door had been broken. Thomas peered through the ragged hole, saw a figure being dragged across the grounds by a pair of guards. It was Amy.

Wild and unruly, she was screaming, "I know you're in there, Thomas! Where is he? Where's my brother!" She fought against the guards, twisting about to no effect, voice raw. "Where is he?"

Thomas felt his knees give out. He staggered, felt the floor shift.

Remember me.

"Rest assured, I have full medical custody of Mr. Lamiell, as arranged with the seminary at Saint Mathurin's."

They were in Dr. Rosanoff's office, as Thomas paced back and forth, avoiding the view from the window. He could hear Amy. She was outside the gate yelling, her voice muffled but insistent.

"You've met Father Patrice?" asked Dr. Rosanoff. "He has a medical background, so he's more sympathetic to these sorts of things. He's overseeing Sebastian's case, and he turned his files over to me. I repeat: Amy is not the legal custodian. She has no authority. True, she can go to a judge, file a T-42, but that would have to go through the medical review board, and that could take weeks."

Thomas stopped his pacing, looked at his father, eyes brimming. "This is not what I had in mind."

"Oh? And what exactly did you *have in mind?*"

"I thought I could help them."

"And that," said Dr. Rosanoff, "is exactly what we're doing. Don't go wobbly on me, not now. We are men of science. We must remain steadfast in the face of irrational claims." He drove the next statement home like an ice pick, stabbing at his son with each word. "We must not falter in our resolve."

Thomas turned away, couldn't breathe. He rested his forehead, suddenly heavy, against the view: rooftops and river, cold to the touch.

Dr. Rosanoff came over, stood beside Thomas at the window.

"Psychiatry is the only branch of medicine that treats people against their will. This is a somber responsibility, a burden that no other field has. And what happened to us? We didn't have the guts. We cut and ran. Like cowards. We emptied our hospitals, closed down our state mental institutions, turned our streets into open-air asylums. We have abandoned society's most vulnerable people—and then congratulated ourselves for doing so. We have abandoned the very people who needed us most. And where are they now? Sleeping in garbage, foraging for food—like animals. We avert our gaze, toss a few coins, pat ourselves on the back for being so progressive when in fact all we have done is taken a giant step backwards. Tormented people, living in alleyways and under bridges, victimized and matted in filth? That's the origin of trolls, Thomas. That crazed man with the long beard, living under a bridge—that figure of folklore is real. He's a lost soul, homeless and caught in an echo chamber of his own thoughts, unloved and ignored. You can read the same descriptions in medieval literature. Of madmen harried by children and feral dogs. This is where our good intentions have taken us, right back to the Dark Ages. Read the Talmud. What is Eli, if not a *shoteh*? 'One who goes out at night, who sleeps in a cemetery, who destroys all that is given him.' We have turned our back on them, and why? Because we didn't have the courage of our convictions."

"I'm not a psychiatrist," said Thomas. He felt as though his chest had been hollowed out with a spoon. "I'm not even a doctor."

"Life is full of unpleasant truths, Tommy. Here's one: madness is not a lifestyle. We aren't helping anyone when we treat it that way. If I had a heart attack, was lying unconscious on the street, I would hope—would expect!—that someone would help me. I would receive emergency medical treatment, even if I was incapacitated. And, if I was lying in my own feces and tormented by voices, I would hope that someone would help me as well, whether I was capable of giving permission or not. We took an oath, Tommy. An oath to help."

"But—that's just it. *Are* we helping?"

"Tough love, Tommy. That's what this is."

Thomas was staring at the front gates below, emptied now of Amy. "Did you know," he asked, "that Connecticut is in the Bible?"

"Connecticut?"

"In the Bible. It's true." Thomas turned, looked at his father. "Did Mom ever take me to church?"

"What?"

"*I said*, Did my mother . . . ever take me . . . to church?"

CHAPTER FORTY-THREE

THE GREY DAYS OF November had given way to
sleet, and the sleet had given way to rain. The incessant drumming of
fingers on rooftops, ice-pelted sidewalks, pockmarked puddles.

Sister Frances stepped out of the doorway, throwing a small square
of light on the wet pavement. She stood a moment under the awning,
rolled her shoulders, cricked her neck. Long day. A pair of detectives
had been interviewing her clients about the string of deaths in Tent
City. Officially, these were still listed as overdoses, but it was clear that
there was something else going on in the shadows. Frances fumbled
with her self-collapsing umbrella—it opened limply, halfheartedly—
and pulled her amorphous cloth bag closer (she'd long since given
up on carrying a proper purse). She began her weary walk to the bus
stop. She was tired, so tired, and didn't see the figure that was waiting
in a doorway. She walked right past, in fact, without noticing.

"It makes no sense," said the figure.

She stopped. "Tommy?"

"I was only a child when she died." He stepped into the watery
light of a streetlamp. "I was only, what? Three? Three and a half? I
barely remember hide-and-seek. How the hell could I remember an
entire musical arrangement? It makes no sense." Then, with a sudden

manic friendliness. "But enough about me! How was your day, Frances? Busy?"

She nodded, slowly. "It was fairly typical. A dozen or so head-to-toe assessments. Trauma referrals and follow-ups. I spent half my time changing dressings and chasing supplies, the other half cleaning needle abscesses and sores gone septic, plus the usual STDs and lung infections." She stepped closer, stared at him from under her umbrella. He looked haggard. "What's going on, Tommy?"

He tried to feign an "I know it's silly, but" expression. "I've been . . . I've been hearing voices."

"Whose?"

"Mine, of course. It's self-generated, like any hallucination. It's my left temporal lobe talking to itself, a minimally invasive form of auditory schizophrenia, probably stress-induced. Very mild. I'm managing it."

"And what are they saying to you, these voices?"

"They—they don't *speak*, they sing. It's faint. Comes and goes. There's music and some sort of choir. Sometimes I hear someone calling my name, softly."

"Your mother took you to church. She must have at some point, even if it was just to light a candle for you."

"But I was so young, Frances. The cerebellum, it isn't developed enough in early childhood to retain memories like that. It's impossible."

"And yet, there it is. Come, walk me."

He joined her under her paltry umbrella, accompanied her to the bus stop, waited with her in the shelter. The fingers on the roof had grown more persistent, more impatient. Rain beaded on the plastic sides, ran down in rivulets.

"It's silly," he said, breath misting in the cold. "I mean, I know what it is. It's a temporary dysthymic disorder. Easily treated with standard sedatives. It's my brain releasing norepinephrine. A reactive auditory hallucination. But still, I thought— I thought maybe it was a memory of my mom."

"The young woman you told me about—Amy, was it? When you were with her, the voices stopped?"

He nodded.

"I think you need to talk to her."

"I can't."

Thomas had been to the gallery to see Amy, had tried to explain that he'd only wanted to help her brother, but he was blocked at the door by Lars. Thomas had shouted past him, yelling for Amy to come out, to which Lars had said, simply, "If you don't leave, I'm calling the police. We'll get a restraining order against you if we have to." *We* will get a restraining order. Not she, *we*.

That rankled Thomas's heart like a sword in a scabbard. Thomas very much wanted to throttle Lars, but of course could not, so Lars was allowed to continue to exist, unthrottled. Instead, groping for pithy and failing, Thomas had shouted in Lars's face, "Go back to fuckin' Sweden, you fuckin' Swede," spitting out his words, "and take your hundred-dollar haircut with you."

"Sweden?" Lars was puzzled by this. "I'm not from Sweden." He had a bruised look in his eyes. "I'm from Minnesota."

Such a mundane answer. It had thrown Thomas off balance; he'd always operated on the premise that everyone's life was built on secrets, and for him to discover that his archnemesis, the stealth Swede, was just some butter-head from Minnesota sent him reeling. One of the women at the gallery, hiding behind Lars, shouted back at

Thomas, "The police are on their way!" Was she bluffing? She was. But Thomas couldn't face being arrested and publicly shamed, so he fled, eyes stinging.

Back at the bus shelter. Waiting with Frances, sidewalks under the streetlamps looking polished on this rain-laden night. "Do you remember the three Christs I told you about?"

"I do."

"One of them is Amy's brother."

"Oh boy."

"It's just—I can't get her out of my head. I can't get the sadness to go away. And even if I could, I don't know that I would want to. I'm not really sure I want to get over her."

"Thomas, you're exhausted. You need rest."

"Can't. It's all under way now! Full steam. Rah rah." He tried to laugh, felt it die in his chest.

"Have you ever considered—" She stopped herself.

"Considered what?"

"That perhaps your father isn't done with you. Maybe the experiment is still running."

And now the laughter did bubble up. "Oh, trust me, I know. That experiment never ended. It won't, until my tombstone has been carved. 'Here lies the Good Son, an hypothesis confirmed.' "

"And Amy? She clearly doesn't want her family to be any part of this. Thomas, you have to end it."

"I can't. It's not that simple." What he wanted to say, what he wanted to cry out, was this: *"I can't, because it's the only chance I have, the only shred of a chance: cure the brother and win back her love."* A ridiculous plan. He knew that. But it was all he had.

"Thomas, in Psalms 34:18 . . ."

"There you go again!" he snapped. "Always dragging God into it." She began to say something, but he stopped her. "God is an evolutionary relic, you do realize that, right? A vestigial organ. Something we've outgrown. Like an appendix or wisdom teeth, but with a higher body count."

"Thomas, there will always be an unanswerable question at the core of everything; there will always be a shoe on the roof. This world of ours is murky and filled with wonders, and there are fibers of mystery clinging to everything. Better to live with this ambiguity than try to deny it, I say."

"And what does any of this have to do with Amy?"

"Everything. Love, like God, is something we believe in but don't understand."

"I don't know why I bother talking to you," said Thomas.

"Likewise," said Frances.

They waited in silence for her bus to arrive. It was a long time coming.

Later that night, back at Kingsley Hall while the rest of the world was sleeping, Thomas searched up the incident Frances had referred to. The story of the shoe on the roof. It was, he discovered, disquietingly true: not a fable nor a fairy tale nor an urban legend, but duly reported. Incidents like this, and there were many, had been dismissed out of hand by scientists—dismissed, but not disproven.

It felt as though he had brushed up against something in the dark.

CHAPTER FORTY-FOUR

IDENTITY THERAPY: SESSION TWO. *Conducted at Kingsley Hall by DR. ROSANOFF with subjects ELI WASSER, SEBASTIAN LAMIELL & JOHN DOE. Thomas Rosanoff attending. John Doe has a copy of the SDM:III manual open in front of him. The two orderlies stand behind Dr. Rosanoff. A VHS player has been rolled into the room on a portable stand.*

DR. ROSANOFF: (*taking his seat*) Gentlemen, there's something I would like to show you (*referring to the VHS player*). But first, I believe Mr. Doe has a question.

JOHN DOE: Well, I'm not sure who this "Mr. Doe" is that you refer to, but as for me, yes, I do have a question. (*referring to the SDM:III manual*) I've been reading your book, and I hope you don't think I'm rude, but the numbers—they don't add up.

DR. ROSANOFF: The numbers?

JOHN DOE: When I tally the diagnostic labels, it doesn't add up. (*flipping through the pages*) There's an updated index after every entry giving the latest stats. For example, you have 22 million people suffering from "socially debilitating shyness." You have 23 million with "sexual dysfunctional syndrome," and 12 million—that's what? 5 percent of everybody in America?—suffering from "generalized anxiety disorder." I added it up, just the major ones, and it comes to roughly 800 million people in the U.S. suffering from some type of mental disorder. That's almost three times the entire population.

DR. ROSANOFF: Mr. Doe, you are neither a statistician nor an authority on psychiatry. We don't have time for this. May we move on?

JOHN DOE: Here, on page 168, Schizotypal Personality Disorder: "Patient displays unusual thought patterns and behaviours" . . . In other words, the patient is eccentric. Is being eccentric a mental disorder? And here, on page 219, Disruptive Mood Dysregulation Disorder: "Patient displays chronic, severe, persistent irritability, with frequent outbursts." In other words, the patient has a bad temper.

DR. ROSANOFF: You're trying to bait me.

JOHN DOE: What about daydreaming? Is that a mental disorder as well? How about imagination? Is that an illness, too?

DR. ROSANOFF: I'm not going to play along.

JOHN DOE: I'm just curious, is all. Or is that a mental disorder as well? Curiosity.

DR. ROSANOFF: You're manipulating the meanings and you know it.

JOHN DOE: Tell me, Doctor, somewhere in this dictionary of dreams, this book of woe, is there an entry for those who have a compulsive need to label others? A mental disorder for those obsessed with labelling mental disorders, and perhaps compiling compendiums about it, like a snake eating its own tail?

DR. ROSANOFF: You do not want to get caught in a power struggle with me, Mr. Doe. Take that as a warning.

Dr. Rosanoff opens a file.

DR. ROSANOFF: Now then, Mr. Doe. We found traces of methadone in your bloodstream. Naloxone as well. Naloxone is used to reverse the effects of a heroin overdose. Why would we find that? Why would that be present in your bloodstream? Please tell me we aren't dealing with some run-of-the-mill, substance-induced psychotic disorder. Tell me you aren't just another street-corner junkie with delusions of grandeur. I mean, you are the Son of God, yes? (*turning to Eli*) Or would that be you?

ELI: I am Christ the Redeemer! I sit at the right hand of God! I sit in righteous judgment!

DR. ROSANOFF: But Mr. Doe here claims that *he* is God. As does Mr. Lamiell. They are making a fool of you, Eli.

Sebastian, speaking softly.

SEBASTIAN: Why can't we all be?

The others turn their attention to Sebastian.

SEBASTIAN: Why can't we all be God? All three of us.

ELI: (*elated*) Yes! Why not? Let's vote! ROLL CALL! Jesus? Do we have a Jesus?

All three lift their hands.

JOHN DOE: (*smiles*) It's settled, then.

DR. ROSANOFF: You can't decide something like that by a show of hands.

THOMAS: (*to his father*) Dr. Rosanoff, may I have a word with you?

DR. ROSANOFF: Not now, Tommy.

THOMAS: (*growing frantic*) It's important. Can we—? It's just (*whispering furtively*), what if he's right?

Dr. Rosanoff turns slowly, looks at Thomas.

—*END OF TRANSCRIPT*—

CHAPTER FORTY-FIVE

"*WHAT IF* . . ." This was a question that has top-pled empires, has overturned civilizations. "What if the world is *not* flat? What if man is *not* the centre of the universe? What if life is an ongoing process, not a divinely stamped creation?" And, as crucially: "What if there is more to us than mere molecules?" *What if* . . .

Dr. Rosanoff yanked Thomas out of the room, was towering over him in the hallway. "Explain yourself," he said.

"What if Sebastian is right?"

"Stop. Think before you say another word."

"I don't mean— I don't mean they're physically the reincarnation of Christ. But I think I've figured out what the problem is. Why aren't they confronting each other? Maybe it's because they *aren't* occupy-ing the same space. They aren't actually claiming the same identity. They're claiming aspects of a larger identity. Think about it. The Trinity, the three aspects of God." His words spilled out, fevered and unchecked, tripping over each other.

"Tommy—"

"No, hear me out, hear me out. Sitting around that table we have the manifestation of all three: the Father, the Son, and the Holy Ghost. With Eli, what do you have? God as an avenging angel. God as *jus-*

tice. And with Sebastian, you have God as *love*. With the magician, you have *mystery* and *magic*. All three, right there in front of us." He was speaking rapid-fire, ticking them off on his fingers. "We have Eli the Father, Sebastian the Son, and John Doe as the Holy Spirit. We have Justice, Love, and Magic. It's all there, right in front of us, if we would only—"

"Get a grip!" There was a flash of rage in Dr. Rosanoff's eyes. "Stop spouting gibberish and listen to me. You are *not* going to get caught up in some sort of induced delusional disorder. I've seen it happen. You get too close and you start sharing their psychoses. Don't ever forget that madness is contagious, Tommy. But that's not going to happen here. Do you understand me?"

Thomas nodded. The fever had passed.

"We are going back to that table, and you are going to stay in control. We are not dealing with anything mystical here. We are dealing with a persecution disorder, a passive delusional personality, and a master manipulator. *That* is your Holy Trinity."

Dr. Rosanoff straightened himself, walked back down the hallway to the room without windows. Thomas, feeling dazed and barely tethered to this world, was about follow when he spun around, expecting to see someone behind him. But there was no one there, only the hallway and a voice asking that same sibilant question: *"Thomasssss?"*

CHAPTER FORTY-SIX

DR. ROSANOFF ENTERED THE room with immense purpose, Thomas less so.

"Gentlemen," said Dr. Rosanoff as he wheeled the VHS player over. "I may not have a degree in theology, but I'm fairly sure that this . . ."

He shoved a videocassette into the machine and hit PLAY. A low-resolution face filled the screen. It was a wino, blood running from his mouth and nose, moaning in pain to the jeers of spectators off-camera.

". . . is something Jesus would frown upon."

The title "HOBO WARS: IV" splashed itself across the screen, as a shakily handheld camcorder found Eli in the middle of the melee, younger, wilder, full of rage. The bleeding wino was thrown back to Eli by the crowd, and Eli hit him again, full force. Bone on face. Down he went. Then two knees onto the ribs. A howling mob, and Eli as an extension of it, knuckles battered, eyes filled with violent zeal.

Dr. Rosanoff killed the power and the screen went blank.

"Should we put that to a vote as well?" He sat down.

No one spoke. Eli was utterly still, almost catatonic. Thomas stared at his father in disbelief.

Dr. Rosanoff turned to his son. "Our Eli is a veritable star on the internet. His earlier work has been rediscovered and reappraised." Then, addressing Eli directly: "They brought you out of retirement, didn't they? Sure, it's all video apps and dark web downloads now, but it used to be good old-fashioned VHS."

The magician slowly got to his feet. "I have enjoyed our time together, Dr. Rosanoff. But I do believe I will be going now."

Dr. Rosanoff smiled at him. "And I do believe you won't."

The orderlies took a step forward, flanking Dr. Rosanoff. He opened a new folder, slid it across the table to the magician. There was a photograph attached, a mug shot.

The magician sat down. Didn't look at the photograph. Didn't need to.

Dr. Rosanoff flipped open the file. "Jeffrey A. Keshen, better known as Jeff. That is you, correct? Middle name Alwyn, from your maternal grandfather, Welsh, I believe. You're thirty-six years old, born in Medford, but raised right here in Boston. You were enrolled at Bay State for two semesters. Started in business administration, and then switched to theology and religious studies at Boston College, dropped out soon after, worked as a children's entertainer for a while, birthday parties, for the most part. Arrested on possession charges, released. Checked into rehab. Discharged four weeks later. Relapsed. Lost contact with family. You have two sisters, one brother, all older. Your father is a retired shop teacher; your mother ran a bakery down on Camden, which is still there, but under new owners. I understand their sticky buns are to die for. Still using your mother's original recipes! Your parents are in Wakefield now, in a senior's residence. Worried sick about their youngest child, I'm sure." Dr. Rosanoff spread his arms. "And just like that, the magic is gone."

Thomas felt his throat tighten. The magician—Jeffrey Keshen—was glaring at Dr. Rosanoff with a defiance undermined only by the wetness in his eyes.

"I've had enough," he said. "I'm leaving."

"No, you're not. There are several outstanding warrants, Mr. Keshen. Parole violations, mainly. Six months served on narcotics-related charges, released on good behaviour, in and out of rehab. Unfortunately, you've stopped checking in with your parole officer. He must be worried sick as well. No doubt he's been contacting your parents and siblings, harassing them every day, trying to track you down. I'm guessing it was right about then that you decided to shed your old identity and assume the aura of God. Quite the step up from where you were, wasn't it? Must have been intoxicating." And then, meeting the magician's glare head-on, "I can't let you walk out of here, Mr. Keshen. I would be remiss in my responsibilities were I to do so, and anyway"—he slid a second document across the table to him—"the matter is largely moot. You've been assessed as a danger to yourself and others, and I've been granted temporary medical custody. I've already spoken with your parole board, so for the next four to six weeks of observation and assessment, you're mine."

The magician turned to Thomas, but Thomas wouldn't make eye contact, couldn't bring himself to look at the man he thought he'd rescued.

"Addiction," said Dr. Rosanoff, addressing the group as a whole, "is not unlike madness. It's an alibi. An excuse. And like madness, it is a choice. To someone overwhelmed with pain and suffering, it may seem like the best choice, the only choice—an understandable choice, even—but a choice nonetheless."

Thomas tried to say something, but Dr. Rosanoff was focused on the defeated magician in front of him.

"Opiates," said Dr. Rosanoff, "such as morphine, OxyContin, Percocet, or—in your case—heroin, help trigger the brain's reward centre, flooding it with dopamine. Stimulus and response. It's the same chemical effect we see with food, sex, love. It's all very simple. Craving, followed by release, followed by a growing dependency. Junkies, binge eaters, sex addicts, they're all cut from the same cloth, all craving that extra dose of dopamine, that extra squirt of chemicals." A sliver of a smile emerged. "But you get your dopamine from religion now, don't you, Mr. Keshen?"

Thomas finally found his voice. "Dr. Rosanoff," he said. "If I may interject."

"Hold that thought."

A worker in splattered coveralls had stuck his head in the door. "Sorry to interrupt, but you asked me to let you know when we were done. We used rubber-based latex, so there'd be less odour. You got pretty good ventilation already, so the fumes and such shouldn't be too bad."

Dr. Rosanoff rose, turned to Thomas. "Shall we?"

CHAPTER FORTY-SEVEN

IT WAS A WORLD gone white. Every surface—the floor, walls, ceiling, doors—had been painted over. Every surface had been rendered in stark eggshell. Bright lights, but no light switches: those were now covered by screw-on panels, also painted white. The amount of illumination in each room would be controlled elsewhere, as would the temperature and background music. Video cameras still peered down from up high. Each room now contained a single bed only; everything else had been removed: dressers, desks, chairs—gone. Even Eli's HOME SWEET HOME had been taken away.

Thomas stood in the maze behind the walls, looking through the mirrored windows. An entire childhood painted over, every trace erased. He felt oddly elated. An empty buoyancy filled his chest. Television monitors had been installed inside each of the rooms as well, up high and protected by mesh. Thomas didn't realize the significance of this until later. The TV monitors had been switched off, for now, the screens reflecting the rooms back on themselves.

"Don't worry, Tommy. We'll move everything back in after this is over. Restore things to how they were." He was trying to reassure Thomas, but it had the opposite effect. He didn't want his childhood restored.

"There were too many variables," Dr. Rosanoff explained, as they peered through the mirrors. "Staying in a room designated for music might influence a subject one way, art another. It's better to simplify, strip it down, reduce any possible outside influence."

The three Christs were waiting in the hallway outside. Every room had two doors, one leading to the outside hallway, the other into the observatory maze behind the mirrors. Dr. Rosanoff met them in the main hall and led them to their newly renovated quarters. The rooms that had once been labelled Library, Music, Bedroom, were now named A, B, and C.

Even with the ventilation on, the rooms smelled faintly of paint thinner. It reminded Thomas of the antiseptic odour of an operating room. It reminded him of Amy's studio. It reminded him of Amy. It was the smell of open-heart surgery.

Dr. Rosanoff herded his three patients into the first room.

"Mr. Wasser, this will be yours, but rest assured the other two are essentially the same. You won't be alone, though. Each room is connected via intercom, so you will be able to hear what is being said in the other rooms, and vice versa. There will be no secrets here, gentlemen. These arrangements are Spartan, I know. But they don't have to be. Anything you'd like, anything at all, we can provide. Ask, and it's yours. All you have to do is denounce the other two men."

Thomas turned, not sure he'd heard correctly.

Dr. Rosanoff continued to a deepening silence. "Deny their claims of divinity, and yours. That's all you have to do. If you're hungry and need something to eat, if you're thirsty and need something to drink, if you'd like the lights dimmer or brighter, if you'd like magazines or a sofa, a Bible or a jigsaw puzzle. All you have to do is say, 'I am not the Messiah, and neither are my friends.' Rights are *earned*, not bestowed. Have trouble sleeping? We can play lullabies over the intercom. Cold? We will give you blankets. A late-night snack? Pancakes or coffee, anything you like, consider it done. Need to use the bathroom? Ask and an orderly will accompany you. You have only to declare that you are not the Messiah. You don't have to believe it—not at first—but you do have to *say* it. Behaviour comes first, beliefs follow. Denounce your claim to divinity and we have staff members waiting to provide you with whatever you desire. Isn't that right?"

The orderlies standing by the door nodded.

Dr. Rosanoff smiled. "God is a habit of the mind, gentlemen. But we can change that." He turned to leave, then looked back. "Oh, and don't try to smash the one-way mirrors. They're under protective plexiglass. They can't be broken." He put a hand on Thomas's shoulder. "Isn't that right, Tommy?"

They left Eli to his room and escorted Sebastian and the magician to theirs. The doors clicked shut, locking them in.

Thomas accompanied his father up the staircase. "But—if there's a fire or, or a . . ."

They walked through Dr. Rosanoff's study to the control room beyond.

"Any interruption to the power grid and the doors open automatically. It's perfectly safe. And anyway, they can leave their rooms anytime they like, stroll around the grounds, the gardens. All they have to do is tell the truth. That's all we're asking for. The truth."

The small control room glowed in the light of the television screens. With Thomas sitting to one side, Dr. Rosanoff rolled his chair up to the monitors: three rooms, stark white, with a patient in each. From up here, they almost seemed interchangeable.

"I'm only interested in what is measurable, Thomas. In what's observable." As he spoke, he toggled the framing of the cameras like a parent fussing over a child's collar on the first day of school. "We can't *observe* someone's mental state, we can't measure 'mind.' What we can observe is behaviour. We can't *weigh* a feeling, we can't *weigh* an idea. Intangibles—such as emotional states, longings, fears, mental processes—we know that these exist because of the effect they have on our actions. We can quantify behaviour. We can observe it, we can measure it, we can alter it. You say their problems lie in their beliefs? I agree. And their beliefs are revealed through their actions. As I said, if you change the behaviour, the beliefs will follow." He rolled away from the monitors, stared his son's doubts into silence. "We are men of science. We do not traffic in intuition; we do not deal in wishful thinking. It's not our job to pat someone on the hand and say, 'Poor baby.' Our job is to make them better. We aren't here to massage someone's ego. We are here to execute a surgical operation, to remove the problem, cleanly, precisely—and without wavering."

Thomas was having trouble breathing. He opened his mouth to speak, but couldn't.

"Our habits define us, Tommy. What is personality? Simply a cluster of habits. Change those habits and you will alter the personality. Parents have been using reward and punishment to shape children's behaviour since time immemorial. Positive reinforcement, negative reinforcement, carrot and stick: we're simply taking a more systematic approach, that's all."

"They'll resist."

"Of course they will. But we know from the Baumeister studies that willpower is finite, that we can deplete it. 'Ego depletion,' I believe he called it. And it might only take something as minor as altering their circadian rhythms."

"Sleep deprivation?"

"If you want to get emotional about it, yes." He leaned in, watched Sebastian for a moment. As always, Amy's brother was rocking back and forth, mouthing something silently to himself. "You want to help Emily's brother? This is how we do it."

"Amy," said Thomas. "Her name is Amy."

But Dr. Rosanoff wasn't listening. "We take a four-step approach with Sebastian. First, we break down his resistance, force him to face his reality, confront his falsehoods. Next, we make him admit his behaviour is irrational. Third, we reprogram. We modify what he says, how he acts. If we can do that, his beliefs will change—and his madness will dissolve."

"And the fourth step?" Thomas had only counted three.

"Repeat, if necessary. What we don't do is medicate. We will not reduce them to biological functions. To do so would be to rob them of their dignity, their autonomy. We treat them like the free agents they are, as individuals who are capable of change. Human beings have an immense capacity to learn, Tommy. They only need the right conditions. I know, I know. Sleep deprivation, sensory isolation, behaviour modification. It may seem harsh. But it works."

So does torture.

The air had become stultifying in the confines of the control room, crammed as it was with microphones, camera feeds, and reel-to-reel decks, but Dr. Rosanoff hardly seemed to notice, captivated as he was by the three figures on the TV monitors in front of him. Thomas could feel sweat forming like condensation in his armpits, on his forehead, in his brain.

"But what if—what if it doesn't work? We can't hold them like this forever. They aren't prisoners."

"Not prisoners, *patients*. And don't worry, we'll cure 'em, son. We'll cure 'em like a side of ham!" He grinned at his boy.

Thomas's objections seemed to be growing ever more feeble even as he became ever more concerned. "But I was trying to take a cognitive approach," he said. "Where *thoughts* come first and the behaviour follows, voluntarily. I was trying to appeal to their common sense."

Dr. Rosanoff wheeled around, peered at Tommy as if over a pair of reading glasses. "And how has that worked out for you?"

When Thomas failed to stammer out an answer, Dr. Rosanoff returned his attention to the monitors. He clicked the intercom to ON, watched the needle bounce on the first crackle of static. Put the mic to MUTE. "I understand what you're saying, Tommy. But you got it backwards. Talking things through is laborious and rarely works. That type of therapy only begets more therapy. The quicker, more decisive approach is to start with behaviour."

"But they were making progress," Thomas said. "If you look through my transcripts—"

"I have," said Dr. Rosanoff. "And what did I find? Conversations. Chit-chat. It's little more than a compilation of anecdotes. Where is the quantifiable evidence, Tommy? Where is the science? The plural of anecdote is not *data*."

Thomas could feel his face burn, was glad his father was too preoccupied with the recording levels and camera angles to notice.

"There," said Dr. Rosanoff. "All set. And now, if you'll excuse me, I have a dose of reality to inject."

But, *What if* . . . "What if they aren't *denying* reality?" Thomas asked. "What if they're trying to cope with it?"

Something the magician had said came back to Thomas with undue clarity. They'd been speaking about Eli and the sadness he seemed to carry within him, even in the midst of rage. *"His problem,"* the magician had suggested, *"is that no one cares about him. Only God."*

And if you take that away?

Dr. Rosanoff brushed Thomas's concerns aside. "If that's a 'coping strategy' it's not going particularly well, is it?"

"What did you mean," Thomas asked, "when you said, 'God is a habit of the mind'?"

"I was making a point, Tommy. Like I said, we are defined by our habits."

A conversation with Sebastian returned, a quiet moment of confession on the drive home after they'd visited the pond at Saint Mathurin's, before the tire had ruptured, before Eli found Connecticut in the Bible, before Thomas had danced naked in the park. Sebastian, looking through the car window reflection at the night-fallen streets, was speaking to the magician as Thomas listened in. He'd only caught fragments of what Sebastian had said: *"When my mother fell ill, I prayed and I prayed. But I couldn't save her, I couldn't save anyone."* Later, the magician would whisper to Thomas, in reference to the scars along Sebastian's forearms, *"I think he cuts himself as a way to make sure he is still there."*

Take away a person's scars and what do you have left?

As these voices swirled around Thomas in a tumult, Dr. Rosanoff pressed the intercom, leaned in, and spoke: "Gentlemen, if you would direct your attention to the TV monitors in your rooms."

Thomas could see all three men look up, startled.

And with that, Dr. Rosanoff pushed the VHS tape into the deck and hit PLAY. A familiar image filled the screens in each of the three rooms, and with it the audio: a voice reminiscent of a ringside announcer proclaiming it was time to rumble. *"Hobo WARRRS: Four!*

More explosive, more dynamic, more eye-gougingly good than ever before!" Dr. Rosanoff slid the volume louder and louder. Crude camerawork. Shaky visuals. The gleeful goading of an off-camera director. And, in the middle, wading through the carnage, was Eli Wasser, "The Hammer of God," pummeling one challenger after another into submission.

The timorous restraint Eli had shown earlier now evaporated and he stood, head back, shouting at the ceiling of Room A in an incoherent jumble of rage. *"Pharisees! Sadducees!"*

On the Room B monitor, Thomas could see Sebastian, eyes clenched, hands over his ears, could hear him repeating a personal catechism, barely audible above the bombast of the Hobo Wars soundtrack: *"God be in my eyes and in my looking, God be in my mouth and in my speaking, God be in my hands and in my actions."*

The magician, however, stood perfectly still in Room C, glaring into the camera while the cruelty continued unabated on the TV monitor over his shoulder. An out-of-focus Eli was now pounding a broken fist into the face of a man who was already down.

"Dad . . ." said Thomas, standing up, feeling queasy. "I really must protest. This is—"

Dr. Rosanoff held up a finger. "Just watch. Watch and learn. Consider this a lesson in tough love."

Eli began throwing himself against one wall and then the other, bellowing like a stuck bull. From the way Sebastian reacted on the adjoining monitor, he must have been able to hear Eli's assault through the walls. He could probably see it as well, the side of his room rattling with every blow. Sebastian held himself closer, rocked more frantically, repeated the catechism with ever more urgency. *"God be in my heart and in my loving, God be in my end and my departure."*

"Enough."

It was the magician. Or rather, it was Jeff Keshen, recovering addict, aging college dropout, former birthday party entertainer.

"I am not the Messiah, and neither is Eli or Sebastian."

And with that, Dr. Rosanoff killed the feed. He leaned in, pressed the intercom. "Thank you, Mr. Keshen."

The sound of Eli sobbing and Sebastian's mantra slowly gave way to silence.

"And that," said Dr. Rosanoff, turning to face his son, "is how it's done."

Thomas fell back into his chair. He felt like he was going to faint.

"Let's play them something soothing, shall we?" said Dr. Rosanoff. "Vivaldi, maybe. Or perhaps some Peruvian pan flute. Grab a cassette. They're on the shelf above the fuse box."

Thomas turned, numb but compliant, picked up several tapes, looked them over. He was about to open one, when he saw the label, written in the distinctly confident handwriting of his father: CHORAL ARRANGEMENT #49.

It took a moment to register. Thomas looked to his father, still numb, and said, "You played church music?" It was less a question than a statement.

"Hmm? Oh, that. Yes, we tried various inputs. Tested different types of music on you to see if there were any measurable differences. We wanted to see whether spirituality was innate, if you would respond to, say, choir music over nursery rhymes. Nothing much came of it, though. We even brought in an Orthodox priest to chant with you, had a rabbi recite the Torah, you even had a playmate who'd been abused by the clergy. We thought it might be therapeutic."

"For him?"

"For you." He looked at Thomas, genuinely puzzled, as though it were obvious. "That was to teach you empathy. Kids from broken homes, foster families. I didn't include it in the book because the results were inconclusive. Now then, about that music I asked for? *To soothe the savage beast.*"

"Here," Thomas said. "Play this one."

Dr. Rosanoff checked the label in the light of the monitor. "Interesting choice. Let's see where it takes us."

Thomas knew. He knew before his father put the cassette in, before he hit PLAY, before the first voice appeared. It was the music he'd been hearing, surfacing like a riddle from long ago. *Where do you bury the survivors?* A choir of voices rising up. What he'd thought was a memory of his mother was only this: a cassette played over the intercoms of his youth while men in white lab coats watched behind mirrors.

"Thomas? Are you all right?"

But Thomas didn't answer. He listened to the music, eyes wet. Smiling. Sad.

"Thomas?"

"It's breast," he said. "Not beast. *Music soothes the savage breast.* You got it wrong."

Something moved then, just below the surface like a vein under skin. . . . Thomas could *see* a memory forming in front of him, lighting up in the neural pathways of his brain, interwoven and intertwined, a vision of dendrites and nerve endings branching outward like skeletal trees, the synapses firing and misfiring, and perhaps madness, like creation, begins on this, with a stutter, with a misfiring of the mind, in the flash-frame lightning of electrical currents, in the voices striving to be heard, desperate messengers rendered mute, mouthing the words, pointing at their throats, as silent and strident as the sewn-mouthed screams of a lost choir, and he could see the conduits opening up before him in the amygdala, could see his thoughts and ideas made manifest, the neural nebulae taking form, stars coalescing, a storm in the cortical tissues, in the limbic nuclei that hold our fears, in the cumulus luminosities that hold our hopes and inward dreams, born of that divine stutter, a misfiring in the brain, the dendrites and neurons reaching outward, ever outward, until they touched the face of nothingness. At which point his knees gave out and his legs fell from under him.

CHAPTER FORTY-EIGHT

NOT FATHER PATRICE—who had studied to be a doctor—but the other one, the younger priest, the one who had leaned forward with a pained expression on his face. What was it he'd said? "Among some members of the clergy, a nervous breakdown is considered a sign of sincerity."

DEPERSONALIZATION DISORDER (from SDM:III, pg. 378): DP Disorder is marked by heightened sensory perceptions and a sense of detachment from one's body. Patients often remain aware that what they are experiencing is altered reality, and this in turn may inculcate feelings of panic. Sometimes accompanied by auditory and/or visual hallucinations, depersonalization disorder can also induce a sense of "heightened meaning," whereby mundane events are imbued with a significance not warranted by actualities.

Dr. Rosanoff, however, had diagnosed simple fatigue. "Go back to your apartment. Sleep. Take a couple of days to reset your brain." But what if Thomas was not suffering from fatigue or a personality disorder, but from a surfeit of sincerity, as he'd been warned about by that priest at Saint Mathurin's, not Father Patrice, but the other one, the younger one?

Everything was tumbling together in Thomas's mind: he could barely recall being helped down the stairs or into the waiting sedan, could hardly recall the slow drive across the bridge, above the river, to his apartment. Could barely remember falling asleep or waking up to darkness.

A text from his father: *"Will send someone to check on you in the morning. Until then, the prescription is rest, relax, repeat."*

And now, here he was, alone in an apartment without Amy—*nothing left, not even her scent*—standing slack-limbed in front of his desk, unsure of what to do. On the shelf above, the lava lamp of the brain floated in formaldehyde, but no visions of neurons and dendrites danced in front of his eyes. He missed these visions already, could see how addictive these hallucinations might become.

The other brain, the educational brain, the plastic brain that opened like a book, sat atop a stack of textbooks. How long since he'd been to class? How long since he'd attended a lecture or been in a lab? Had it been only a week or two? It felt longer.

Barefoot in boxers, hair dishevelled, Thomas padded across the open-concept of his tubular world, rummaged around in his fridge— leftover fish sticks and milk only slightly past the expiration date. He drank from the carton, sniffed the fish sticks. Decided against it. He could hear the murmur of voices next door, conversations on the other side of the wall—and a postcard on the counter, demanding of him only this: REMEMBER ME.

Madness is a phone that keeps ringing until you are compelled to answer. The murmurs on the other side of the wall grew louder. Thomas tried to ignore them, even hummed a low, droning note to drown them out, to no avail. He finally threw on a bathrobe and stomped out of his apartment to pound on his neighbour's door.

A face appeared, confused and blinking. The man had clearly just woken up. "What do you want?" He was trying to sound gruff, but the quaver in his voice betrayed him. Thomas could see the cellphone at the man's side, thumb poised above EMERGENCY CALL.

Thomas shook his head, stepped back. "Wrong door." No apology. He crossed the hall, pounded on his other neighbour's apartment.

"Keep it down in there!" he shouted.

No answer.

He hammered his fist again and heard a dead bolt turning. An elderly woman peered out from behind the chain. She looked frightened.

Dammit.

"Wrong door," he said.

The hallway became distorted, like the entrance to a fairground fun house, the floor and ceiling torquing against their own lines of perspective. Thomas stood, listened. Nothing. But as he reached for his own door handle, it seemed to pull away from him even as his arm elongated to reach it. He heard his name again. Faint, but undeniable. Thomas wheeled around, hoping to nab the culprit, but there was no one there. Only an empty hallway closing in on itself.

I can't even blame this on the fish, he thought, and then laughed. Loudly. Too loudly. *Fuck you, voice in my head.*

Thomas retreated into his apartment, locked the door, began turning on lights until the windows became mirrors. He took a deep breath, and then—

A knock.

Thomas froze. Stared at the door. Another knock, and this time he knew it was no hallucination. *Who could it be, this time of night?* How incredibly inconsiderate. "Go 'way!" he shouted, but it came out chafed and unconvincing. So he tiptoed across on exaggerated steps, unlocked the door, flung it open to confront his tormentors.

A pair of beaming smiles greeted him.

"Good evening!"

A well-scrubbed woman in a dark woolen skirt and an equally well-scrubbed man in a suit and tie stood on his threshold. The woman cradled a stack of religious pamphlets against her chest, the young man held a Holy Bible in both hands, title out.

Thomas leaned out of his door, looked down the hallway and then back at the pamphleteers. "It's late. How did you get in?"

"We were buzzed in."

"By who?"

"They didn't say." The woman smiled as though their entry were a sign from God, a minor (but significant) miracle rather than a lapse in judgment by one of the tenants.

"We were dropping off literature."

"Sliding it under the doors."

"And we couldn't help notice—"

"Your light."

"It was still on."

"And we thought maybe we might share the gospel of Our Lord Jesus Christ."

Thomas stared back at them, as though from across a vast divide. They were waiting for his answer. "You want to talk about God," he said.

They bobbed their heads with disarming enthusiasm.

Boy, did you pick the wrong fuckin' door.

With a manic grin, Thomas said, "Do I want to talk about God? You bet I do! Come in, come in!"

Thomas hustled them inside before they could object. "Have a seat." He pulled up a pair of chairs to his cluttered kitchen counter.

"You wanna talk about God? I know all about God. Wait here."

He hurried across the brightly lit living room to his desk, came back with the floating brain under one arm. Their smiles had taken on a more strained appearance.

"I can show you God." He unscrewed the top of the jar, reached in, and slooped the brain out onto the kitchen cutting board. "Here. In the right temporal lobe. That's where spiritual beliefs are generated. You've been looking for God? Well, there he is. And the devil? He's even deeper down, buried in the darkest reaches of our inner medulla. Here . . ." He pulled out a large knife, the same one Eli had used to slice vegetables. "Let me show you."

But the Witnesses had already fled, if they ever existed at all.

"Hey!" shouted Thomas as he ran after them. "It's not like I'm using a Ginsu knife! Those things can cut through anything!" Nothing. He was left hollering down an empty hallway to an audience of one.

CHAPTER FORTY-NINE

IT REMINDED THOMAS OF a Bedouin camp. The heat of day. The haze of dust. The smoke uncurling above the cooking fires.

What's it like to be a bat?

Thomas pushed through the narrow confines of Tent City. Along the way, he gathered a surreptitious following, men who shadowed him with dark intent. He didn't care. He had left his wallet in the car and the car in a secure parking garage. Thomas pressed on, propelled by a single question that chewed on his bones: *Why did they say "bat"?*

He feared he already knew the answer.

Thomas found them in their narrow canyon between the tenements, selling their wares. Fistfuls of money passing hands, crystal meth and OxyContin, hollow-cheeked customers and open sores, a pair of brothers presiding: Gus and Desmond, dancing in a den of thieves.

When they saw him coming, they momentarily panicked, expecting Eli to appear as well. But it was only Thomas.

"Why did you say 'bat'?" he shouted, forty paces out, closing the gap with every step. "Why did you say 'bat'?"

"Bat? What the fuck are you—"

"When Eli was here, when the magician turned over the tables. You said, 'What are you, a bat?'" Thomas was out of breath. His face was raw and red.

Gustus shrugged. "It's somethin' they say down here."

"Why?"

The two of them might have knocked Thomas down then and there, but the spectre of Eli lingered.

"Because . . . I don't know."

"It was Charlie," said the other one. "The night he died. He was shouting, 'I'm not a bat! I'm not a bat!'"

"People could hear him yelling," said Gustus. "Thought it was funny. It's what people say now when you go crazy down here. Charlie must have been on something. He OD'd, but it wasn't us. That goofball couldn't pay. We comped him a couple times, but not that night. Not the night he died, yelling out, 'I'm not a bat!'"

"It was the devil," said Des. "Running loose in Tent City. That's what they were sayin', anyway. Someone dressed in black."

"Not in black," said Gustus. "In white."

Like a doctor. Like a priest.

"Whoever it was visited Charlie under his tarp. That's what people are saying. Don't know why Charlie was yelling like that."

But I do.

"He was asked a question," said Thomas. "He was scared and he was trying to answer it. This—this person who visited Charlie. Did he have a widow's peak? A streak of white in his hair?"

"No idea. Didn't see him."

Thomas turned and faced the crowd that had gathered behind him—a crowd that was dangerously close to becoming a mob. He could see several men hanging back, waiting. *People die in Tent City all the time.* But Thomas held his ground, addressed the crowd directly. "I come here under the protection of Eli Wasser, the Hammer of God! What you do to me, you do to him!"

And with that, Thomas waded into the crowd, defying the men in the shadows to stop him. No one did.

CHAPTER FIFTY

BERNIE SIGHED.

Professor Cerletti had been calling, trying to find out what Thomas was up to, and Bernie had let the phone in the hall go to voicemail. A few moments later, Bernie's cellphone trilled. Then a text. Next thing, Cerletti would be dropping letters in Bernie's mailbox or sending out a fleet of carrier pigeons.

"Thomas has disappeared," went the message. *"What is going on?"*

But of course, Thomas hadn't disappeared; he just wasn't attending Cerletti's seminars, hadn't submitted an abstract or any updates. To a professor, that was the same thing as falling off the edge of the known world.

Bernie, in the small room he rented in the access alley behind the semiliterate Dunkin' Donuts sign. Bernie, with his partial view of Fenway on the other side of the turnpike. A world away from Thomas, a world away from Kingsley Hall.

Bernie opened his fridge for the fourth time, even though he'd memorized every packet of ketchup, every pickled egg, every limp salad roll. He considered a midnight run to the pizza place near the bridge, decided against it; was probably closed by now anyway. He stood at his window instead, staring out at the glowing billboards of

Fenway rising above the warehouses like stone tablets. He couldn't see the stadium from his thin slice of alley—it was cut off from view by the turnpike—but he could hear it. Night games were the worst: the crack and roar of a run brought in, a base stolen, an anthem ending. Why was Professor Cerletti so obsessed with Thomas's latest experiment? Faint alarm bells were ringing in the back of Bernie's head. Had Cerletti stumbled upon the MRI log, noticed the late-night entry from three weeks before? Or (more likely) was he simply keeping close tabs on Thomas in the hopes of snaring the damnable son of his former protégé, Dr. Tom Rosanoff?

Bernie: alone, exhausted, unsettled.

On the long trudge home, across the bridge onto Massachusetts Avenue, he thought he saw someone who looked like Father Patrice crossing the street below. Father Patrice, unindicted, still free. Hadn't he been a doctor as well? The two worlds seemed interrelated: hospital wards and confessionals, parishioners and patients. Was that why Bernie had gone into medicine in the first place? Was it because of Father Patrice? And where had he been, all these years? Not that it mattered; the man Bernie saw hadn't been Father Patrice but only the haunted memory of him, tripping down the alleyway. And what was Dr. Rosanoff doing in Tent City anyway? Bernie had spotted Thomas's dad leaving the streets of the down below. Why?

CHAPTER FIFTY-ONE

"A Bedlam baptism?" Professor Cerletti chuckled. "Let's not get ahead of ourselves."

The student lowered her hand, mildly embarrassed.

"We'll get to that, I promise. But first—"

With a showman's flourish, he pulled aside a draped cloth to reveal an electroshock machine. "Straight out of Frankenstein, I know," he said with a small laugh. The table was set at a 45-degree angle so that the patient could lean back into it. "Once the wrists and legs are restrained, the table is unlocked and then swung back to a fully perpendicular position, at which point electrodes are attached to the patient's temples."

The students were backlit by high windows. An assemblage of silhouettes, watching.

"Electroconvulsive therapy," said Professor Cerletti, "better known as electroshock, conjures up images of the 'bad old days.' Clenched jaws. Compression fractures. Cracked vertebrae. But that's changed. It's much more humane now. The public is still a bit squeamish, of course, so it's not something we like to advertise, but electroconvulsive therapy is still a commonly prescribed procedure. And perfectly safe. Today, we can pass 400 Volts directly through the human brain without so much as a single chipped tooth."

Cerletti tapped the screen on his tablet, launched a PowerPoint presentation on the whiteboard behind him. The opening images were of Victorian woodblock depictions of an insane asylum.

"The squeamishness is understandable, perhaps. Electroshock treatments were developed out of earlier 'terror-inducing therapies.' An example of this is the Bedlam baptism you were asking about earlier. The world *bedlam* itself comes from Bethlehem. More specifically, the Bethlehem Asylum in London, which was part medical centre, part carnival sideshow. Members of the public could pay a penny to watch the raving antics of the lunatics—from a safe distance, of course."

As the professor spoke, a series of increasingly horrific images appeared.

"Here we have an early form of hydrotherapy. The patient is locked into a cage and then dunked into water, repeatedly. The idea was to bring them to the brink of death—and then pull back."

The woodblock images had given way to black-and-white photographs from the 1940s and '50s. Patients being bound, eyes wide in fear, as they were submerged in large vats. A Bedlam baptism, as it was known.

"Death can be very therapeutic. Tends to strip the madness away. It was terrible, of course. And inhumane. But it was also . . ." he chose his next word carefully, ". . . cleansing."

With that, the PowerPoint ended and Cerletti turned the class's attention back to the electroshock table. "This is not a lecture on the history of psychiatry. That's beyond my purview. But it does bring us up to the present, and this lovely instrument here." He placed a fatherly hand on the unit hooked up to the table. "Small. Compact. Elegant in its simplicity. The patient is strapped in and a series of pulses are passed through his or her brain. This triggers a seizure, which in turn has a calming effect on the patient. Works like a charm, it truly does."

A raised hand. A question about its application.

"Today? Mainly for clinical depression," said Cerletti. "But this treatment can also be used for bipolar disorders, schizophrenia, even anger management. A typical course might run six to twelve treatments, bilateral. Or unilateral, with the current passed through only one lobe, usually the right cerebral hemisphere. As I said, extremely effective and completely safe."

"Then why the restraints?"

It was a voice from the back of the room. Cerletti squinted into the darkness. "Thomas?" The professor's lips tightened into what might easily have been mistaken for a smile. "The prodigal son returns. I was wondering when you would show up. Thought we'd lost you forever. Still hanging with the undergrads, I see. You've skipped our last three appointments, haven't submitted even the trace of an abstract. Is there a reason you're auditing my class?"

Thomas made his way down the aisle toward the electroconvulsive unit. "If the procedure is so safe, why do we need to strap them down?"

"Class, Mr. Rosanoff is asking why, given that this procedure is so benign, we are required to restrain the patients. I'm afraid it's often necessary to treat people involuntarily. Following proper judicial proceedings, of course. With some patients we may need to apply electroshock treatments twenty or thirty times over the course of a year. Some of them lash out, become violent. Their fears are completely unfounded, but unfortunately—"

"May I?" Thomas walked onto the stage, composed and calm. A façade.

"Of course. Be my guest." Professor Cerletti threw a smile to the audience.

Thomas looked out at the class. "I took my lab from Professor Cerletti on this same topic many years ago."

"Oh, not so many. You make me sound old."

"Not old," said Thomas. "Distinguished." They both had a chuckle over that one. "The restraints are easily applied," said Thomas. "Allow me to demonstrate. Professor? Just the wrists. I won't bother with your ankles."

"Of course." Cerletti leaned back against the table, placed his arms down at his sides. "Oftentimes the patient is sedated prior to this," he said. "As you can see, it's a simple hook-and-latch."

Thomas threaded the leather straps through and tightened them, first one wrist, then the other.

"And even if I struggle"—Professor Cerletti demonstrated this—"there is no damage to my wrists."

"We then apply gel to the contact points," said Thomas. He brought a tube of gel over, dabbed a bit on both of Cerletti's temples. "This is to prevent the skin from burning."

"Exactly. Now, please undo the straps."

"It's a funny thing," Thomas said, addressing the class. "Many, many doctors have prescribed this treatment, and yet I don't know a single one who has ever volunteered to try it on themselves." He turned to Cerletti. "Why is that?" Then, leaning in so close that only he and Cerletti could hear, he whispered, "I know what you've been doing in Tent City, you fucking murderer."

Cerletti opened his mouth, eyes bulging, tried to speak, but was left dumbstruck. Had they tested the professor's galvanic skin responses, the results would have been palpable.

Thomas attached the electrodes to Cerletti's temples, turned to the machine, set the dial. "Class, pay attention."

And with that, Cerletti yelled, face pink with perspiration, "Stop this! Right now! Right this instant!"

"Let's begin with, oh, 200 Volts. Perfectly safe." He put his hand on the switch.

The students shifted in their seats, exchanged looks, not sure what was going on. They were waiting for someone to tell them what to do. Was Cerletti's reaction part of the demonstration?

Cerletti began to shriek—there was no other word for it—spittle flying, neck twisting as he threw himself against the restraints, trying to wrench his wrists free. "You little cocksucker! Let me out right now, you little fuck!"

The class looked on, agog, and before anyone could react, Thomas flipped the main switch.

Cerletti, in tears, tensed up, wincing in anticipation of . . . nothing. The expected jolt of current never came.

Thomas leaned down, picked up the unplugged cord, said to the class, "First, do no harm."

He left the stage, and then, almost as an afterthought, said, "Before I forget, would someone please release Professor Cerletti?"

CHAPTER FIFTY-TWO

DR. ROSANOFF STRODE DOWN the hallway, scattering students and staff, his lab coat billowing behind him like a cape. He'd been called away in mid-interview (a follow-up to the *Psychology Today* profile) and he wasn't happy.

He threw open the door to the staff room with one straight-armed shove, zeroed in immediately on Anton Cerletti, sitting distraught in the corner.

This room rarely saw police officers. Usually, budget allotments were haggled over, doctoral candidates discussed and dismissed, absent colleagues mocked. Not today. Thomas was at one end of the table, flanked by officers who were evidently taking a statement, and Cerletti was at the other end. Cerletti started to get up when he saw Dr. Rosanoff coming at him, but was told, "Sit *down*."

Professor Cerletti did as he was told.

"You're not pressing charges."

Cerletti looked up at Dr. Rosanoff, flustered and afraid. "I don't think I have a choice."

"You're not pressing charges. Understood?"

"It was an assault. There are witnesses."

"A misunderstanding. A classroom demonstration gone awry.

Thomas is an exemplary student, under a lot of stress. Med school will do that to you. It was a misunderstanding, nothing more."

"But he . . . he tied me down."

"You volunteered."

"He flipped the switch."

"There was no power. He assumed you were demonstrating the panic that a patient might exhibit." Dr. Rosanoff cast a glance to the police officers in the other corner, then back to the man cowering below him. An Ichabod figure. A lesser Caesar. "For that you called in the police? You prick."

Cerletti, eyes up, beseeching. "I didn't call the police. He did."

Dr. Rosanoff stepped back. "What?"

"He's making wild accusations. He"—Cerletti's voice became hushed, desperate—"he's saying that I've been killing homeless people with injections down in the, in the slums." He tried to laugh it off, but his laughter came out tinged with hysteria. "He's telling the police I'm a murderer."

"Ask him!" It was Thomas, yelling from the other end of the table. The officers tried to calm him down, but he persisted, hurtling his accusations across the room. "I know the exact date of the first occurrence. It was the same day Amy and I broke up. I walked around in a daze for hours. I don't remember where I went or what I did, but I remember the date. It's burnt into my memory. Ask him where he was on the seventh! Ask him!" It wasn't clear whether Thomas was talking to the police officers or his father. "Ask him! That was when the first body was found in Tent City. That was no overdose, that was Professor Cerletti!"

"Thomas!" Dr. Rosanoff shouted. "That's enough!"

Cerletti tugged on Dr. Rosanoff's lab coat. "Your son's having a breakdown. He needs help. I was nowhere near there on the seventh. I was four hundred miles away, giving a lecture at Hopkins. The other dates as well. I can account for my schedule." Although somewhere in his murky recollections, Cerletti was faintly aware he couldn't account for every date. He remembered a long walk in a cold mist one evening and a familiar figure in the streetlights ahead of him. . . . But as quickly as the recollection arose, it fell away.

Dr. Rosanoff stepped in, closer than necessary, looming over Cerletti. "You want to talk to the authorities? Let's."

"Tom," he pleaded. "I don't have a choice."

"We always have a choice, Anton. That's all life is, a series of choices. And here is mine. If you press charges, I will cooperate, too. It's only fair. We can both speak to the authorities, about all sorts of things. Cabbages and kings, Anton. And a certain arrangement you set up with the pharmaceuticals. The tests you ran, pulling patients off of sertindole to trigger psychotic reactions and then treating the results. You wouldn't be hiding the suicide stats to get FDA approval, would you, Anton? Of course not. Sadly, the press might not see it that way."

Professor Cerletti blanched. "Tom, please . . ."

"Borison and Richards? They weren't in half as deep as you. And they got fifteen years. Each." A long pause. "It doesn't really matter who called the police, does it? You won't be pressing charges regardless, will you?"

Cerletti shook his head, mouthed the word *No*.

"It was a misunderstanding, wasn't it, Anton?"

He nodded, eyes down.

Dr. Rosanoff smiled with all his teeth, tapped his open hand against the side of Professor Cerletti's face, a gesture that might have appeared friendly from afar but here had a definite sting to it. "Was that so hard? As for this craziness about Tent City, I'll deal with that. Don't worry. No one is going to blame you for the death of a couple of junkies nobody cares about."

But on this Professor Cerletti disagreed. "That's not true," he said softly. "Thomas cares."

Once the officers had taken the professor's statement and received Dr. Rosanoff's assurances regarding Thomas's mental health, father and son walked in silence down the long hallways of the university's east wing.

Thomas suddenly stopped. He looked at his father. "It wasn't Cerletti. It was you."

"What are you talking about?"

"It was you all along. Bernie saw you down by Tent City. Plus, you treated Charlie at the shelter. And you treated Eli. Those weren't murders. Those were drug tests gone bad."

"This is ridiculous."

"The drug companies. How much are they paying you?"

"Oh for chrissake, Thomas. Any involvement I have with the pharmaceutical companies is to *remove* people from their meds, not to kill them. I stand in opposition to the overmedication of our population, remember? It hasn't made me popular with Big Pharma." And then, the kicker: "I was at the same conference Anton attended. I gave the keynote address. There were five hundred people in that audience. Are you going to accuse all of them as well?" He pulled out a pad and pen, scribbled something across it, tore off the page, and handed it to Thomas. "100 milligrams. Twice a day."

And he left. Thomas watched as his father disappeared into converging lines of perspective.

"Thomassss . . ."

"Stop talking!" he yelled. But the hallway was empty of everything, even echoes.

That night, Thomas walked back and forth across his apartment, fitful, fidgety, taking pills by the fistful, washing them down with red wine directly from the bottle. The postcards on the counter asked their question, demanded an answer: REMEMBER ME. Except . . . it was no longer a question. It was a command. And it struck Thomas again how everything can hinge on a single turn of punctuation, how *Remember me?* becomes *Remember me.*

He threw back the wine and the pills, swallowed hard.

"Do I know you?!" That was what Eli always yelled—*"Do I know you?!"*—except when he hadn't.

It stopped Thomas cold. *Required reading.* That's what Cerletti had told him.

A question that wasn't a question. *Do I know you?* And suddenly everything fell into place, like a tumbler turning in a lock.

I know exactly who you are.

CHAPTER FIFTY-THREE

"IT'S LATE, I KNOW, but I need your help." Thomas was trying not to shout to be heard over the voices jumbling against each other in his head.

Bernie, on the phone, groggy. "Thomas? Is that you?"

"It's late, I know, I'm sorry. But I need your help."

"It's okay." Bernie swallowed a yawn. "I had to get up to answer the phone anyway." Thomas could hear him fumble for his glasses. "What is it? Did Igor screw up again?"

"No, it's not that." The voices were growing louder now, were clamouring for attention. Not voices. Memories. Fragments of conversations, coming back in sharp relief.

They agreed to meet halfway, on the bridge. A faint mist hung over the water and the lights along the river glowed in halos of fog. Thomas tried to remain calm, but as he walked toward Bernie, he began to yell, voice cracking. "How did you know the name of my hamster?"

Bernie came over to him, wrought with concern. He could see flashes of anguish, perhaps even madness, behind Thomas's eyes. "What are you talking about?"

"My hamster. How did you know about my hamster?"

"Thomas, everybody knows. Your life is on public record, remember? When you called, you said you needed my help. With what?"

"The truth."

"Truth?" said Bernie. "What is truth?"

Thomas could feel his certainties waver. Was the name of his hamster even in his father's book? His thoughts eddied like water circling a drain, and the look of concern on Bernie's face was heartbreaking. It hit Thomas just then how few friends he really had. Perhaps only one.

"I'm—I'm having trouble," he said.

"Thomas, we need to get you home."

And then . . .

There it was. A faint twitch of the lips, the hint of a smile, there and then gone. A hell of a tell, that one.

Thomas's gaze hardened. "The night Amy and I broke up . . ."

"The night she dumped you."

"Where did you go?"

"I don't recall. It was, as they say, a little drunk out that night."

"Not after, before. When I phoned you. Where were you?"

"I don't know. Somewhere."

"You were out of breath."

"I'm always out of breath."

"You were downtown."

"Fine." Bernie sighed. "I was visiting an Asian massage parlour. Happy now? Not all of us can have your success with the ladies. Some of us are downright lonely."

Thomas stepped closer. "Bullshit. *Do I know you?!*' That's what Eli always shouts, what he always asks. But that's not what he said when he met you, is it? He shouted, 'I know you!' and you looked scared. I thought it was because Eli was loud and full of fury. It wasn't. You were worried he recognized you. He'd seen you before. You told me you'd spotted my dad down by Tent City, that you avoided him. I asked myself what my dad was doing down there. I should have been asking what *you* were doing down there. My father was scouting test subjects for a highly unethical drug regimen. You? You were scouting subjects of your own, but not for medical tests. It was for something much worse than that. Tell me I'm wrong, Bernie. I fucking dare you to tell me I'm wrong!"

"Is that what this is? You want some sort of confession? This isn't church, Thomas. Go home."

He turned to leave, but Thomas grabbed Bernie's overcoat. Navy blue, not black. But who would know the difference in the dark? And when he shed his overcoat, the white of his lab jacket would emerge.

"What's it like to be a bat, Bernie? *What's it like to be a bat?*" Thomas threw the question at him. "That was required reading. I never bothered with Cerletti's assignments, but you did. You were always the better student, Bernie. And it must have made an impression on you, that question. How can we really know what it's like to be someone else? *What's it like to be a bat?* That's what you asked, wasn't it? Before you killed them."

When Bernie spoke, his breath was barely a whisper and full of mist. "I was just culling the herd, Thomas."

"Jesus, Bernie."

Bernie, eyes smiling, full of tears. "Every story needs a Satan. Every gospel needs its devil."

The memories were crowding in, coming quicker. *"I always forget you're a former Catholic, Bernie." "There's no such thing as a former Catholic, Thomas."* And when their God helmet had first worked, when they thought they'd succeeded, Bernie had been jubilant: *"Imagine the look on the priests' faces! Imagine their reaction when we prove that God is merely a trick of the mind, that no one is watching out for us."* Visions of dendrites and neurons radiating outward. And buried in the brain, the almond and the seahorse: fear and anxiety nestled in beside memory and self-control. They bleed into one another. *Remember me. Remember me.*

Thomas on the bridge, reciting Bernie's own words back to him: " 'The greatest tragedies can exist right beside us and we might never know!' Those weren't Cerletti's words; those were yours."

The voice of Thomas's father coming back to him: *"We thought it might be therapeutic." "For him?" "For you."*

"When I was little," said Thomas, "I played with a boy who'd been abused by the priests. That was you."

A sad smile surfaced in Bernie. "You didn't even remember my name."

"We'll still be friends, right?" That's what Bernie had asked the last time they saw each other as children at Kingsley Hall.

"They put me in foster care," said Bernie. "The priest was quietly reassigned and I was forgotten. The only thing I had going for me— the only thing—was this." He tapped his temple. It was a gesture he'd learned from Thomas. "I *thought* my way out of the life I'd been given. And when we met again, after all those years, I kept waiting for you to remember me. It never happened, not even a glimmer. I wasn't even in your father's book. I was edited out. The Gospel According to Bernie wasn't deemed worthy of further study."

Thomas felt the world rise and fall beneath his feet. Mist curling above him, a river of ink below, and a single question left to ask and always the hardest to answer: "Why?"

Bernie in Tent City: facing fear. The pulse increases, blood pressure rises, palms grow clammy. The symptoms of fear are a physiological response originating in midbrain. Bernie, hands shaking when he takes out the syringe. *We're all just molecules*, he tells himself. Bernie, taking off his overcoat, adjusting his lab jacket. *People trust doctors the way they used to trust priests*. The elderly man trembled as Bernie tied the rubber tourniquet, tapped out a vein. "You're responding to fears you didn't know you had," Bernie explained. "There is something in my voice, my smile. There's part of your brain, even one as atrophied and addled as yours, that is still picking up on signals, on tiny changes in facial expressions, in the slight shifts of tonal quality in my voice. That prickly sensation on your skin? That's your amygdala trying to warn you. Everything we are, everything we are capable of, sadness and anger, panic and fear, lives in the synapses, in that tiny gap between the thalamus and the amygdala." He smiled. "Remarkable, isn't it?"

The primordium of fear, the primordium of love, the primordium of rage. These three we are born with, but the greatest of all is fear.

"Why did I do it?" asked Bernie, standing on the bridge, staring into Thomas. "I was trying to get God's attention. But there was no response, Thomas. No answer, only an overwhelming absence. And I knew."

"Knew what?"

"That He doesn't exist. Or doesn't care. And either way, the result is the same. There is no one waiting for us at the top of the tower, Thomas." And with that, Bernie swung his body over the side of the railing.

"Don't!"

"Think of it as a Bedlam baptism," said Bernie. And he stepped off, into nothingness.

PART FOUR

IF BY CHANCE YOU SEE

CHAPTER FIFTY-FOUR

BERNIE DIDN'T DIE. He couldn't even do that right. He was fished out of the water, sputtering and coughing, by a good Samaritan who waded in to save him. Bernie was rushed to Massachusetts General Hospital in the early stages of hypothermia.

Thomas had watched in horror as his friend disappeared into the water, the splash closing around him, the current carrying him away. He'd staggered back, called 911. "A body is in the river. He's—he's gone."

"Who? Did you know him?" the dispatcher asked.

"No," said Thomas, hollow-chested. "I didn't know him . . ." He turned off his phone, stepped back.

Thomas wasn't aware that Bernie had surfaced, wasn't aware of any of that. He knew only this: Bernie was gone, and the experiment had to end.

At Kingsley Hall, the light in the corner tower was off. Thomas's father was sleeping, and the night staff that let Thomas in were held to silence by a finger to his lips.

"Shhhh," he said. Only that.

Up the stairs to his father's study and the control room beyond. Thomas, turning off the monitors one by one. And back down the stairs to the main hall and another door, one leading into the labyrinth of mirrors behind the walls. Thomas, slipping in, locking the door behind him.

He passed the one-way mirror that looked into Eli's room. Eli sat on his cot, restless and awake, his wrists once again attached to a canvas belt around his waist. (Eli had been put back in restraints following his outburst during the Hobo Wars incident.) The lights in the rooms had been dimmed. Someone must have recanted.

Thomas came to Sebastian's window, opened the door quietly, entered the room. These doors locked automatically from the outside, and Thomas was careful to leave it open behind him. He had come to take Sebastian away.

"Wake up."

Sebastian blinked himself awake to find Thomas standing above him in the half-light.

"This—this is all your fault," said Thomas. "You realize that, don't you? Everything that's happened. This entire experiment, it was set up solely to cure *you*. And you didn't even have the common courtesy to get better."

Sebastian tried to speak, but Thomas stopped him.

"Where do you get off, claiming to be Jesus H. Fucking Christ? What arrogance."

Sebastian tried to sit up, but Thomas shoved him back down.

"Tell me your name."

Again Sebastian tried to rise. Again he was shoved down.

"Tell me your name."

Sebastian looked up at Thomas with the tremulous gaze of a kicked dog. "I am Jesus. Son of—"

"Tell me your name."

Thomas now pulled Sebastian up by the scruff of his bathrobe. He was surprised—thrilled, in a way—at how weak Sebastian was, how easy it would be to mistreat him, to hurt him, as though that were what he was made for.

"Pain can be therapeutic," Thomas said, and with that he ran Amy's brother headlong into the one-way mirror, headlong into his own reflection, the two rushing up to meet each other. A loud thud. The glass rattled loudly in its protective case. Nose and lip, spraying blood, droplets like paint, a perfect red. Thomas drove Sebastian full force into the mirror again. And again. A faint moan, nothing else.

"Take a good look!" Thomas forced Sebastian to face himself. "This is not the face of God. This—this is who you really are. A fucking imposter."

Sebastian's lip was split, his mouth was filling with blood. In the next room, the magician sat up, suddenly alert. "Sebastian?" He put his ear to the wall. "Thomas?"

In his own room, Eli was awake as well. "Sadducees!" he roared. "Release him!" He didn't know who was in Room B with Sebastian, but he assumed it was the devil. And he was right.

Thomas could hear Eli's muffled yells next door, but he didn't care. He dragged Sebastian from the whitewashed confines of the room, splattered now with Pollock sprays of blood, and forced him down the narrow maze of hallways to the bathroom. "Ever heard of a Bedlam baptism?"

Sebastian was crying now. So was Thomas.

Thomas kicked open the bathroom door, ran Sebastian into that mirror as well. But this one was not encased in protective plastic, and it shattered with a crash, glass cascading onto the floor. Sebastian went down, blood streaming from his forehead.

Out of breath, Thomas locked the door, turned the bathtub faucet on full, closed the drain. Over the tumult of water, he yelled again, "Tell me your name!"

Sebastian began to sob. "I am the Son of Man."

"Your real name. Tell me your real name!"

"Stop . . . please . . ."

In Room C, the magician was yelling. He had heard Thomas's voice. "Thomas! What's going on?" He ran his fingers around the edge of the door but could find no way to open it. It was sealed, almost seamless.

In the next room, Eli struggled against his own restraints, twisting the straps into the flesh of his wrists. "Serpents! Serpents in the House of the Lord!" The straps twisted tighter till his hands turned red, almost blue. He was fighting his restraints like a man wrestling with madness, until—with a rend—the clasp broke, the belt fell away, and Eli was free.

He threw himself against the door, shoulder first. "Sadducees!" he bellowed. He raised his foot, slammed it directly into the plexiglass of the one-way mirror. The glass might have been covered in protective casing, but the wooden frame it sat upon was exactly that: a wooden frame. It splintered on the third pile drive from Eli's leg, the entire window propelling outward, into the narrow hallway behind.

It was this noise that woke the orderlies, who in turn woke Dr. Rosanoff. They had first thought someone was breaking in—they didn't realize that someone might be breaking out.

Thomas had forced Sebastian into the tub. He was so feeble, this thin Messiah, so insubstantial, this failed priest. Sebastian went under, sending water over the side and shards of glass swirling across the tiled floor.

He came up, gasping for air.

"Who are you?" Thomas demanded.

"I am Jesus, Son of—"

Down again, with Sebastian's hands clawing at the air.

Back up. Same answer. Down again.

At the sound of the window being kicked out of its frame, the magician shouted, "Eli?" Hitting the one-way mirror in his own room with both hands, he cried, "Eli! Let me out!" The turn of a lock and Eli burst in, bewildered and enraged. "Where is he?" he roared, but the magician had already pushed past, and was running down the narrow maze of hallways to—dead end—he turned, ran into Eli coming up behind.

Back in the bathroom, Thomas had given up. He turned off the water, sat on the closed toilet, head down.

Sebastian, bathrobe sodden, slid out from the tub and onto the floor.

Thomas began to laugh, a manic exhalation of defeat that originated in his stomach and radiated outward through his chest and throat. It was the laugh of a condemned man, of a sinner in love with his sins. *All for naught, all for naught.* Thomas picked up a drinking glass from beside the sink, scooped some water out of the bathtub, drank deeply, eyes closed. He filled the glass again, handed it to Sebastian, who was now propped up on the floor against the side of the tub.

"I don't know about you," said Thomas, "but I could use a real drink right about now. Wine, please, if you're up for it."

Voices clamoured on the other side of the bathroom door. It was

Eli and the magician. As the magician grappled with the lock, Eli was thundering away about Pharisees and pharaohs.

At this point, what did it matter?

In the distance, behind the outer doors, other voices, equally frantic. The orderlies were trying to get past the first obstacle, into the maze, as Dr. Rosanoff, in silk robes, urged them onward. Boxes within boxes.

The door to the bathroom shimmered violently, rattling on its hinges; Eli was apparently trying to break through this one as well. Thomas looked at the shards of mirror and pools of water on the floor. What did it matter?

And then . . .

Sebastian's hand came up, trembling, holding out the drinking glass that Thomas had given him. The water inside slowly transformed. Thomas watched in disbelief as it turned into wine in front of his eyes, the crimson uncurling like smoke into water, like dye from a dropper. But no. Not wine. Blood.

Sebastian's wrists had been slashed, and he fell, dropping the water glass at the very moment the bathroom door blew inward. Everything went silent—a vacuum that ended with a crash of voices. Thomas felt as though he were coming up for air. He grabbed a towel, put pressure on Sebastian's wrists—and was immediately yanked backward as though on a rip cord. It was Eli, pulling him back. Eli, the Hammer of God. Eli, with one eye clouded, but the other perfectly clear. He clasped a meaty hand on either side of Thomas's head, squeezed—hard. "Sadducee!" he yelled. "Worm! Judas! The Kingdom of Heaven is at hand! Howl! Howl at the judgment of the Lord!"

Eli dragged Thomas across the tiled floor like a rag doll, as the magician worked frantically to stem the flow from Sebastian's wounds, twisting the towel into a tourniquet. The orderlies were still a long way off. Thomas was on his own.

"An eye for an eye!" Eli bellowed. "Eye for an eye!" And he pushed his thumbs up, under Thomas's gaping gaze. "Physician, heal thyself!"

Thomas could feel the pressure under each eye socket. He could feel it coming, and he spoke: one word. The only word that could save him: "Mercy."

"Pharisee!"

"Have mercy . . ."

Eli glowered down at Thomas, then released him from his grip. Thomas toppled onto the floor.

The door that led into the maze behind the mirrors flew outward as Dr. Rosanoff and the orderlies leapt back. It was Eli, carrying Sebastian in his arms, a blood-soaked towel knotted around dangling wrists. Eli, unrestrained.

And somewhere in the distance, the sound of sirens.

CHAPTER FIFTY-FIVE

HUMAN DESIRE MAY BEGIN in the hypothalamus, but it spreads out from there, saturating the entire brain. Fueled by dopamine reward circuits and opiate-like endorphins, love and desire unleash a wave of neurochemicals into the brain's synapses. The strongest of these is oxytocin. One might say that oxytocin is the chemical formula for love. When a mother gives birth, oxytocin floods her brain, creating both a sense of euphoria and a powerful feeling of bonding. Oxytocin turns off our higher critical functions, dampens our sense of pain, reduces feelings of trepidation. This is the same exact neurochemical that is released in women during orgasm, equally intense, equally irrational—but not in men, alas. When we speak of a woman's postcoital "glow," we are speaking of oxytocin.

And not only with love, but with food as well. They all flow from the same chemical craving, the one found in gamblers and alcoholics, in heroin addicts and pack-a-day smokers. Indeed, love may be the original addiction, a chemically induced form of madness. From endorphins to dopamine, love was the brain urging itself onward with that same frantic message: *Hit me. Again. Again.*

From the first tingle of interest—the dilated pupils, the heightened sense of arousal—to the surf-crash of sexual climax to the postcoital cuddling, Thomas could chart the rise and fall of a lover's hormones with a scientific precision. He could chart it in Amy's warmed facial features and mottled skin, her shallow breathing, the growing urgency. It was the ebb and flow of desire. Chemistry in action.

"Thomas, what are you thinking about?" she had asked once, sleepily, when she saw him studying her face.

"Just how beautiful you are."

Those relaxed facial muscles? Oxytocin, definitely oxytocin.

But what Thomas saw now was the opposite of oxytocin: not love but rage, pure and undiluted.

She came at him from across the emergency room, eyes crazed. In old movies, a lady would beat her frail fists against a man's chest before collapsing into his embrace, but not Amy. She went right for the throat, right for the eyes, right for the heart. It was only the state of her nails, cut short for kiln work, that saved him from lacerations.

It took Dr. Rosanoff and two security guards to pry her away, and in the tussle Thomas caught the faint scent of paint thinner. Her hair was falling out of her scrunchy over eyes raw with grief—and in that single flicker, it was almost worth it, just to be close to her again, even in anger.

"You asshole son of a prick!" she screamed, lunging again at Thomas.

"Calm down," said Dr. Rosanoff. "If you want to see your brother, you have to calm down."

Nurses crashed past with a gurney, shouting instructions in the chaotic hallways of the hospital. Other emergencies, other lives. Sebastian was already recuperating.

"Your brother is under the care of my personal physician," said

Dr. Rosanoff. "We're moving him to a private suite, where he will be well taken care of."

She turned, hatred in her gaze. "You did this," she said.

"I did this?" Dr. Rosanoff raised an eyebrow. "This isn't the first time, is it? He's tried this sort of thing before, hasn't he? Perhaps *you* did this, Amy. Perhaps society did it. Or perhaps, just perhaps, he did this to himself."

"Fuck you." She pushed past him to the admissions desk. "I'm family," she said. "I want to see him. Now."

Sebastian was sitting up in a softly lit room, wrists bandaged, clean gauze and fresh stitches crocheted along his forehead and lip.

Amy's voice caught in her throat.

Her brother looked at her as though seeing her again for the first time. He smiled faintly. "Amy," he said.

"Sebastian?"

He nodded.

She rushed over, held him. "I've missed you," she sobbed. "I've missed you so much."

CHAPTER FIFTY-SIX

THOMAS STAYED WITH THEM through the night and into the day. On seeing her brother returned, Amy's rage subsided. She was now focused on keeping him here, in the real world, with her. *We, the wounded, the damaged, the unrepairable.*

Thomas watched as Amy tended to her sedated brother. Hushed voices. Medicines and meals rolled in on trays. Pillows and pills and slow unsteady walks to the en suite bathroom, IV wobbling alongside, a small nod to Thomas as he passed.

The sun through the window gradually shifted, throwing light across the floor and then reeling it back in. It felt as though Thomas were caught in a time-lapse photograph, a study in sun and shadow, and when Amy finally acknowledged his presence, it was only to say, "You can go now." It was the closest she would come to saying, *"I forgive you."*

At Kingsley Hall, Thomas walked down the long, echoing corridors, across terra-cotta tiles and up a sweep of stairs. The manor was quiet, as though slumbering, and Thomas entered his father's study without knocking. No one was there, and Thomas picked up the wastebasket from beside his father's desk, entered the soft glow of the control room beyond. The clipboards and binders, the reel-to-reel tapes and videocassettes: it all went into the wastebasket. Thomas even pulled the Post-it notes off the consoles and crumpled them into a fist of paper, tossed them in with the rest.

But then something caught his attention. Not a presence, but an *absence*. (And it is absences that are always more unnerving.) He looked at the monitors. The whitewashed rooms were empty. Eli and the magician were gone.

"Thomas?"

He turned, found himself face-to-face with his father. Thomas placed the wastebasket to one side, stared into the still-life images of empty rooms on the monitors. "Where are they?"

"It's nice to see you as well, son."

"Where did they go?"

"Jesus One and Jesus Two? I had them committed. Long-term, under my care and custody."

"You can't."

"I just did."

"The magician—"

"You're referring to Mr. Keshen."

"I am."

"Then use his proper name. Or Jeffrey, if you prefer."

Thomas turned his attention from the monitors. "The magician was never a patient at San Hendrin. He's not a threat, not to himself, not to others. The review board, the ethics committee, they'll never allow it."

"The ethics committee?" He laughed. "I *am* the ethics committee. And your friend is going to remain under my care for as long as deemed necessary. The experiment isn't over, Tommy. It's only just started. One down. Two to go."

Thomas bolted, taking the stairway two steps at a time, almost tripping, down the hallway and out the door, scrambling to his vehicle.

The admissions nurse at San Hendrin looked up to see a frenzied young man sprinting toward her, incongruous amid the calming hues and wafting music of a modern mental facility. Thomas ran to, and almost into, her desk. "Rosanoff," he said. "Thomas Rosanoff. You have two of my patients"—he looked back to see if anyone was behind him—"a Mr. Wasser. Eli Wasser. And a—a Mr. Keshen. Jeffrey Keshen. They were admitted, under my care. Here. This is my driver's license, that's my medical ID. Thomas Rosanoff. See? Right there. Harvard Medical."

"But they're in seclusion, as requested. Until the sedatives take effect, we won't be able to—"

Thomas stretched his body across the desk, looked at her computer. "That's them," he said, finger on the screen. "Right there. Rooms 22 and 24. I'm signing them out. I'll need a—a requisition form. Ah, a twelve-sixty-one—"

"Sixty-two."

"Right. And I'll also need a—"

Thomas looked back, saw his father striding down the hallway toward him, flanked by his two orderlies. Thomas grabbed the keys from the nurse's post and ran. Behind him, he could hear his father shouting, "Thomas! Stop!"

Down one hallway, up the next. Searching for Seclusion Room 22. Thomas turned a corner, backtracked, counted down the doors as he passed, found the one he was looking for. It had a thin window, wire-meshed. Thomas fumbled with the keys, tried one, then another, dropped them in a jangle, snatched them up again, and that was as far as he got.

One of the orderlies pulled Thomas away, held him against the wall.

Dr. Rosanoff closed in. "Thomas," he said, out of breath and ragged from exertion. "I don't know who you are trying to impress with these antics. But it has to end."

But before Thomas could respond, the other orderly whispered, "Dr. Rosanoff, I think you should see this."

Thomas's father peered through the narrow window, then pushed on the door. It swung open. The room was empty, unlocked.

"Where is he? He must have been moved to another . . ."

Eli!

Thomas raced to the next room, with Dr. Rosanoff and the orderlies in pursuit. But Thomas slowed as he approached the door. They all did. They could already see it was unlocked—and open.

Eli was gone.

Gone where?

Having spoken at length and with increasing increments of irritation, Dr. Rosanoff found himself in the facility's surveillance room, with Thomas and the two orderlies crowding in behind him as San Hendrin's head of security scrolled through the footage. They could see the magician sitting on a cot, arms crossed by a restraining device, more commonly known as a straitjacket. He sat so still that even with the tape on fast-forward he barely moved, only small jerky movements, and then—

"Stop! Right there. He's doing something." Dr. Rosanoff moved closer to the monitor, watched as the magician rose to his feet. The straitjacket fell away. The effect was so startling they jumped back.

The magician then looked directly at the camera. He reached out his hand to a place below the lens, and as soon as he did, the security camera cut to the white noise of static.

Everyone was speaking at once, voices overlapping.

"What the hell . . ."

"He cut the feed. How?"

"No idea."

"Where did he go?"

"There!" said Thomas, pointing to the camera in Seclusion Room 24.

A different monitor. A different Messiah. Eli in his own strait-jacket, writhing on the floor, eyes rolling back in his head, a lion in chains roaring at the world.

"The door handle," said Thomas. "Look."

They could see it jiggle once, twice, and then—a fan of light spilled across the room. Eli fell silent. The magician entered, sat down beside him. He spoke to Eli, and Eli became calm. Rising up once again, the magician walked toward the camera, stared directly into the lens, directly into their eyes.

And this time he didn't need to reach out his hand. The image on Eli's camera cut to sudden static as well.

"He must have shorted something when he yanked the wires out of the first camera, some kind of trick." The security supervisor began flipping switches, more or less at random, hoping to reboot the cameras, but there was nothing. Only static.

Dr. Rosanoff stumbled backward, looking like a man who had been hit in the throat.

The orderly beside him smiled; it was the faintest of flutters, there and then gone. "Looks like your experiment got away from you," he said.

CHAPTER FIFTY-SEVEN

THE PEWS WERE MOSTLY empty. Family and friends were up front, shaking hands and making conversation. Stained glass and the waxy smell of candles flickering in the nave. Wishes, set alight. Our Lady of Constant Sorrow.

"Do you believe in the Seven Sacraments?"

"We believe in the Seven Sacraments."

"Do you believe in Christ Everlasting?"

"We believe in Christ Everlasting."

A baby in a lace gown, gurgling and full of smiles, is lowered toward the baptismal font. The priest dips his hand into the water, trickles it over the child's forehead, makes the sign of a cross as he speaks.

"Go in peace, and may the Lord be with you."

He passes the child to Amy, equally radiant, who passes the child to the child's father. That would be Lars, from the gallery. The handsome man from Minnesota, so deeply, doomfully in love. (He is not her One True Love, either, the one waiting for her beyond words. Should we tell him? Would it matter?)

Thomas, in his white coat, medical satchel by his side, watched this anachronistic ritual from the back row. He'd been invited, almost didn't show. He was on his way to the shelter for his weekly rounds, trying to pretend he'd forgotten the date of the baby's baptism, when the sound of church bells brought it all back to him. He couldn't escape those, even if he tried.

Amy came down the aisle afterward, smiled at him. There was affection there, maybe even the remnants of something else.

"You came," she said.

"Beautiful child."

She looked back to the receiving line that had formed around the infant, parents and colleagues cooing over the newly anointed, congratulating the father, posing for photos. But Lars was distracted by Thomas's presence and he kept a wary eye on them.

Amy turned her attention back to Thomas. Pale eyes and hair that refused to hold a part. "Look at you, all grown up. A real doctor."

"That's what they tell me."

"GP?"

"Community health."

"I didn't know you needed a PhD for that."

"You don't."

The plastic tag on his shirt read: T. ALEXANDER.

"I heard your father was let go," she said.

"Removed from the ethics review committee, yes. He's on a forced sabbatical, under review. He'll be fine, though. He's editing the expanded SDM manual, working on a new study, keeping busy. And Sebastian? How is he?"

"Good," she said a little too quickly. "Better. He couldn't be here today. He's starting a new shift up at the plant. Dad got him the job. Assembling box springs, but he hopes to move up. And anyway . . ."

She looked around at the stained glass windows and cruciform corridors, "I thought maybe, with everything that happened, it might be a bit, you know . . . He asks about you."

"He does?"

She laughed. "No, not really. But I'm sure he thinks about you, as if in a dream."

It's a hard thing, giving up one's faith, whether in crucifixes or molecules. Thomas took her hand, looked at the fingernails, was reassured to see that they were still cut short, still showing stubborn signs of paint along the edges. He had no doubt that if he were to bury himself into her arms and hold her, eyes tightly closed, that he would smell toothpaste and Dove. Perhaps even traces of turpentine and tea. He let her hand fall away.

"I never did thank you," she said.

"Thank me? For what?"

"For caring about him."

"I don't know that I did."

"You must have," she said, her laughter returning. "That's the only explanation that makes sense."

They were calling for her now. *"Where's the mother?"*

"I have to go," she said.

They shook hands, awkwardly, in that half embrace of ex-lovers, and she walked away from Thomas into the stained glass sunlight to where her family and friends were waiting. It seemed as though she were far away, as though he were watching her through the wrong end of a telescope. Halfway down the aisle, she stopped and turned, gave him a small almost secretive wave. The faintest of expressions flitted across her face, but she was too far away and the light was in his eyes—and it might have been love, or the traces of, or it might have been nothing. Nothing at all.

Later, when Thomas arrived at the shelter, Frances said, by way of greeting, "You're late."

"You should be glad I showed up."

"Just grab a bedpan," she said, and then, sensing something—not sadness, exactly, but something like it—she asked, "Are you okay?"

"I am."

"How's the noggin?"

"Better. I'm taking Risperdal, mild antipsychotic, low dosage. Symptoms are under control." The music in his head had almost entirely disappeared. That's the problem with modern medicine. It works.

"Bedpans," she reminded him. It wasn't a question.

"You're a mean old woman," he said. "Anyone ever tell you that?"

"Only you. All the time."

CHAPTER FIFTY-EIGHT

IT WAS ONLY WHEN Thomas went to report Bernie's death that he discovered Bernie was still alive. This was soon after Eli and the magician had disappeared.

The media would dub Bernie the "Tent City Killer" and would dredge up horrors from Bernie's own past, the uses and abuses of authority, of trust, divine or otherwise. Bernie was sent for psychiatric assessment, but he wanted to face an open court. Professor Cerletti testified at the hearing. He'd assessed Bernie as mentally unfit to stand trial, but the courts remained unconvinced. "He was my star student," said Cerletti, "and it breaks my heart."

When Thomas visited Bernie at the San Hendrin mental facility, the staff kept them on opposite sides of the glass, even though Bernie had never shown any evidence of violence. Even his crimes had been largely passive, relying on a soothing voice and medical injections deftly delivered, not brute force.

Bernie's voice was frantic. "I've seen the brain scans," he said to Thomas. "The psychopathy isn't there. There's nothing wrong with my brain. Don't let them commit me." And then, growing angry, growing sad, he said, "I am *not* a sidekick. I am not a supporting character in the Story of You. I will not be locked up and forgotten like some lunatic."

But there was nothing, nothing, nothing Thomas could do. And every time he went to visit Bernie, he left feeling despondent—with his friend suspended between competing judgments, caught in limbo. At those times, the anguish of Saint John of the Cross came back to Thomas, and the lines that Bernie had recited, not so long ago: *"If by chance you see him I love the most, tell him I am sick, tell him that I suffer."*

Outside in the dusty heat of summer, a city bus rattled past smokestacks and warehouses, straining uphill and then fighting its own momentum on the way down. Sebastian was inside, dressed in factory blues, toolbox on his lap.

The driver looked at him in the bus's rearview mirror. "You seem familiar. Do I know you?"

"Maybe," Sebastian said softly. "I used to be somebody."

And the bus trundled into the haze.

Thomas never spoke with Sebastian again, or Eli. He missed Eli, his rampaging voice and thundering invective, his sly humour and tender mercies. The *shoteh* who came out from under the bridge.

In the weeks that followed, the heat would give way to rain and with it the usual permutations and combinations: fitful winds followed by muggy drizzles, humid and heavy, which promised a relief that never came. At Hynes Station, the commuters hustled past, pouring in and out, ignoring a small card table that had been set up beside the entrance. With head down and palms flying, a raggedy man in frayed clothes was playing three-card monte, keeping up his patter as the pedestrians pushed past. "Find the lady! There she goes, round and round, no one knows." Sucker bets, down by the station.

Thomas watched from across the street as the man's hands moved in a blur. The most effective magic is always close up: the card disappears and the coin reappears before your very eyes. "Find the lady! Place your bets!" The monte-card dealer glanced up, caught Thomas's gaze. But it was someone else. Not him.

Thomas never saw the magician again, but he kept searching for him nonetheless, down by the tracks, late at night, or in the park on sunnier days when he thought he might see him surrounded by children as he performed small feats, sleight of hand. And though he knew he'd never find him, he kept looking, and is looking still. The Boy in the Box, chasing echoes down endless hallways, trying still to close that gap.

And there he is now, pushing his way through the dishevelled shelters of Tent City, down to a makeshift medical clinic where patients crowd in. An old man with festering wounds. A woman, infant on hip. Chest infections and hearts beating out of time. And Thomas in the middle, opening his satchel with a sigh, taking out his stethoscope, leaning in to listen. A doctor, lost in a sea of humanity.

CHAPTER FIFTY-NINE

"LIMITED-TIME OFFER! Call in the next ten minutes and you will get *two* Ginsu knives for the price of one. It slices, it dices, it cuts, and it peels! And every Ginsu comes with a money-back guarantee. If you are not completely satisfied, you can return it for a FULL REFUND. Shipping and handling not included."

In a dimly lit bar in a dimly lit city—it doesn't matter which city, and it doesn't matter which bar—an infomercial is playing to an empty room. On the television screen, the woman holding up the product has a decidedly strained look on her face. She turns to her cohost for the demo.

"Eli, over to you!"

Eli, in an ill-fitting suit, hair slicked back, beard neatly trimmed, attacks his assignment with gusto.

"That's right!" he bellows. "Only $29.99! Order now and we'll throw in our patented salad shooter at no extra cost! It's delightful and diversionary! Every Ginsu knife is made of the finest tempered steel. They can cut through anything!"

He begins sawing through a tin can.

"Metal. Copper. Frozen pork chops. They can even"—he holds up a heavy frying pan—"cut through cast iron!"

The panic in his cohost's eyes is self-evident. "Um, no," she says. "No they can't."

Eli ignores her, launching at the frying pan with his knife, pieces of metal flying up, as his cohost looks into the camera, almost pleading. "Order now . . . please?"

Above the set, in the studio control room, the director has called for camera two. "Stand by, Camera Two." On the monitors, Eli has made a sizable nick in the cast iron.

The editor at the switching board shakes his head. "Jesus. . . ."

"I know, I know," the director says. "But you should see how sales spike whenever he's on. It's a miracle."

A NOTE FROM THE AUTHOR:

ON THE BLENDING OF
MONTREAL AND BOSTON

THE SHOE ON THE ROOF was originally set in Montreal, a city rich in Catholic lore and academic traditions, but I soon realized that the story only works in a place where there are private mental health facilities. I tried again and again to rework the narrative to make it fit, but it couldn't be done. And so, reluctantly, I packed up the characters and their belongings in a U-Haul and moved them to Boston, a city similarly rich in Catholic lore and academic traditions. Thus, McGill University became Harvard, the Saint Lawrence River became the Charles, Notre-Dame Basilica became Our Lady of Constant Sorrow, and the Sisters of Charity became Carmelite nuns. At some level, though, I've always felt there is still a great deal of Montreal in this story, as though the two cities have blended into one, creating a fusion of the two. But I could be wrong.

Will Ferguson
September 2017

ACKNOWLEDGMENTS

THIS BOOK BEGAN WITH a story my mother told me. My mom, Lorna Louise Bell, worked as a psychiatric nurse at the Weyburn Mental Hospital in the 1950s under Dr. Humphry Osmond. She often spoke about her time at Weyburn, and the stories she shared with us were, by turn, unsettling, heartbreaking, occasionally uplifting, and at times inspiring. She mentioned psychological experiments that occurred at facilities in the U.S., where mental patients suffering from the same identity delusion were brought together and forced to confront their doppelgängers. The roots of these experiments can be traced back as far as the 1660s and the Case of Simon Morin, as cited in this novel. A similar encounter between women who believed they were the Virgin Mary occurred at a mental facility in Maryland in the 1950s, and the unexpected cure that resulted from this was later reported in *Harper's Magazine*, which directly inspired psychologists such as Dr. Milton H. Erickson (whose experiment in bringing competing Christs together succeeded) and Dr. Milton Rokeach (who failed). Although inspired by these stories, *The Shoe on the Roof* remains a work of fiction.

Several people helped me with this manuscript. My oldest son, Genki Alex, read the first drafts and provided invaluable advice and feedback. He also took a rather snazzy author photo. My brother, the playwright and author Ian Ferguson, provided great help in sorting out the story in its early stages. And my friend Karen Jorgensen, a painter, explained how one might go about searching for "perfect blue." She also showed me around her artist's studio, even letting me smell her paintbrushes at one point. As fortune would have it, Karen's daughter Kelsea Gorzo, whom we've known since she was in kindergarten with Alex, is now studying neuroscience at the University of Calgary. (The mouse brains experiment described in this novel is taken directly from Kelsea's own experiences, right down to the seventy-two hours she spent watching "mice videos.") I should also thank Doru Gorzo for his hospitality and patience with me as I endlessly quizzed his wife and daughter about their work.

Dr. Jaideep Bains at the Hotchkiss Brain Institute kindly gave me a tour of his lab, answering my questions, however inane, and explaining in layman's terms what all the various equipment does. It was very helpful, and I thank Jaideep and everyone at Hotchkiss for allowing me to peek over their shoulders and scribble down notes while they worked. (I should also note that the Bains lab, though equally cluttered, is far tidier than the one presented in this novel.) It goes without saying that I am *not* a brain surgeon or a scientist, and any errors or oversights in how I presented the fields of neuroscience, neurology, psychiatry, or physiology are entirely my own and should not be ascribed in any way to anyone who helped me along the way.

The Alberta Foundation for the Arts provided crucial support for this project, and I thank the foundation sincerely for this.

Several works proved instrumental in researching *The Shoe on the Roof*, too many to list here, but I would like to note: *The Spiritual Brain* by Dr. Mario Beauregard and Denyse O'Leary, which provides a cogent look at the interface between neuroscience and faith, and *Mapping the Mind* by Rita Carter, which remains one of the best overviews of neuroscience on the market. The expression "book of woe" is a reference to Gary Greenberg's *The Book of Woe: The DSM and the Unmaking of Psychiatry*, which makes for sombre reading. Bonnie Fournier's wonderfully frank and often funny memoir, *Mugged, Drugged and Shrugged*, of her time spent as a nurse on the streets of Vancouver's Downtown Eastside provides a fascinating look at the front lines of mental health care, addiction, and homelessness. And although Dr. Rosanoff's views are grounded in the behaviourism of B. F. Skinner and the reality therapy of William Glasser, *The Shoe on the Roof* is not meant to be a comprehensive critique of either.

Two people loaned me their names for characters in this book: publicity maven Frances Bedford (who is not a nun, lapsed or otherwise) and historian Jeffrey Keshen (who is not, as far as I know, a recovering heroin addict with delusions of divinity). Thank you both! And Bruce Bennett as well.

I'd also like to thank everyone at Simon & Schuster Canada for their unwavering enthusiasm: President and Publisher Kevin Hanson; Editorial Director Nita Pronovost, who did a splendid job editing the manuscript; VP of Marketing Felicia Quon; Managing Editor Patricia Ocampo; Publicity Director Adria Iwasutiak; and Publicity Manager Catherine Whiteside. There's a reason Simon & Schuster is the fastest-growing publisher in Canada! I should also thank copyeditor Joshua Cohen for his meticulous work. (Any quirks or inconstancies in style and usage are wholly my responsibility, however.)

Finally, I thank Terumi and Yuki Alister deeply for their love and support while I was writing this strange book. *Arigatō ne!*

ABOUT THE AUTHOR

WILL FERGUSON is the author of three previous novels: *Happiness*, a comedic story about a self-help book that actually works, and thus destroys the world; *Spanish Fly*, a con artist coming-of-age tale set amid the jazz halls and dance clubs of the Dirty Thirties; and *419*, a story of heartbreak and revenge in the international world of cyber-crime, which was awarded the Scotiabank Giller Prize. Ferguson's travel memoirs include journeys across Japan, Rwanda, and Northern Ireland. A three-time winner of the Stephen Leacock Medal for Humour, Ferguson has been nominated for both a Commonwealth Writers' Prize and the IMPAC Dublin Award. He lives in Calgary with his wife and their two sons.

Simon & Schuster Canada
Reading Group Guide

THE
SHOE
ON THE
ROOF

WILL FERGUSON

QUESTIONS FOR BOOK CLUBS

1. Sister Frances tells Thomas that "Science can only take us so far. . . . There will always be something just out of reach. Something elusive. We might as well call it God." What does *The Shoe on the Roof* ultimately say about the tension between science and faith?

2. After Thomas and Amy break up, Thomas complains that love serves no evolutionary purpose, but merely produces "temporary madness, when all is said and done." How are the ideas of love and madness intertwined in *The Shoe on the Roof*?

3. How does Thomas's childhood as "the Boy in the Box" shape him? Does it change how he relates to others?

4. What role does Sister Frances play in Thomas's life? What influence, if any, does she have on Thomas?

5. Religion plays an important role throughout the novel. How does religion shape the lives of each of the characters? Is it for better or for worse?

6. Not wanting to live under the shadow of his father, Thomas adopts his mother's surname and, in doing so, alters his identity. How does the importance of names affect Thomas and other characters throughout the novel?

7. Thomas is simultaneously drawn to and infuriated by Eli, Sebastian, and the magician. Discuss why there is a push and pull between Thomas and his test subjects.

8. Thomas believes that "injustice, like longing, gravity, taxes, or air, will always be part of our world, not an anomaly." What do you make of Thomas's view on life, considering everything he has gone through?

9. According to Bernie, we are born with three emotions: fear, love, and rage. Discuss the significance of these three emotions in Thomas's subjects: Eli, Sebastian, and the magician.

10. Does Thomas's experiment fail? Do you think that Eli, Sebastian, and the magician can all be God? Why or why not?

11. Discuss the significance of the title *The Shoe on the Roof*.

ENHANCE YOUR BOOK CLUB

1. Now that you've finished the book, reread the parable of the shoe on the roof at the beginning of the book. How does this relate to the themes of the novel?

2. The novel addresses addiction and homelessness, two issues that are prevalent in many urban areas. After reading about the lives of these characters, has your opinion of addiction and/or homelessness changed?

3. In his author's note, Will Ferguson explains that the novel was originally to be set in Montreal. Do you think this story could have taken place in your city? Why or why not?